When Jack entered Judith's judicial chambers, he thought his eyesight was going again. It turned out to be the lighting. The overhead fixture had been turned off and the room lit only by the brass lamp on Judith's desk and a standing lamp by the couch under the windows. The room had been done in a masculine décor, paneled in dark mahogany, furnished in the same wood with brass fittings, green leather on the couch, greener drapes, and the deepest green lampshades.

The only feminine touch in the room was a wilted rose on Judith's desk. Its silver vase stood out against the brass like a planted clue in a crime scene.

When Jack entered the dim chamber, Judith was on the couch in her stocking feet and reading glasses, with a big leather book propped on her raised knees. A glass of red wine stood on the rug alongside her. When she saw Jack, she closed the tome, not with a snap but gently. She wore a rumpled grey skirt and a burgundy blouse with two buttons open at the throat. When she swung her legs around to face him, she looked like a goblet of claret herself.

"Hello, Jack," she said.

"Time for a new rose, Judith. That one has seen its day."

She contemplated the sad flower on her desk. "I have a little trouble letting go, sometimes. You know that, don't you?"

Defending Her Honor, page 186

Books by Richard Fliegel

The Next to Die
The Art of Death
The Organ Grinder's Monkey
Time to Kill
A Semi-Private Doom
A Minyan for the Dead
The Man Who Murdered Himself
Clerical Errors: Tales of Murder and Ministry

Defending Her Honor

Chelmsford Press   Briarcliff Manor, New York

Chelmsford Press
Briarcliff Manor, New York

ISBN-13: 9780615887418
ISBN-10: 0615887414

Thanks to my friends Michael Holzman and Jane MacKillop, without whose help this book would never have seen print.

Defending Her Honor

A Thriller in Chambers

by

Richard Fliegel

1

Her Honor Judith Frick is propped against a pillow, reading pretrial motions, when he enters the bedroom in a bathrobe and ski mask.

The robe is worn white terry with the Royal Dutch cruise line logo on its pocket. The mask is new black wool.

Her Honor is 52, without surgery but with brown curls darker than they used to be. She's wearing a flannel nightgown. Underneath is a different story, though there's no way he can see that yet. Her hair sticks up in the back from the headboard, whose brass bars annoy her spine. She turns to adjust the pillow, sits back, and finds him standing in his woolen mask like a lost ski patrol.

"What do you want?" the judge demands, over the rim of her reading glasses.

Uninclined to hysterics.

The clock on the nightstand reads 10:54. She still has a motion to exclude in her briefcase, open on the rug below a stack of files on a scalloped pillow. She slips the page she has just read into its cardboard folder.

He pulls aside the quilt. "Mon yer black," he orders through the wool.

She blinks. "My what?"

He moves faster than she expects, catching her ankles and pulling down sharply, so she flops back on the mattress. That knocks the breath out of her.

"Wait—"

But he doesn't. His arm snakes across her, reaching for the bedside lamp. Click! Its trembling shade goes dark.

She tries to sit up, but he pushes her down, his face close to hers. She arches her back. "Please—"

Smirking through the weave. No other word for it. "F' what?"

"I'm on my glasses."

That's different. He snatches them out from under her and drops them onto the nightstand. Light from the TV tints the lenses blue.

A three-piece suit is still talking about NANI loans. For an instant she hears, No assets no income. But she can't keep listening when he shoves her legal briefs out of his way, scattering them over the sheets. A cover page crumples under her hip. Sweeney v. the State of. She twists, trying to lift her weight off the paper, but he presses her down, climbing on top again.

He drags the flannel hem over her hips, revealing black lace panties. "Moping for a little excrement tonight?"

"Don't be crude." She flushes. "You're hurting me."

His body shifts, reaching for her hand. The weight of his ribs across her stomach makes it hard to fill her lungs. He catches her right wrist in his left fist and gropes in the pocket of his robe, pulling out a swath of pink chiffon he tries to wrap around her wrist. But he doesn't have the angle for it, and after two attempts he flings the thing at her. It floats over the tangled quilt and sticks to the nap of her nightgown.

"Eye it yourself."

"What?"

He rolls up the ski mask, revealing his chin, soft mouth, and stained front tooth. She'll have to make an appointment—

"Tie it, I said. Tightly." Getting the adverb right.

He gestures for her to knot the scarf around her own left wrist, which she does, drawing the gauzy bond tight. She winds the loose end around the brass pole on the left side of the headboard and twists onto her back to thread it through the central poles. Then she wraps it around the thick pole on the right side of the bed. She loops the loose end around her own right wrist but can't draw the knot tight enough, using just her teeth.

He reaches over to finish the job, lying on top of her as he grunts and strains to manipulate the fabric. Her face is pressed against the hairs twisting out of his bathrobe. He lifts his torso, just a bit, but it gives her a chance to shift her hips, and as she does, she kicks him, hard, in the shin.

"Fuck!" He whispers, reaching for his leg.

"Sorry."

"I'll bet." He rubs the bone vigorously. His elbow catches a green bowl at the edge of the mattress. It slides against the quilt and pitches over. Gobs of strawberry gelatin fly off the bed.

He leaps out of the way as the glutinous mess slips past his feet, and the empty bowl tumbles over the carpet. Its contents wiggle obscenely, staining the rug, with ivy and geraniums entwined in its wool. His face is red as columbine, red as the jello, when he pulls off his ski mask.

"Now see what you made me do?" He's breathing hard again.

So much for the platinum gym card.

She has to sit up to see over the edge of the mattress, but can't get up far enough with both wrists tied to the brass. She wriggles her right hand free of the knot without much trouble—he never was a boy scout—and props herself against the poles, ignoring the pressure on her backbone now. Globs of strawberry twinkle all over the rug like ripe berries in the ivy.

Does it stain? Judith thinks so. But she sees his face and lies.

"It's not that bad."

"So what are we going to use?"

"There's a bowl of chocolate pudding in the fridge."

"I didn't see it there."

"On the bottom shelf, behind the eggs."

"Were you hiding it?"

"Of course not. Would you like me to get it?"

The scarf around her left wrist is still knotted securely. "I'll go," *he says bravely.* "On the bottom shelf?"

"In a plastic bowl. The red one."

She calls the color after him, since he's already left the room. Over the murmur of the TV set, she listens to his feet on the carpeted stairs and then the noises from the kitchen as he bangs around, opening the sub-zero and searching through the jars of mayo and sauerkraut, the bottles of orange juice, white wine, and beer. She hears a crash—louder that it ought to be, whatever he's knocked over, reaching past the leftovers on the bottom shelf for the red plastic bowl of chocolate pudding.

Shattered glass. Then a thud.

"Walter? Are you all right?" *She tries to sit up straight, but the scarf around her left wrist is cinched pretty tight. It digs into her flesh, cutting the circulation to her hand. She flexes her fingers, which are puffy and stiff, when she hears his footsteps on the stairs again, slower than they sounded on the way down.*

When he enters the bedroom, he's in the same shabby bathrobe but a new mask. The black wool is gone, and in its place he's wearing the plastic face of Charlie the Chickadee, with a rubber band caught in his hair. The bird's stiff yellow head-feather and goofy grin look ridiculous over the terrycloth under his chin.

"Where'd you get that silly thing?"

No answer.

Beneath the hem of his bathrobe, the judge sees khaki trousers. She thought he was wearing his plaid pajamas, but she can't take her eyes from the mask. "Did you actually buy it?"

He moves closer to the bed.

11

She can't see any expression behind the Chickadee's grin except for his eyes, and there is definitely something odd about them. She tugs at the cover with her unbound right hand, but there's only so far it will go.

"Walter?"

He sits down on the edge of the mattress, near her face. He picks up one of the pillows and smoothes it across his lap. He ruffles its scalloped border with his fingertips, when the judge notices that both of his hands are free.

"Didn't you find the pudding?"

A spot of bright crimson glistens on the white terrycloth sleeve. No, more than one. A spatter.

"Is that ... blood?"

He brushes the flecks off his forearm.

She has seen blood before. Evidence. Her Honor Judith Frick, Judge of the Superior Court, has presided over criminal and civil actions. She has examined dried blood through plastic bags, tagged with the signature of the officer who collected it and the criminalist who analyzed it. Inspecting it with judicial detachment, evaluating its relevance and the chain of custody, in the daylight of her courtroom. In her bedroom, by the light of her lamp, it looks shockingly garish.

That's it—the color. His brown irises shouldn't be so dark.

She backs against the headboard and raises her right hand for protection. Her left is still bound to the bedpost. The eyes in the plastic slits are fixed on her, and the Chickadee's unwavering smirk looks downright creepy. Her voice sounds dry, when she hears herself ask, "Is it yours?"

He picks up the pillow and places it carefully over her face. She tastes the cotton pillowcase and feels the spongy foam inside it pressed against her teeth. She calls out Walter's name, loud as she can, though she can't manage the syllables and knows it isn't Walter on the far side of the pillow.

She flails her free hand, trying to strike the man, to punch his elbow and forearm, but he snags her right wrist and holds it against the mattress until it goes numb. But Judith can hardly feel that. She can't draw a breath through the hundred-thread cotton, and its whiteness in her eyes turns to black.

2

The world burst back into focus with a silent flash—a fat man in a wrinkled suit on one massive knee, weighing down the mattress at her feet. His lens stared right at her, ogling her armpits and the damp breasts clinging to her nightgown. A red-green imprint still floated in the air, when his flash exploded again. Her Honor felt another presence on her right periphery, smelling of sweat and camphor. Four fingers pulled the flannel hem down over her hips. The nails were cropped to the cuticle line in a clear polish, and the voice was firmly female.

"Okay, that's enough."

The knee came up, and the mattress. "I just got two."

"Two of those are enough, Hank."

A loose-limbed blonde was sitting on the bedside, squinting. Her eyes were green with a smear of blue-green shadow badly wiped off her eyelids. Peach lipstick was still caked in the cracks of her mouth, which was grimly determined and vaguely familiar. Her hair was pulled back in a ragged ponytail bound in a tortoise-shell clip. She wore a Gold's Gym T-shirt, faded gray and stained under her armpits, as if she had jogged all the way from South L.A. to the house in Cheviot Hills.

Judith's eyeballs throbbed as they slid back and forth. The floating after-image turned yellow-white but flashed across the blonde's face whenever Judith blinked. "That man just take my picture?"

Whose voice was that? Hoarse as a wino's. Her throat felt stuffed with straw. She tried to rise from the mattress, to prop herself on one elbow. But her left hand held her down, still bound by chiffon to the headboard.

The blonde set a palm on Judith's free shoulder, settling her down. "It's his job, Your Honor. Just one more shot, of the scarf. Are you all right?"

Judith didn't know. Her left arm was numb above her head. The whole left side of her body felt petrified.

"Could I have a glass of water?"

"Frank? Get us something to drink, please."

There were all sorts of men behind the blonde, standing around Judith's bedroom. Opening her drawers, eyeing the brushes on her dressing table, kneeling on her carpet. Frank brought a glass from the sink in the bathroom, and the blonde held it up to Judith's lips. The water tasted ice-cold when she sipped it.

The blonde set the glass on the night table, using the doily under the lamp for a coaster. "My name is Newman. Lieutenant Patricia Newman. A doctor's on the way, right now. You've been through a traumatic event." She spoke in a rhythm, deliberately calm, as she tugged at the fabric swelling the judge's wrist. "Someone did a job on this, didn't they?"

"It's a square knot," said Judith, twisting round her elbow. "A simple double loop. Left over right, then right over left."

Newman spread the loose end over her palm and traced a broken line in the fabric. Curved like a moon. Teeth marks. "Did you tie this yourself?"

Judith flushed, nodding.

Newman stuck a ballpoint pen into the heart of the knot and worked it until the scarf came loose. The skin underneath had been rubbed raw, but the real pain gripped her armpit when Judith lowered her arm.

"Easy," said Newman. "Let me help."

She cradled the injured forearm and laid it across Judith's stomach. The nap of flannel made her wrist sting, but the words were starting to register.

"A police lieutenant?"

"Can you flex your fingers?"

She could—stiffly, but the blood was flowing into them again. A man on his knees was crawling backwards, scraping dried jello off the rug and saving it in a plastic bag. Judith drew a breath that turned into a shudder. "Is he ... is this a crime scene?"

Newman nodded slowly.

Judith couldn't recall something that happened to her. She saw a pair of khakis, not pajamas, and felt a brush of wiry hair against her cheek and mouth. She tried to chase the feeling out of her mind but suddenly pictured—

"Walter?" She sat up, and felt a pair of needles knit up her eyebrows.

"We have him downstairs."

"Is he all right?"

Squinting. "We'll know more when the doctor arrives."

Was she raped? Judith shifted her thighs. No soreness or pain. Was the doctor coming for Walter, then? The lieutenant looked past her uncomfortably. Something was not being said.

"I'm a judge," said Judith.

"I know that, Ma'am. I testified in your court. Not like this." Her gesture took in her outfit—a T-shirt and bicycle shorts, track shoes without socks. "I was out for a run when I got the call. When they told me whose home was broken into and how they found you, I didn't stop to shower and change."

What time was that? The clock read two-forty.

Newman followed her gaze. "Nothing like a run to help you sleep," she shrugged. "We all have our little habits."

It was almost a confession, carefully worded to show respect with something else in the tone. Disapproval? If those cracked lips had curled in any direction, Her Honor would have known how to respond, but Newman was working hard to conceal any hint of an attitude. Judith studied her face, all angles and eyes. And finally placed it.

She saw Detective Newman's green eyes lined in fresh mascara, her lips rouged carefully in a workday rose. She wore a cream silk shirt with a rounded collar and ivory jacket with matching skirt hemmed an inch above her knee.

Newman was already up-and-coming at the time; you could tell by the way she tucked in the hairs of her upswept coil, or sat in the witness box with her hands in her lap, like a schoolgirl who knew her legs looked good in a pleated skirt and knee socks. She wore her going-to-court suit proudly, like a uniform with a new stripe sewn on the sleeve. Except the stripes were hidden in the linen now. She had earned her plainclothes jacket and was in no hurry to change back into blues.

"The Scanlon case."

Newman turned her head to profile as if she were a suspect in a line-up.

The details of the case rushed back into Judith's mind:

Isador Scanlon is a homeless head-case off his meds in Rite-Aid. It takes three officers to subdue him in the aisle and drag him, kicking and biting, to the parking lot —where they teach the man a lesson with their nightsticks and shoe leather. Two rookies and a sergeant. Newman is still a sergeant herself, who reviews the drug-store's video and challenges the defense claim that Mr. Scanlon was subject to excessive force by the training officer. What was his name? Not Hoffman exactly, like Heffner or Heffalump. Herman Hoeffler.

15

Judith might have forgotten what she did the night before, but she remembered every motion of the Scanlon case.

Sergeant Patricia Newman draws every eye as she steps up to the witness box. Her demure ivory outfit only serves to accentuate her natural advantages. The upswept bun shows off her long, white neck. The hem of her skirt and the low but pointed heels frame a shapely pair of calves. Even the soft fabric of her blouse draws attention to her figure, which the ladies journals once called 'high-bosomed' and the men's magazines call 'stacked.' The clip of her heels on the courtroom floor, and the swing of her hips as she slides onto the hard wooden bench, all convey more confidence than any officer ought to assume in Judith Frick's courtroom.

Her Honor interjects a few pertinent questions of her own.

Sergeant Newman concedes that police officers do sometimes over-react. Unless you've worn a uniform, it's hard to imagine how often cops are provoked. She honestly couldn't say how long she herself might have stood for the kicks and bites of Mr. Scanlon, whose decision to spit out his meds that morning was responsible—wasn't it?—for the fit he threw in Rite-Aid. Hermie Hoeffler had a moon-shaped scar on his right palm from Mr. Scanlon's teeth. It might not be the ideal response we hope to see from the police, but it's understandable—isn't it?—how a person might react with a little too much zeal, in dragging a wild-man away from law-abiding citizens.

'And the epithets?' asks the A.D.A. 'What about the things he swore at Scanlon, when he spat at him on the ground?'

'Jokes,' Sergeant Newman swears under oath. 'Hermie Hoeffler spits and makes bad jokes when he's pissed. He's never had a dry sense of humor.' Her grin brings the jurors in on the joke.

Judith is not amused. That's what she says, in four crisp words, and that's what they say about her, for a year, in the squad cars and locker rooms of the precinct houses. 'Her Honor is not amused.' Shorthand for all the support and understanding blues never get from the bench. Followed by your choice of expletive. Their nickname—the Frick—is none too respectful, either.

Now this same Patricia Newman was assigned to investigate Her Honor's home invasion? Or was it worse than that? For the first time since she opened her eyes, Judith shivered and reached for the quilt at the foot of her bed.

"You've been promoted."

Newman murmured, "To Homicide."

16

With a hint in her voice … of pride? Or a threat? Judith guessed there was more vanity under that ponytail than the sweaty shirt and sneakers implied.

"Congratulations."

The Lieutenant nodded and stood, releasing the edge of the quilt under her thigh. "We'll take a statement from you later," she said with a glance that added, *when you've had a chance to make yourself decent.*

Judith felt a wash of relief, followed by a blast of fatigue. The muscles in her jaw and neck felt like rusted cables. She couldn't wait to get these people out of her bedroom. And Walter? Was he even still in the house? A lump rose from the bottom of her throat, cutting off her air. She opened her mouth and wheezed, forcing the clammy breath out of her lungs—

"There is one thing I need to ask, while it's still fresh in your mind."

And filled them up again. "Go ahead."

Newman's eyes narrowed, though she asked casually, "When exactly did you tie yourself to the bed?"

3

"My wife doesn't want to fuck me," Jerry Schiller said, as he closed one kitchen drawer and opened another.

He was talking to "Mac" Macaulay, the coroner's five-foot-two assistant, whose chief contribution to their working relationship was that he rarely had anything to say. Macaulay's mother had probably given him an actual first name, but since he never said an unnecessary word, no one knew what it was. Now little Mac just grunted, kneeling over Walter Frick's dead body, trying to take the liver temperature without disturbing the steak knife stuck upside down in his solar plexus.

Jerry Schiller on the other hand was called "Four-One-One" or "Four" for short, since he was always full of doubtful information. This came in two varieties: unsolicited accounts of his personal challenges, and odd facts he had picked up on the Internet. He was also a first-rate criminalist, which counterbalanced a host of personal quirks. His lips moved as he silently counted first the forks, then the spoons, and then the silver knives, which did not match the steak knife between the dead man's ribs.

When he finished, he jotted down his counts and said, "Sheila does—fuck me, I mean, not want to—but it's only because she doesn't want me to go out and fuck anybody else. But, you know, there's nothing less erotic than a woman who doesn't want to fuck you. I have to think about somebody else, just to get a hard-on. So she's sitting on top of me, not wanting to be bouncing up there, and I'm lying under her, thinking of somebody else. And that's what they call love-making."

Ninety-two point four," said Mac, reading off his thermometer. A dead body loses heat at a constant rate, a degree and a half per hour in normal room temperature. The Frick kitchen was a little cooler than seventy-six degrees, so the difference between ninety-two-point-four and ninety-eight-point-six degrees Fahrenheit meant the murder had taken place almost four hours earlier. Sometime around eleven o'clock.

"I'm not proud of myself," said Schiller, "but what can I do? When I see that flat look of boredom in her eyes, and know she doesn't want to fuck me, I lose all interest. I'd rather fuck a duck. Did you know that certain breeds of ducks can screw right in the air, on their way to South America? They don't even have to touch down to do it. Now that's what I call a mile-high club."

Little Mac grunted, which could have resulted from resettling himself alongside the body. Schiller heard it as a sympathetic cluck of agreement.

"Too bad we're not ducks," shaking his head. "What's good for the goose and all. Though geese are not really ducks, are they?"

Little Mac made no reply.

"I thought not. Too bad for the ganders," Schiller sighed and turned at a squeak of sneaker on the stairs behind them.

The kitchen tiles were stained brown, when Patricia Newman came downstairs. She stood on the final step, peering down at the goo that had pooled against the riser. Four-One-One saw her face and grinned. He squatted down, touched the stuff and held up his gloved finger for Newman to sniff. She just stared at it, so he stuck his finger in his mouth and licked his lips.

"Pudding." Cracking a broken smile.

Newman's nose wrinkled as she surveyed the room.

The kitchen was done in California Spanish contemporary, which meant baskets from Oaxaca, fabrics from Bolivia, ceramic tile from Peru, and a steel sub-zero fridge with double-thick glass in its door. The stove was a black restaurant range big enough to fix a family of twelve each a different dinner, while as far as she knew, there were only two of them living in the house. There was a pine island in the middle of the room with a sink and chopping block built into it. Walter Frick's body lay beside the island, face up, in his plaid pajama bottoms and nothing else—except a steak knife with a wooden handle sticking out of his belly.

It was a round belly. The man could've used a Stairmaster. The serrated edge of the knife rippled upward from his waist, facing his solar plexus.

"What can you tell me, Four?"

The criminalist pointed at some bright drops on the floor. "Those are blood," he told her. "You see how round they are? Passive stains, pulled straight down by gravity. From their splatter I'd say they fell about thirty-six inches from the wound. But these"—indicating a couple of drop-shaped stains a few inches away—"are projected. The tip of the teardrop always points away from the position of impact. So, if we follow them back, and watch where their lines cross those on the far side, Mr. Frick must've been standing here, with his assailant right in front of him."

"Close?"

19

"Enough to stick him in the belly without more projected stains that we see here," said Schiller. "A friendly little stab, from a foot or two away."

Newman nodded. She was used to hearing him talk like this, as if the dead man were not a few feet away, staring at the ceiling.

"Think he knew the stabber?"

Schiller shrugged. "Eleven o'clock in his kitchen?"

They both knew that homicides in a private residence usually point first to the spouse. The exceptions—a home invasion, say—left a mess of broken glass, forced locks, and shattered doorjambs. Except for the blood and chocolate pudding, the Frick kitchen looked awfully neat.

Newman nodded gravely. It made her ponytail bounce up and down behind her. "This how you found the place?"

The criminalist waved at a door in the rear of the kitchen, with four panes of glass in a white wooden frame. "The back door was open when we got here, and the dog was in the yard. That's what got a neighbor out of bed to complain—the dog barking its balls off in the yard, which, they said, never happens. The duty officer sent around a cruiser, who got no response to the front doorbell, peeked through the kitchen window, and called in the marines."

He meant the Crime Scene Unit and Lieutenant Patricia Newman from Homicide. "Any sign of a surprised burglar?"

Schiller's head wobbled. "If anybody broke in, he didn't come to steal. No reason to hang around the kitchen, if you're after the plasma screen in the den."

"Is it still there?"

"Plugged in and mounted on the wall."

"What about the alarm?"

"It wasn't set." She gave him a hopeful look, until Four said, "But I wouldn't read too much into that. Most people don't set their security alarms 'til they're ready for bed, when lots of folks forget, or don't bother. Especially smokers."

"Are they smokers?"

"One of them is, or was. There's tobacco ash on a flagstone just outside the door and three squashed butts in the flowerbed."

"How do you know there's one smoker?"

Four gave her a patient smile. "Why would anybody light up in the cold?"

"Their spouse doesn't like smoke in the house."

He nodded. "Smokers don't set the security alarm until after they've had a last chance to step outside."

"And fill their lungs with one last snort of noxious carcinogens."

"That's one way to think about it."

"Okay," said Newman, in deference to Four's own fondness for cigars. He had given her a talk about them, hadn't he? On Winston Churchill Blenheims, named for his grandfather's castle, where Sir Winston was born? Schiller thought he had, but before he could check, she said, "So, no burglar alarm. Are you sure the back door is the point of entry?"

"If you're thinking break-in. The first floor windows are all secure, and the front door faces a public street. Nobody's going to break in that way, when they have a nice, convenient back door to pop in peace and quiet."

It did look private. "Any evidence of forced entry?"

"Take a peek."

It wasn't an invitation, if she wanted to hear any more. He followed her to the door, but when Newman knelt to inspect the lock, Schiller kept standing.

"Pulled my groin in the can," he said, rubbing his thigh.

She opened the door, preventing his explanation. Then she shut it again, testing the knob, doorframe, and jamb. "The glass panels aren't broken. The wood isn't split. But what are those marks?"

Leaning over her shoulder, Jerry caught a whiff, sharp and sweet. Perspiration. "Scratches, I'd say."

"Could the lock have been picked?"

He squinted and shook his head. "You see their direction?"

"What direction? They're all over the place."

"Instead of focused inside the lock and around its edges. You can't open a door by poking it with a stick."

Newman accepted his offered hand but rose to her feet without leaning on it. She reached down with the same hand to brush off her knees.

"So the lock wasn't picked?"

"Someone might've tried, who didn't know how, or who wanted to make it look like he didn't," Schiller said. "Nobody had to break in. Why should they? Nothing was stolen. Just to talk?"

"Maybe to murder," said Newman. "Someone with a grudge—an ex-con getting even with Her Honor, or a neighbor jealous about her petunias."

"Premeditated?"

"Maybe."

"The killer didn't bring a weapon."

"You're sure of that?"

"The knife came from the drawer. I counted."

He glanced toward the drawers until she opened one. It had a set of matching silverware arranged in felt-lined compartments, forks, knives, and spoons. Schiller shut that drawer and opened the one beside it, revealing a gift box of gleaming steak knives with wooden handles and serrated steel blades.

"The same set," Newman observed, comparing their grips to the one rising from Walter Frick's corpse.

"The same *pattern*," Four corrected her. "The killer could've brought a matching knife, if he knew what they looked like. If he had dinner here, let's say."

"Except he didn't?"

Schiller loved these tutorials. "There are sixteen forks in the silverware drawer. Fifteen soup spoons, sixteen teaspoons, and sixteen silver knives, with rounded tips. The steak knives belong to a separate set, you see, in the next drawer over. But only fifteen knives are in there now."

She looked at the victim. "And one makes sixteen."

"Right," said Schiller. "Which means the killer didn't bring a weapon. Because who goes through the drawers when you've got a knife in your pocket?"

"Nobody."

"And why go searching for any kind of knife, if you've brought your own Glock? Or even, say, a blackjack?"

"No reason at all," said Newman, looking increasingly perplexed. Had the killer come to the house unprepared? Or was it an impulse killing? Four had a theory—he waited for her ask, but she just said, "So nobody broke in and nobody brought a weapon. Is that what we've got?"

"Two points already, wouldn't you say?"

"Walter Frick—what? Knew his killer and let him in the door. Then watched him go through the drawers 'til he found a knife he liked and stuck it into his host's belly? That's what you're trying to tell me?"

He was a little offended by her tone, but at four o'clock in the morning he could make allowances. "It's one possibility. Take a closer look at the victim."

He strolled over to the body, clasped his hands behind his back, and leaned over the belly wound. It was still seeping into the clotted hairs, turning the white ones dark. Little Mac had already finished with the *corpus*; Newman knelt in the space the coroner's assistant had occupied.

She saw a dead body, face up, with a knife in its belly.

"Notice anything?" asked Four, hovering. His nostrils flared just inches over the knife's handle—his way of giving a clue.

Newman peered at the entry wound. The knife was less than a foot long from its handle to the entry point in Walter Frick's pale flesh. Its wooden handle was fastened to a steel serrated blade, which looked finely sharpened and substantial. But—he hoped she noticed— its jagged edge did not point down, toward the belly. It pointed up, toward the victim's heart.

He was gratified when the lieutenant ran her gloved finger along its cutting edge. Sharp enough, through the rubber.

"It does the most damage that way," Schiller said in confirmation. "An upward stroke, between the ribs, angled close to the heart."

Newman tried to picture it. "The killer held the blade upside down?"

"Probably," said Schiller. "They could've stabbed him from above while he lay on the ground, holding the knife in his fist, like they do in Slasher films. But Frick would have to be flat on his back, and how did they get him to lie down? Little Mac found no sign of blunt force trauma. I'd guess an assailant stood in front of Frick, holding the thing like they do in a knife fight, with the business edge up."

"You're not thinking a gang killing?"

"Not unless the Harvard Club threw down against Yale. Kids on the street don't turn the blade around. You need some know-how to do that. A little medical knowledge, or criminal experience—some kind of training to get past how they do it in the movies. Check out the angle of penetration."

The blade was standing up, but not at ninety degrees. It tilted slightly to his left—which meant a right-handed killer must have stood face-to-face, close enough to stick the shaft into the victim's gut.

"Now, who do you think Walter Frick trusted enough to do that?"

Newman's eyes went to the ceiling. "Not her?"

23

"You're the one who talked to her. Do you think she could?"

Newman studied the rafters. Her Honor *could*. But would she? Knowing what she did about forensic science and police procedure, how could she imagine getting away with cold-blooded murder?

Schiller read the question in her face. His shoulders rose and fell. "Lady praying mantises start eating their hubbies before they're even done mating. Eating them alive. That's why I buy 'em dinner, first."

4

"I told you, already," said Aisha Adams, laying her big hand on Jack's forearm. He felt the tips of her stick-on nails but could make out only a sparkling blur of bright colors. "Trust me, baby. Nobody's come out yet."

Aisha was a big-boned girl with a pretty face—that's how Maggie described her. As far as Jack could tell, she used to have a very pretty face, before someone stained it across her jawline from neck to cheekbone with what looked like a splash of *café au lait* against her bittersweet chocolate complexion. What had splashed across Aisha's face had not been milk but something that smoked when you lifted the stopper from its thick glass jar. He had Maggie's word on that, but Jack was in no position to question Aisha's credentials as a driver or anything else, since their arrangement was working out better than he expected.

"I heard a bell," Jack insisted, squinting.

"In-side," said Aisha, her voice fading as she turned her head toward the interior of the café. "Your omelet's on the counter, waiting for a pick up."

He heard the zip of nylon and pictured her crossing her long black legs. She had given up hot pants at least, though her running shorts hardly covered more territory. Still, the halter with Kobe Bryant's number on her back fit in better on Montclair Avenue than the sports bra and peek-a-boo shorts she liked to wear on the stroll.

"I ordered a scramble."

"That's what you said to the girl. Only you pointed to the omelets on the menu. Which one you think she scribbled on her pad?"

Jack sat silently for a moment, blinking behind his black wraparounds. He had to stop pretending he could see more than he could—to stop believing what he wanted to be true. The waitress came back with a Mexican omelet, a rolled corn tortilla and a cup of mango salsa. She set them down in front of him on the table, close enough for his fingers to feel the warm edge of the plate.

"I'll get you some more coffee," she told Aisha. "What about him?"

"Ask him yourself," said Aisha. "He's blind, not deaf."

"I'm fine," said Jack, as if he had been asked, though the truth was he didn't know how much was left in his cup. He ran his pinky along the inside until it touched liquid, lukewarm and halfway down. Fine enough.

The waitress moved away and the daylight grew brighter. Jack saw blurs of white and silver moving past with the purr of expensive engines, and blobs of pink and brown passing by on the sidewalk. Snatches of conversation resolved into voices at the tables around them. A mother and daughter behind them were arguing about a little black dress with a satin bodice that was or was not too tight.

He heard Aisha scrape the wrought iron legs of her chair on the patio flagstones. Turning around. "What is it?"

"Jesus, Jack. I'm just making myself comfortable."

"You are not. Tell me what you see."

"Just some guy going by."

"What kind of guy?"

"Young. Okay, maybe he's sexy. All right?"

Jack listened to his sandals slap the pavement. "No way."

"Uh huh. Slim and trim. Works out. With a three-day beard and a black t-shirt that has a thirty-eight and a rose—"

"From a tour? Maybe Guns 'n' Roses?"

"Could be."

"Thirty-five? Forty?"

"Thirty. With crinkly blue eyes and wavy brown hair."

He listened harder, to the pace—shuffling by, slap-slap, slap-slap. Impossible. Then he heard a squeak. "Pushing a stroller?"

She didn't sound surprised any more when she said, "That's right."

"Nobody's sexy with a stroller. There's no way to look cool when you're pushing a two-year old down the block." The kid in the seat started kicking and cooing, which quickly turned into squirming and squealing. Jack grinned. "Either one of the wheels has turned inside out, or Mr. Filf has a potty problem. Either way I'd guess he's sinking fast on the sex-o-meter."

"That's some paternal instinct, you've got," said Aisha.

"A poor thing," he conceded, "but my own."

Across the street, the doors flung open and a crowd of kids ran out through the chain-link fence of Lincoln Elementary School. Their parents sat waiting in minivans and SUVs, like an expeditionary force preparing to invade the private homes north of Montana Avenue. Except most of the vehicles had rolled out of— and would return to—those million-dollar driveways, once they picked up the kids running through the gate like rats from a fumigated building.

Jack heard the kids laughing and complaining as they paired off for play-dates, karate and ballet classes. When the last of them had been seat-belted into luxury trucks and vans, Aisha stood, five foot ten in her spiked heels.

"Come on, tough guy. Nothing more to see here. Let's move."

Jack shook his head. "Not today, Aisha."

"You want another cup?"

"Maybe. But you don't have to wait. I'll see you tomorrow, at the house."

He heard her foot tap. "You're staying without me?"

"That's right."

"No, that's wrong. Unless—you got a date?"

"I wouldn't call it that."

"You going to meet a woman?"

"I guess." Though *meet* wasn't the right word exactly.

"Then that's what you call it. Hell, that's what I call a *blow job*. Five minutes, maybe, but it's still a date."

"I'm not paying you for five minutes. I'm paying you by the hour—"

"To keep you from walking into the street."

"To keep me company. And I won't be needed your services this hour. You'll still get paid for the rest of the day."

"In that case," Aisha swung her big purse over her shoulder, "you can keep your secret, Jack. Nobody needs to tell me twice, when I'm getting paid for doing nothing. I'll pick you up tomorrow, like you said, ten o'clock at your place."

Aisha waved at the waitress and strode down the sidewalk, swinging more than her bag. Stripes of purple and gold bounced with her limbs. Then the world closed in around Jack again, a haze of bleary color streaked by the shaft of light from a water glass. He lifted his wraparounds and rubbed his eyes.

Without Aisha, Montana Avenue was a cacophony of noises and odors he couldn't quite identify. A crash of metal could be life-threatening or the lid falling off a garbage can. It might have been easier if Jack had been born blind, with forty-two years to learn Braille and make better use of his hearing. He had spent nearly all of his first four months on disability in a hospital room or the tiny backyard of his house in Venice, waiting for his sight—until Maggie Malloy decided it was time for him to get out and hired Aisha to help him do it. To *force* him to do it was more accurate, but by now even Jack could see the wisdom in Maggie's matchmaking.

27

With a ragged blotch on her face and neck, Aisha couldn't earn on the streets—and Jack hadn't ventured past his mailbox. It hadn't taken a week to get used to her. Now, within minutes of chasing her off, he felt Aisha's absence as soon as the waitress set down the check. It arrived in a metal cup, near his elbow. He could put his credit card in and sign the printed slip, but how was he supposed to figure twenty percent for a tip? Sitting at a table on Montana Avenue was the first time Jack had been out on the street, nearly blind and entirely alone.

But he wasn't alone for long. Ten minutes after Aisha sashayed down the block, he heard the tap-tap-tap of expensive heels and a shapely blur of pearl-grey silk occupied her seat.

"Hello, Jack," said Judith in her best courtroom voice.

5

Jack would have recognized that tone anywhere. He had heard it every day that he worked for the District Attorney's office, and every night for the final three months, once things got sticky between them.

Mrs. Walter Frick had been Ms. Judith Harrow, then. She used a soft, personal whisper when they first met, and a hard, professional voice to cross-examine suspects on the witness stand. When he heard her *I'm-just-curious* voice on the other side of his bed, he knew their nights of lovemaking were numbered. Jack would never have brought that up now, so why was she using her courtroom voice on sunny Montana Avenue? Judith had phoned *him*, not the other way around. He knew enough to be sure she hadn't called out of nostalgia. She wanted something from him. But what did she expect to get, using her courtroom voice?

"Hello, Your Honor," said Jack. "Want a coffee?"

Judith shook her head and bit her lip. Something she used to do when she said more than she intended. She must have known from his face that she hadn't started well. She settled in her seat, raised her chin, and tried again. "How *are* you, Jack? It's been some time, hasn't it? I heard about your accident—though that's not really the right word, is it? You're a national hero."

The voice was better this time, softer, but she was talking too fast. Flattering him. "I never got to meet Oprah."

She flushed. "A local hero, then. The Times covered it, didn't they?"

"Page twelve," he said. "You noticed."

"I looked for it," she confessed, "once I heard about it at the courthouse. You went in after a child, they said. Is that true?"

Jack thought he would want to talk about it, but he didn't, really, when it came right down to it, sitting across a café table from Judy Harrow Frick.

"What did you come for, Judith? I'm glad to see you again, of course—I should say, to hear you. I'm sure you look terrific. You always do. But there's a reason we're here today, isn't there? Or you would have said *yes* or *no* to coffee, one way or the other. You didn't even hear my offer to buy you a cup."

"I heard it, Jack. I'll have a tea, if it means that much."

She was using his name, repeating it, because she knew what it did to him. Jack shook his head. "We could chit-chat, if you like. Talk about Walter first, his bank and your calendar. I could tell you my story about busting up a meth lab. But you wouldn't be able to focus on any of it, would you?—while you worked around to something. So why don't you tell me what's on your mind?"

"Don't be so suspicious, Jack. Can't I just feel like seeing you, as one old friend to another?"

"Is that really the case you want to make?"

She laughed, but it didn't come off. She sounded nervous, as if he might say *No*. "You could always see through me, couldn't you, Jack?"

A subtler attempt to flatter him. Jack had to hand it to her. She had shrugged off his rebuke with a fake little smile. Either she regretted some part of their life together, or she needed him badly. But what could she possibly need from him now? His curiosity was getting the better of him.

"Not always," he insisted under his breath and tried to make out her expression. He could imagine every line of her face but couldn't read her reaction—until she reached across the table and tapped his wrist. Her touch was light as a falling leaf, but the shock of it ran up his shoulder. "Not all the way through."

She shivered, despite the warm afternoon. "All right, Jack, I'll tell you," she said, "whatever you want to know."

"You need something, don't you? That's why you're here?"

"That's right," she said, looking away, though she needn't have bothered. He couldn't see her eyes anyway. The laughter was gone and the courtroom voice was gone, and for a moment she sounded like herself at the end of a trying day. "I do need help. And there's no one I can turn to except you."

He would have laughed, if he could. But he didn't have the breath, and she didn't give him the chance.

"They think I murdered Walter," she said. "Can you believe it?"

"Your Walter?"

"He's *dead*," Judith said, with a stifled sob. "Someone broke into our place and caught him in the kitchen."

"And killed him on the Spanish tile? Why would they do that?"

"A burglary, I guess, or something to do with his business."

"Is that what Homicide thinks?"

"They're working a couple of theories," Judith told him. "But their questions have taken a turn, and I see the way they look at me."

"Who?"

"A fresh young thing—Patricia Newman. Do you know her?"

Jack shook his head. He had heard about Newman, when she made lieutenant, but they had never worked together, and you never really knew another officer until you walked alongside her rubber soles.

Judith made a noise in her throat. "Very careful, very smart, but not very likely to succeed. I'm afraid she doesn't approve of me."

"Of the Honorable Judith Frick?"

"We have some personal history," Judith confessed, "which shouldn't make any difference, of course. But in this case, it does."

"Judith," he said, "I'm practically blind. Haven't you noticed? I can barely make you out, across the table."

"I heard, Jack. I'd still rather have you on a case, blind as a mole, than any other investigator. But I'm not asking you to do anything that might jeopardize your disability. You don't have to take on the case, or even look into it."

"Then what?"

She swallowed. "Just *talk* to this woman Newman and let her know about me. My likes and dislikes, the kind of thing we used to do together, when you and I were ... "

"Screwing?"

"I was going to say intimate, but that's the general idea. Lovers."

The word sounded fanciful. "Is that what we were?"

Judith hesitated. "We can't go into it now, Jack. Please—just tell her what you remember of our time together. What I liked, the things we did."

"In the sack?"

"The bastard came into my bedroom, Jack! And scared me half to death. Put a pillow over my head and left me tied to the bedpost."

"That must have been awful," Jack said, then added, "though not an entirely unfamiliar position."

"That's why I need your help," she said earnestly. "You know these things about me. Newman knows I tied the knot, but not when or why. She thinks I stabbed Walter with a steak knife from the kitchen drawer, went upstairs, and tied myself to the bedpost to make it look like an intruder."

"While I know that you've been tying yourself in knots for years," Jack replied. "Is that what you need from me? An alibi in bondage?"

"It wasn't all my doing, as I recall, Jack. You got pretty worked up yourself." Judith rubbed her wrist wistfully. "Your knots were gently but firmly tied. There must have been something behind them."

"There was," he said, "at the time. You don't need any help from me. Just show her your lashing and half-hitch."

"But I do, Jack. You're the only one who can convince her I didn't kill Walter, because you're the only cop who knows from first-hand experience what used to happen behind our bedroom door. You do remember, don't you?"

Of course he remembered. How could he forget? Their sex life had taught him more than he cared to admit about his own desires. There was nothing wrong with it, she used to insist, when two adults consented and nobody got hurt. Plenty of powerful men sought relief from their responsibilities by asking a dominatrix to take total control. Why shouldn't a powerful woman want the same escape?

"You will help me, won't you, Jack? Because I'm afraid that Lieutenant Newman doesn't approve of a woman in my position enjoying a little submissive time or even—heaven forbid!—some careful strokes of discipline. And her personal disapproval might land me in a very public prison."

Jack would have liked to see the fine lines of her face when she said that. They might have told him what to believe. Her voice sounded strained enough, with that catch in the back of her throat. The fact she had turned to him meant she was certainly desperate. And yet, if his time with Judith had taught him anything about her, she wasn't saying more than she was.

"I should do this little favor for you, because—?"

"Because at one point we meant something to each other, didn't we? You know me better than anyone, Jack. You know I didn't kill Walter. That's the truth. And if there's one thing you love more than you ever loved me, it's the truth."

6

Jack had an easier time than he expected getting in to see Lieutenant Newman. She had a glass-walled office in the Westside Division headquarters on the second floor, over the beat cops. There were half a dozen detectives on the floor, including a couple of sergeants, but no one was surprised when she took the case herself. Every badge in the station knew the story of Patricia Newman's testimony on behalf of Sergeant Hoeffler and the reception it received from fricking Frick. Now they were watching, quietly waiting for the tables of justice to turn.

He expected her to smell fresh-scrubbed, of soap. But there was something else, floral—lavender. Toilet water? Or simply shampoo?

"You're Jack Stryker, aren't you?" Newman said, when he sat in a wicker chair in her office, wearing his dark glasses. The Lieutenant came out from behind her desk to shake his hand. She was wearing a white blouse with a beige skirt. The matching jacket hung behind her door. When she sat on the front edge of her desk and crossed her legs demurely, Jack noticed the strangest shoes—brown blurs with heels that clicked against the wooden desk, and orange tips.

He had left his cane downstairs with Aisha, who was kneeling on a hard bench, reading wanted posters off the public board. But even on his own, without a cane, Jack couldn't duck the inevitable question. No sooner had he settled his weight into the straw visitor's chair than she asked, "Is it true? Did you really waltz into a crack-house with a shoulder-holster forty-five to pull out a hooker's Bi-O-U?"

Bio-Owe-You—a child for a marker. By her voice he couldn't tell if she thought it the courageous act of a hero cop or the reckless move of a cowboy-in-blue. The story was already losing details. He found them cooking crank, not crack. Jack raised his dark glasses and squinted at her.

"A nine-mil. Beretta. What gave me away?"

"I looked you up." She tapped a file on her desk that must have been his, though he couldn't make out the label. No sign she caught the joke he made—a little dry maybe, but still, no sign. He let his glasses drop to the bridge of his nose. "How are your eyes?" she asked, too late.

"The doctors keep saying *patience,* as if they expect a recovery."

What he actually saw was a blonde halo ringing a blur of pink and cotton-candy sugar blue mascara. A flicker of green when her eyes moved and a gash of red lipstick when she said, "You have to stay positive."

"I'm a great hoper," said Jack. "Any anybody."

"If you don't mind, I have a few questions about the incident."

He had run into this before. Professional curiosity. Cops wondering why he had done what he did, and whether they might have done it too. Mostly the answer was *no*, and they looked at him suspiciously. The truth was that he did mind, but Jack could put up with two or three questions, if they earned him a few in return.

"Such as?"

"Who was the mother of the kid in the lab?"

"A strawberry named Cherise."

"Your C.I.?"

He shook his head. "Just a crack whore working a doorway to score her next hit. You must have a few of those around, even here on the west side."

"Not really," said Newman seriously. If she was making a wry face, Jack couldn't see it. "An old friend, maybe, from your days in Vice?"

"No one I knew."

"She must have known you, though. A whore doesn't come up to a cop and ask for his personal help without some reason to believe he might be receptive. She might go into the station, if she's desperate enough, and file a complaint with the desk sergeant ... but to approach a plainclothes detective on the street? You must have some acquaintance in common, at least."

"Maybe we do," he agreed, to shut her up.

"Maggie Malloy?" asked Newman.

She knew about her too? "Maggie doesn't associate with that kind of girl."

"But you do, I understand. With all kinds. Enough to raise a few questions."

"If you've been through my file, you know that Internal Affairs cleared me of any impropriety. It was a bogus charge from the start. They made a lot of noise, but when they looked into it, they concluded there was no truth to it."

"They said there was no *evidence*," Newman corrected him, "that you gave anyone advanced warning about the raid. Except Ms. Malloy had her gloves on, and the girls were fully dressed, playing bridge, when they broke down the door."

"Pinochle," he said. "Not bridge. You'd better check your file."

"I read it pretty carefully," Newman told him. Then she said in a different voice, "Is there something wrong with my feet?"

Can blind men stare? Jack took a shot. "Toenails?"

"Yes. They're polished."

"Orange?"

"Cantaloupe." She recrossed her legs. "Your career got off to a strong start, didn't it? I might have called it *impressive*. A special investigator for the D.A. by the time you were twenty-eight."

"I caught a few breaks in my salad days."

"Luck had nothing to do with it," Newman insisted. "An outstanding arrest record, with commendations from your training officer and patrol sergeant. Detective Sergeant by thirty-two ... and didn't I see a medal of valor somewhere?"

"I don't know what you saw."

"It's right here." She drew a page from his file. "You pulled a wounded officer out of the line of fire."

"Anybody would've done the same for his partner."

"No, they wouldn't. They shouldn't. It's against policy—even reckless. A good way to lose two officers instead of one."

What the hell was she driving at? This interview wasn't going the way Jack planned. He looked at the window but saw only bright panes of light. "To tell you the truth, Lieutenant, I can't remember what I was thinking. It was a long time ago."

"Ten years."

"Feels like forty."

"Those were the Jews in the wilderness."

"Right. Mine weren't as dry."

"Water under the bridge, is that it? Because the part I don't get is the next step. Why does a young cop on the fast track to the brass suddenly resign from the D.A.'s office? Tanking his brilliant career?"

"I never said I was ambitious, did I? Or smart about department politics. I was looking for a change of pace, that's all."

"In Vice?"

"You meet a better class of people in Vice."

"Better than what?"

"Better than the white collar cases the D.A. had me working. At least in Vice you know when a citizen's screwed."

Newman never blinked. "But you didn't stay there, either."

"I got restless," said Jack. "Did you ever work Vice, Lieutenant? It gets to you, watching people succumb to their weaknesses. At least it got to me, busting them for acting on impulses they couldn't

35

control. It might not be a problem for someone like you, with no personal weaknesses of her own."

"I never said I had no personal challenges." Newman flushed. "Though I'm not about to start listing them now."

"Then why don't we talk about Judith Frick?" Jack suggested.

"Speaking of personal weaknesses?"

"If you like."

She didn't seem surprised. Or opposed to the idea. Jack went on, "You're working her husband's homicide, I understand."

"From the judge herself? She told you that?"

"Yes. As a friend."

"Another acquaintance," Newman noted, "who came to you – for what? Legal advice? Or is there something else she asked you to tell me?"

"Sorry, Lieutenant," he shook his head, "but she didn't kill her husband."

"You have her word on that?"

"Her history," he said. "We worked together in the D.A.'s office. Judith was an A.D.A., out of Hastings. I was a senior investigator."

"Sounds cozy," said Newman. "Work a lot of nights together?"

"When we had to," said Jack, surprised by how quickly Newman was jumping to the right conclusions. "Days and nights."

"I'll bet she asked a ton of questions," Newman said.

"Trying to learn her craft."

The Lieutenant shook her head. "That's one thing Judith Harrow never had to be taught. Craft."

Jack sat forward in his wicker chair. "Why are you so sure about her – so sure she did her husband? If you had any physical evidence, she'd be under arrest by now. What are you going on? Instinct?"

"Did she tell you how we found her?"

"Tied to the bedpost?"

"She told you that too? You must be old friends."

"I've seen her there. In fact," he added, "I've put her there."

"You have."

"Oh, yes. Long before she knew Walter. Or had any reason to establish an alibi. You know why? Because she likes it."

"Not being able to move where she wants?"

"Not having to decide what happens next. She does a lot of deciding all day long, a lot of judging. It relaxes and excites her for somebody else to decide."

"That's her excuse?"

"Her personal history. Yes."

"You think it proves ... what? That she's a kinky lay? Or that she didn't murder her husband?"

"I think it makes her less likely as a suspect."

"Less likely than who?" Newman demanded. "A stranger in a bathrobe and a Charlie the Chickadee mask? Who entered the house without breaking a windowpane, stabbed Walter Frick with a kitchen knife, and bound his wife to her bed? Who stole nothing from the house but slipped out again without leaving a trace? Is she really less likely than *him*?"

"Nothing was taken?"

"Not the silver from the kitchen drawer or the TV from the den. There's a jewelry case in the bedroom and a safe in her husband's office filled with cash, securities, and documents. A nice little pile of cash."

Jack said, "I keep a couple hundred myself, in case of an earthquake."

"Not forty thousand dollars, you don't. In hundred-dollar bundles."

"Walter was a banker."

"I heard," said Newman, "but aren't they supposed to keep money in the vault? You don't need forty thousand to tip the pizza boy."

"Not even on the west side?"

A crease of red—maybe a smile. Quickly covered over.

Jack said, "Walter could have surprised a thief when he came down to the kitchen. They scuffled, snatched a knife from the drain board, and Walter caught it in his gut. I wouldn't try to unhook the TV with a bleeder in my kitchen."

"You wouldn't, maybe, but our hypothetical intruder didn't have your sensitivity. The kitchen door was six feet away, but stabbing Mr. Flick didn't spook him. According to your bosomy buddy, the evil Chicakdee went upstairs and put a pillow over her face. With Mr. Frick dead on the kitchen floor and the Missus out cold, our intruder had plenty of time to look around, didn't he? Enough at least for the jewel case, in plain view on the dresser. Guess what was missing."

"A cuff link?"

"Not a pin. Diamond earrings and pearls inside. Still in their shiny places when we went through the house."

"Judith must have told you that."

"Why? Didn't she tell you the same thing?"

"I never asked."

"You *are* an old friend," Newman said, "but if you know her so well, you must be aware how easily she plays men like you. Wasn't there any sign of that when she made her mark at the D.A.'s office?"

Jack couldn't help remembering all the mornings they had showed up after nine, entering the office one by one so nobody would notice them arriving together. All the afternoons they slipped out early or stayed late but did no office work. Judith might not have been the hardest working A.D.A., but she always managed to land the big cases—by which she meant the high profile crimes, prosecutions most likely to be noticed by the press and senior jurists. Jack himself had helped her secure some of those assignments. Had she really planned it all?

He refused to believe it. Her success was a natural response to her talent and intelligence, her charm, good looks, and the rest of the package. Judith hadn't hooked up with him to advance her career. He couldn't quite remember how they came together, though he didn't recall pursuing her either. One night she hadn't been there, and the next night she had. That was how Jack remembered it—wasn't that how it happened?

"Uh huh," Newman said.

"You have your suspect," said Jack. "That's all it is. Someone to look at."

"Right. And if we don't push these first few days, the evidence will disappear. We're not going to let that happen, Sergeant, out of deference to Her Honor. If she stuck Walter Frick, we'll nail her for it."

"I'd bet you would, Lieutenant. *But what if she didn't?* What are you going to tell the victim's widow, if the case goes cold on her husband's killer because you were so focused on Frick?"

Newman's eyes shone like pearls stained with rings of green. "It won't. Because we're not. She's sold you a bill of goods, Stryker. You might have your reasons for sucking it up, but we don't."

"What makes you so sure she's lying?"

Newman produced another file from the bottom drawer of her desk. She opened its cover and set both palms on its first sheet. Jack couldn't make out the smeared print.

"Did you ever hear of Sergeant Herman Hoeffler?"

Jack nodded. He had never met Hoeffler personally, but he heard the story, all right. Every cop in Los Angeles did.

"And you're still asking questions to help her out? She hasn't by any chance hired you, has she? To do a little private snooping? Because the last time I checked, you were still on disability. There are rules about those things."

"And you're the gal to enforce them?"

The left foot arched in her sandal. "Do you have a problem, Sergeant, with female senior officers?"

"No, Ma'am, I don't. Nine times out of ten."

"I hope you don't. Because this is my investigation. If you step on my painted toenails, you can kiss your badge good-bye. And your pension. I'll have your ass so fast, you'll never hear me coming. With or without your seeing-eye dog."

7

"Of course she thinks Judy Frick is a liar," said Maggie Mayfield Malloy, as she squeezed a soapy washcloth into Jack's ear. "Number one, she hates her. Number two, a murder conviction of a sitting judge is a real career booster. Number four, Pat Newman is a pain in the ass. You know how she's treated my girls."

"You forgot three."

"Number three, Lieutenant Newman really hates Judge Judith Frick."

"That's the same as number one," Jack said.

"That's how much she hates her," Maggie said, wringing out the washcloth and using it again to wipe off his face.

Jack was in a tub in a second floor bathroom of the house in Hancock Park, with both eyes shut against the soap. It hardly mattered if he opened them, since all he could see was a red mass of hair and Irish green eyes. Her hair was a brighter red than it once had been, and her skin a ruddier pink from the whiskey, but Maggie's eyes were still dark as peat-bog and twice as likely to draw a man under. They rested on you easily, as if she could tell just what you wanted and how much you could afford. Jack usually enjoyed her confident gaze, but Maggie used a coconut Castile bar soap that stung like a bastard if it got in your eyes.

"Because of Sergeant Hoeffler?"

"Hermie Hoeffler was a decent cop," Maggie said. "No big hero, but somebody you could depend on."

"In other words, when you bought him off, he stayed bought."

Maggie poked his shoulder. "Sit back."

Jack did, and the washcloth swirled through the black and grey hairs of his chest. Maggie was really good at working up a lather.

"Judy Frick put him through a wringer," she said. "The brass didn't see the case her way, but you know how those blueballs shrink up when they're squeezed. They put him on suspension. Hermie was a big, dumb kraut with too much pride to stay on his knees. He said he'd rather end his career than have them kill it slowly."

"He quit."

"Or else Frickin' Frick drove him out. Depending on how you felt about him."

"Is that all of it? Or is there something more?"

"Like what?"

"Judith thinks that Newman disapproves of her. Because of the bondage games." He put his wrists together.

"Some women are like that," Maggie conceded. "Judging everyone. You'd think the young ones would have open minds, but some of them look up to an older gal who they think should have broken free of the rules. And they're disappointed to discover that nobody likes to feel free all the time."

Jack dropped his hands. "*You* don't think Judith is lying, do you?"

"How should I know? She's your old girlfriend. You ought to know better than anybody else how she wakes up in the morning. All I'm saying is, I wouldn't jump to any conclusions because Patty Newman said so."

She reached into the soap-scum between his knees. He waited as she found what she was feeling for. It turned out to be the soap.

"How is Miss Adams working out?"

"Aisha? She's great. She drives me everywhere, looks out for falling objects, and knows the lyrics to every song the Black Eye Peas ever sang."

"That's how she kept warm on the street, singing to herself and dancing."

Jack nodded. "She's got a feel for the job. She seems to know when I need help and when I want to try something myself."

"Hooking is good training for all sorts of things."

"You never hired her here, I noticed."

"She came to me with that face."

"No one wants to sleep with a disfigured girl?"

Maggie's eyes crinkled when she smiled. "You don't know your fellow creatures, do you, Jack? Plenty of men get turned on by visible signs of abuse. But I don't want that kind of client around my house. You never know when they'll decide to start acting out their fantasies."

Jack felt a familiar impulse to apologize for his sex, but there was nothing he could say that Maggie hadn't heard a million times. For a few minutes he rested against the tub with his eyelids fluttering, until he felt her warm breath in his ear.

"Okay, Jackie boy. On your feet."

He gripped the side and stood unsteadily on the porcelain. Maggie wrapped a beach towel around his hips and offered her sinewy forearm to help him out of the tub. He refused her arm, stepping over the wet tiles onto the mat, which felt furry between his toes.

"Something's dripping."

Maggie draped another towel across his shoulders and massaged it into his hair. "I think you can take it from here," she said, rising from her seat on the side of the tub. "The comb is on the sink, under the mirror. But don't spend too much time admiring yourself. Janie Mae will be here for you any minute."

"I didn't ask for Janie."

"No? I thought you liked her."

"I like you."

Maggie shook her head. "You can't afford me."

"Oh, I'll pony up. Whatever it takes."

"Well, I can't afford *you*," Maggie said and laughed, with no real pleasure in it—the noise she made when a customer told a joke.

"Ever again?"

"We'll have to see about that."

Before Jack had finished running a comb through his hair, there was a soft knock and the door opened. But Janie Mae wasn't behind it.

"Ready?"

"Dry as a martini," Maggie said after a pause. "Jack, do you know Rosalind?"

He reached out his hand and felt her spiky hair— blonde, by the blur he could see. He ran his hand down the side of her face, felt cheekbones, the soft fuzz at her jaw-line, the fragile bones of her clavicle, small breasts, prominent ribs, out-thrust hip. Rosalind stopped his hand there, but not before he had put together a pretty good picture. She was slim, maybe thirty, in a white silk shift that showed off her shape more fetchingly than nothing at all.

"Nice to meetcha, Rosalind," said Jack.

The blonde looked doubtful. "Can he find his way down the hall?"

"All the way down," said Jack.

Maggie put a hand on his arm and asked, "Where's Janie Mae?"

Rosalind shrugged. "Never showed."

"Didn't she call?"

"Or answer her phone. Chevy said to tell you. And Mr. Wiggly is waiting."

Maggie's green eyes narrowed. "That isn't like her at all."

42

8

Janie Mae Olmstad was really more interested in Hannah Arendt than she was in Heidegger, but gossip usually stole the show, even in Philosophy. She had waited after class to ask her question, but the gangly kid with frizzy hair had taken up too much of the prof's time with his own theory of responsibility for anyone else to get in a word. Now, as Janie Mae hurried to the parking structure, she went over how she could pose her question to show she was asking to get more out of the lecture, and not because she had blown off the reading.

She could understand Arendt's hooking up with him in the first place—the smart young lady and the famous older man. Just calling him Martin must have been a thrill. Thoughtful Hannah would have made some allowances in the sack, but the coupling had advantages for both of them. Martin hadn't even joined the Party yet. But afterwards? After the war, when she heard at Nuremberg all that had happened and knew what he had done as Rector at Freiberg? How could a decent Jewish girl forgive the nasty old Nazi, once all the grisly facts came out? When you read his ideas against his actions during the Third Reich, they didn't seem so purely philosophical.

She thought to write that down for later, an idea for her paper. Her notebook was right on top, but her pen had fallen to the bottom of her book-bag. She was reaching around, feeling for its clip, when the indicator dinged and the elevator slid open.

Empty.

Where had she parked? On the seventh floor, back aisle, northeast corner. She had to thumb the button three times before it lit. As the door closed, she heard a shout and saw the gangly kid waving his arm for her to hold the elevator. She could have stuck out her foot and caught the door, but why should she? His monologue made her late for work again. He was proud of how he had held the floor, challenging Dr. Lutz, and would probably pick it up again to show how smart he was— hitting on her in the only way he thought he had a chance. She smiled at the idea of his reaction if he knew where she was working. That would shut him up *profoundly*, as he liked to say. Now he could wait for the next elevator.

The floors dropped away. Three. Four. Five. After you left the ground floor, no one was going up.

They had given Arendt such shit for *Eichmann in Jerusalem*. So little sympathy for the victims, such a cold eye on the crowd, like a cop who can't stand to hear the story of a rape victim. Janie herself had listened to all kinds of grief, but she was getting paid for it, and it was certainly easier to say *Poor baby!* and rub a man's back than some of the other things they wanted you to do. They missed the main point entirely at the time. It wasn't overlooking the crimes of the war to notice how close the man on the street was to committing them himself. Anybody at all could suddenly act like a monster, given a little encouragement and opportunity. Janie Mae or any of Maggie's girls could testify to that. It took a woman to say it, was all.

The seventh floor was deserted, this time of night. She had been forced to drive all the way up when she arrived on campus at six, when most of the undergraduates were eating their dinners or smoking dope in the residence halls. Now, however, when classes were done and the commuter students had mostly gone, her steps echoed off the concrete walls as she trotted down the back ramp to her Beamer. It was a nicer car than most of the kids in her class could afford, but it was one of the private rewards Janie Mae used to keep herself going. She had needed to find a way to pay for tuition, and her first job at the copy center hardly covered her books. Maggie made her a better offer. The hours were more flexible and the work more enjoyable, since Maggie never forced them to go with anybody. She just calculated the ratio of come to compensation in a cost/benefit analysis that was hard for a practical thinker like Janie Mae to resist. She would have to apologize to Mr. Wiggly, who always waited for her on Wednesday nights, but she knew how to make it up to him. Maggie might have a few short words for her, but Janie Mae didn't expect half an hour's lateness to make a dent in her evening's paycheck. Isn't that precisely what flexible hours were for?

On second thought, she completely understood Hannah's thing for Martin. Had politics ever made a difference when it came to sex? Bill Clinton's guy, James Carville, hit it off with that Republican Mary Joe Maitlin. He even married her, didn't he? They say opposites attract, and who could be more oppositional than a Nazi philosopher and a Jewish New Yorker watching the Nuremberg trials? Of all her own clients, who did Janie Mae like best? Okay, the big, blue-eyed Norwegian, but after him came the nebbish accountant from Orange County, who always called her Lady Jane and tipped like a drunken Kennedy.

Croaker, he called himself. If that was even a name.

She heard something *click*.

The lighting was crappy on the back ramp. The fixture above the northeast stair had no working bulb. Janie hit a button on her key; her Beamer beeped and flashed its taillights in greeting.

She scooted in behind the wheel, threw her books on the passenger seat, and fit the key in the ignition. The dashboard lit, her seat tilted, and the cross-belt tightened. The stereo played Radiohead's *Karma Police*. She listened to Thom York's falsetto and sang along "arrest this girl, her Hitler hairdo is making me ill." Janie turned around to check before putting the car in reverse.

And jumped.

There was someone in the back seat, sitting in the shadow. He leaned forward, and she saw the grin on his Charlie the Chickadee mask.

9

Gloria Cordesman wakes up in her bedroom in Mandeville Canyon dreaming about bath towels and beach towels. Jonathan is coming to stay for a week with his new girlfriend Sheridan, and Gloria has bleached the green bath towels she normally hangs in the guest bath. She can give them beach towels, of course—she has plenty of those—but ratty old beach towels aren't the same as bath towels, are they? Not as plush, not as comfy, not as soft on your tender parts when you step out of the shower. If she asks Harry, she knows what he'll say. A towel is a towel, Glory, something like that, or worse, It's just a bit of rag to dry yourself off. Which is why she never asks his opinion on questions about the kind of home she has made for him and the kids.

He never appreciates it, but what does that matter? She does what she does because she's that kind of woman, not because he's that kind of man. For a moment Gloria wonders if any man is really that kind of man, any straight man, at least, but she lets the thought drop when she remembers that she still doesn't have any plush new bath towels for Jon and Sherry, who will be arriving Friday.

What does Harry care about? Bonds and securities? What bond is closer than the one between father and son? And how much security could anybody really enjoy, if the best she can offer their elder son is a forest green towel with blotches of white, like clouds passing over the treetops?

She could run out to Bed, Bath, and Beyond and pick up some new bath towels. Peach, like the bath mat and the new cover on the toilet seat. Only, if you hope for a match, peach with peach, you have to get it exactly right, or the bath towels clash with the hand towels, the hand towels with the rug, and everything clashes with the fuzzy cover on the toilet seat. She should've gotten something neutral, like beige, ivory, or ecru, or something that contrasted nicely. Burgundy. But it's too late for that now. She can't get bath towels and a rug and a toilet seat cover in the three days before Jon and Sherry drive up in their Subaru, hot and tired from the drive, probably wanting a cold iced tea and a bath.

"Harry?"

She shakes the feather quilt next to her but it gives way under her hand and she realizes no one is under it. The digital reads seven-fifteen. Harry is up already? There must be something wrong with him, his stomach again probably. She told him he should check with

47

the doctor, he might have a spastic colon and they could do something about it instead of just swallowing bottles of antacid and groaning through the night. She usually finds him curled up on his side of the bed after a night with his spastic colon, if that's what it is, and now there's nobody under the quilt.

It takes her a few minutes to wrap herself in her flannel robe, the one she bought for herself after Harry bought her the flimsy one that matched the see-through negligee she never wears and never will. Was that thing supposed to be a gift for her? It isn't flattering, for one thing. How could it excite him, unless the sight of saggy tits is enough to get him going? That isn't a line of reasoning she enjoys exploring, so she puts it out of her mind, just as she put the negligee and flimsy robe out of sight, in the back of her lingerie drawer. Harry still asks about it, but even he knows it's a joke by now, the negligee showing chunky thighs under a robe that hides nothing at all. A flannel robe in eggshell plaid—now that's a gift she would have appreciated, if he had the taste to choose it. But of course a man who buys a hot pink thing that barely covers her bottom can hardly be expected to put it back on the rack for a comfy flannel eggshell robe instead.

She finds him in the living room on the multi-pillow-back couch, with the chocolate-brown and white linen pillows surrounding him like cotton balls in a pillbox. Sitting on the edge of the cushion with the remote in his hands, staring at the fifty inch flat screen TV mounted on the wall. His eyes are open, staring at an image that should fill the screen. Except there is no image on the TV screen— just a shoebox of flickering noise, of colored dots that keep appearing and dissolving while he watches them pop, as if his whole life were about to appear or had vanished before his eyes.

"Harry," says Gloria, louder than she intends.

No answer.

'Harr?" She repeats quietly, reaching for his arm.

It feels stiff in her hand.

He doesn't make a sound or turn his head, and it dawns on her for the first time they might have something more to worry about than clashing peach dye lots in the crapper.

10

The Hancock Park neighborhood of West Los Angeles was created in the 1920s by G. Allan Hancock, who grew up in a house near what is now the La Brea Tar Pits. Captain Hancock inherited four thousand acres of Rancho La Brea from his father, Major Henry Hancock, drained it of oil, and subdivided the land for residential development. The Wilshire Country Club leased one hundred acres, and the families who moved into the grand homes nearby shaped the history of Los Angeles. Chandler, Crocker, Doheny, Duque, Huntington, Van de Kamp, and Van Nuys all built houses around Hancock Park, designed by the region's most celebrated architects.

Those homes were set back from the street, behind wide lawns without fences to divide them. The rooms inside were numerous, spacious, and well appointed. Telephone and power lines were buried beneath the ground. The result remains an urban landscape of dignified restraint, confident of its architecture, proud of its history, and comfortable in the privacy it still affords its residents.

In one of those grand houses Maggie Malloy opened her business, counting on the reputation of the neighborhood to convey a discreet message to her clientele. The wide front lawn below her porch was kept immaculately mowed, with a tasteful array of white lilies surrounding the steps. The front door was rarely used, in any event, since most of the comings and goings used the alley behind the house. This was very convenient for the sort of customer Maggie liked to attract. The garage behind the house made it difficult for any snooping eyes to jot down a license number or snap a photo of a gentleman caller climbing out of his E Class.

Maggie Molloy's favorite room in the house was the front parlor, which had been a receiving room for the mistress of the house in the early twenties. Maggie updated the furnishings in her own quirky style, covering the Queen Anne chairs with a contemporary jacquard, refinishing the woodwork with a high gloss lacquer, replacing the full-length mirror with a beveled, rose glass that needed no floral frame. This was where she had the first Galois of her day, tapping the ash into a crystal tray with a blood-orange fingernail, watching the smoke curls float out the bay windows. Through the plantation shutters she saw white iris and calla lilies reaching for the porch, while rich green grass behind them caught sunbeams in the dew. Maggie liked to close her eyes and listen to the sprinklers clicking back and forth. The girls knew not to disturb her when she sat with her ledger book propped in her lap, breathing in the fresh-mown lawn, while the clock on the mantle ticked the minutes to seven.

That only made it more unusual for Maggie to walk into the front parlor in her Japanese robe and slippers to find rumpled Mr. Wiggly snoring in her favorite armchair. In a hoarse whisper she called, "Chevalier!" and then, finding her full smoker's voice, rasped out, "Chevy! Get in here!"

A moment later a six-foot-three black man with a shaved head bounded into the parlor in what seemed a single *jete*. He wore a white chef's apron over his rippled torso, cargo shorts, and flip-flops. In his right hand he held a spatula gilded in egg yolk. Chevalier de Plaisir had come to L.A. to dance like Fred Astaire but found his place in Maggie's kitchen, scrambling breakfast, bouncing rowdies, even dusting the high shelves now and then out of Esperanza's reach.

"Who is this?" demanded Maggie, turning her palm to the chair.

Chevy peered at the sleeper. "Mr. Wiggly, isn't it?"

"Have you any idea what time it is?"

He glanced at the clock on the mantelpiece, then at his wrist-bound Swatch, and adjusted the hands on the mantle. "Seven?"

"In the morning! In my parlor. What's he still doing here? Besides dribbling snot on my jacquard."

Chevy picked up a satin pillow from the roll-arm sofa and stuffed it between Mr. Wiggly's cheek and the patterned cloth of the Queen Anne armchair. A pool of saliva darkened the crimson satin.

"I think he's waiting."

"For what?"

"Miss Olmstad. For his date last night."

"Janie Mae never showed up?"

Chevy shook his head as Mr. Wiggly drew up his knees and resettled. "It don't look like it to me."

Maggie tried to remember – how much did she have last night? Just a couple of Irish coffees after dinner and a few shots at the bar with the gent who owned the mattress store and kept offering her a discount. What was his name? Seligman? Maybe more than a few shots. But somebody should have told her that Janie Mae never clocked in. "Did you try calling her?"

"Am I my sister's keeper?"

"The answer to that should be *yes*, shouldn't it?"

"Only four times. Cell and home. Nobody answered. Rosalind said she told you."

Maggie vaguely remembered that. "What about her girlfriend ... the China doll?"

"Suziko Mori is Japanese. And Korean."

"*Mori?*"

"She might not have been born with that name. My mama didn't call me Chevalier either."

Chevy had been cast in two films when he first arrived in L.A., but he couldn't come on camera. He was shy that way.

"I don't care if she's comatose, Chevy. Aren't they cousins or something?"

"Sisters, they say, in Sigma Chi or the Delta of Venus, depending on the night. White wool sweaters with Greek letters stitched carefully over their boobs. Rah-rah-sis-boom-bah! But strictly for the johns."

"Don't they live together?"

"Yes, Maggie. I believe they do."

Janie Mae had introduced Suziko to the trade, had *turned her out* in the quaint phrase of the brothel business—the pair of them together at first, working parties and three-ways. There was even a specialist customer who paid double to pleasure himself while he watched the twosome wink and moan in the throes of fake passion.

"Is she missing too?"

"Suziko? I don't know. Didn't Janie Mae say she was going to Vegas for a couple of days?"

"Not to me."

"To me, either. But that's what Rosalind said."

"The China doll is a flake," said Maggie, "but Janie Mae isn't. She juggles a lot between school and work but always remembers to call in, whenever she might be late. Now you're telling me lshe never showed or called last night? That doesn't sound right at all."

"You want me to check it out? Ring her condo's doorbell?"

"Don't you have work to do here?"

He raised his spatula. "Omelets to order, for twelve. Who'll wake up, one by one, pissy as wine vinegar."

Maggie knew what she would hear if the coffee hadn't perked. "Food comes first, Chevy. Nobody works convincingly on an empty stomach. But Jack is with Rosalind, isn't he? Why don't you scramble those eggs, bang on his door, and ask him to look in on Janie Mae, as a favor to me?"

Chevalier shook his head. "Can't do that, Maggie Mae. Jack got picked up half an hour ago by an Amazon in a Buick. Who didn't

51

even bother coming by the alley. She left skid marks in the driveway."

11

Rae's Diner on Pico Boulevard is hardly wider than a train car. Booths for four and tables for two ring the stools of the main counter, where workingmen order mugs of black coffee and the 2-2-2 special—two eggs, two pancakes, and two strips of bacon or sausage. Families and older couples gravitate to the booths, while younger couples and singles occupy the smaller tables inside the front window. At the end of the row of booths is an odd little table large enough for three. Because of its shape and position in the diner it's usually the last one occupied. But that was where Jerry Schiller liked to eat his breakfast, spreading out the morning paper on the trapezoidal table-top, running his fingertip over the crossword puzzle while he sopped up fried eggs with a piece of sourdough toast. The crossword clues got his brains boiling, Jerry liked to say, and the papers spread over the funky table helped him forget he was eating alone. Sex wasn't the only thing Jerry's wife didn't care to do with him anymore.

Nobody ever bothered him. The hardhats had seen him often enough to ignore him, and the waitress brought around a coffee pot to refill his mug without disturbing his concentration. So Jerry was surprised to see a six-foot black woman in a short leather skirt making her way down the aisle without a glance at the roomier booths. And he was forced to look up from his crossword puzzle when she stopped at his oddly shaped table, pressing her thighs against the edge of his newspaper. Jerry was even more surprised when she stepped aside to allow Jack Stryker to slip into the seat across from him. Then she plopped down beside Jack, unfolding her legs in the aisle near Jerry's ankles.

"Hullo, Four," said Jack.

"Hello, Jack," replied Jerry, though his gaze rested on Aisha—or rather on the scooped neck of her halter top and the line between her boobs that disappeared into it. She was not what he'd call *a pretty girl* with that blotch across her cheek, but as she settled into her seat and resettled beneath her thin cotton halter, she had what he considered an energetic *charm*.

"Jerry," said Jack, "meet Aisha," patting her elbow. "My driver."

"Your driver?"

"His seeing eye dog," said Aisha. She tilted up Jack's sunglasses and Jerry saw the pupils flickering behind his lashes.

Jack resettled the frame on his nose and Jerry started remembering. "You were in some kind of accident, weren't you?"

"Some kind."

"No accident," said Aisha. "A meth lab went boom." She opened her hands to illustrate the noise. Her fingers spread, big as starfish.

"You blew it up Rambo style?" said Jerry. "I think I heard about that."

"Everybody has," said Aisha. "At least everyone he introduces me to."

"I don't blame him," said Jerry.

She gave him a quizzical look, then a smile, when she figured out the compliment. She tried twisting it into a frown, but not fast enough.

"Jerold Schiller."

"Charmed." Aisha folded her hands.

He looked at them, swallowed, and blinked at her. "Frogs can't swallow without blinking. Did you know that?"

She kept her eyes wide. "No, Jerold. I didn't."

"It's true."

The waitress came by with a little green pad and golf pencil. She didn't need it, Jerry knew, the pencil or the pad. Leticia remembered everything. But the cook must have needed it to make up his orders, scrambled or poached with home fries. There was always a circle of green slips hanging over the griddle like dragonflies over a poppy field.

"I'll have what he's having," Jack told Letty. She didn't jot it down.

"Coffee for me," said Aisha. "Black." Then to Jack, "Can you actually see what he's having?"

"Yellow and white, right? Sunnyside up. I'm betting that brown lump on the side of the plate is bacon or sausage."

"Nope."

"Not potatoes."

"Toast. But you're getting closer. Soon you won't need me at all."

Jerry thought *he* could find a use for her, but said, "Is that why you're here, Jack? Dropping by the diner for an eye exam?"

"And breakfast."

"You come here often?"

The question was addressed to Aisha, who said, "First time for me."

"They make a nice meatloaf," Jerry told her. "For dinner."

"You just mentioning that?" said Jack. "Or are you asking her out?"

Jerry flushed. "We're just talking."

"Let's talk about something else," Jack said.

Jerry took a mouthful of egg and toast. "Like what?"

"Judith Frick."

"Can't," mumbled Jerry. "Open 'vestigation."

"You went to the house, didn't you? With the crime scene unit? And somebody from the coroner's?"

Jerry nodded, swallowing yolk. He looked at Aisha. "Macauley."

"How is Little Mac?"

"How is he? The same. Little. Don't schmooze me, Jack," said Jerry. "You're keeping me from my puzzle. Tell me what you want, already."

"Not much. Just a few fast answers."

"Why ask me? I'm not the detective in charge."

"Newman blew me off."

"You've met the Princess already? And you're still asking questions?"

"I'm a curious guy. The Lieutenant thinks Judith killed her husband, doesn't she?"

"That's one possibility."

"But there are others, aren't there?"

"There are always other possibilities," Jerry said, "until we find out the truth."

"You and I know that. But it doesn't sound like Newman wants to."

"I thought you were on disability," Jerry said, scooping a spoon of marmalade from its pot and holding it between them. He imagined what the orange glop must look like through a fried cornea.

"I am," Jack said, "but it's been a couple of weeks. I'm restless for a crime scene."

Jerry snorted, and a drop of coffee caught his nostril. "No can do."

"Sure you can. One or two things you need to clear up. Take another impression in the yard."

"You think we missed something? That you'll spot? Forgive my noticing, Jack, but you can't tell toast from bacon."

"A consultation, then."

"Go right ahead. Consult me."

"I mean you could consult me. I know her, Jerry. Her Honor. I knew her pretty well, upon a time."

"Do you know anything we don't?"

"If you tell me what you know, I can answer that."

"Jeezus, Jack. It's not your case."

"I promise not to solve it." He raised his palm as if taking the oath and crossed his heart for good measure.

Neither one of them was Catholic.

Jerry said, "No forced entry. Nothing stolen. The missus is upstairs, tied to the bed, while the mister is down on the kitchen floor with a knife in his ribs. She's got a story about a masked intruder, but we don't find any sign of one. And as it turns out"—blushing for Aisha's sake—"Her Honor admits she tied her own wrists to the bedpost."

"Both of them? That's hard to do."

"One wrist, I guess."

"Almost a confession," Jack said. "She told you so herself?"

"Not me," said Jerry.

"Newman. Why do you suppose she did that?"

"What?"

"Told her."

"That she tied the knot herself? The judge wasn't in her right mind when she let it slip. Swimming into consciousness."

"Sleeping pills?"

"Someone put a pillow over her head."

"And you figure – what? She tied herself to the bed and dropped a pillow on her face? Or she put the pillow over her face and then tied herself to the bed?"

It didn't work either way. Jerry felt his cheeks grow hot and lost his appetite.

Aisha laid her hand over his fist, covering it. "The car's out front," she said. "I'll drive."

12

When the bailiff called the courtroom to order at ten o'clock sharp, Judith Frick took her seat at the bench with her usual flourish of robes. Women judges had an edge on the men when it came to making an entrance, she thought, thanks to a lifetime of practice in handling skirts. Bruce C. Golden, the Managing Judge of the Superior Court, had taken her off the schedule at first. She might need a few days out of the headlights, he said, mixing the image of a startled deer with the text of a scandal sheet. But Judith had touched Bruce's bicep ever so lightly through his striped shirtsleeve and insisted she needed to work to keep her mind off her loss. She let her voice drop on the last words, as if the effort to get them out had winded her. Brucie had cupped her elbow to say, *Of course, dear, whatever helps.*

It might have helped if she had been able to review the pretrial motions before hearing oral arguments in the Whistler homicide. She had been reading those pages when Walter entered the bedroom in his silly black mask. Smeared ink collected in the creases under her hips, where he pressed her into the mattress. Now, as she took those crumpled sheets out of her briefcase and smoothed them over her desk, they trembled in her hands. She rested on her elbows and folded her fingers over the wrinkles, leaning slightly forward to pay closer attention to what their authors had to say.

The issue before the court concerned the admissibility of witnesses whose names appeared on the prosecutor's list. That much she had gathered before Walter entered their bedroom. Bernard Whistler was to be tried for the murder of his investment counselor, Philip Hazlitt, who had reportedly lost or stolen a considerable amount of Mr. Whistler's money. The District Attorney's office had submitted a witness list that included a number of names whose relevance had been challenged by the defense. Today's hearing was to determine the admissibility of those witnesses, whose only knowledge of the crime, as far as Judith could remember, had been gained at a party in the Hotel Pierrot on the evening of Mr. Whistler's arraignment.

Judith tried to push another question out of her mind: how much did the lawyers she would face in court know about the horror on her kitchen floor? How much discretion could she expect from Lieutenant Newman, the loyal friend of Herman Hoeffler?

Judith felt a buzzing at the back of her skull, above the starched collar of her white silk shirt. She recognized it as the first hum of a migraine that typically kicked in later in the proceedings.

"Mr. Prosecutor," she said, to dislodge the A.D.A. from his conversation with a junior associate at his table. Judith knew the lead counsel, Lester Talbot, to be a career man in the D.A.'s office, who had made an impressive early start with multiple convictions in commodities fraud but whose recent cases had not provided equal opportunity for high-profile prosecutions. The Whistler case held a certain potential for public interest, given the notoriety of its victim, but Judith was determined to keep the case in her courtroom, rather than allowing its arguments to be picked over by hyenas on the six o'clock news. For that reason she had closed today's hearing on pretrial motions, a decision she thought especially foresighted as a vein began to throb above her ear.

"Good morning, Your Honor," began Mr. Talbot, rising from his seat but holding his place behind the table. "The question before us today, if I understand the challenge, concerns the People's use of certain witnesses on our list. I'm sure the defense would like a preview of the case we intend to present" – with a nod in the direction of the defense table – "but the People prefer to save our arguments for the trial, when they can be heard at the same time by the jury."

"Your Honor," said the defense attorney, a distinguished gentleman with curves of stiff white hair sweeping back to his shoulders. He had started his career defending anti-war protesters in Oakland, but the politics of his defendants had changed with their causes and complexions through his career. His name was Randolph Raines. His voice was a stream bubbling over smooth stones, and his suit cost more than the paneled walls of the courtroom.

Nevertheless, Judith waved him back into his seat, addressing the A.D.A. herself. "I'm sure you would prefer to keep it all to yourself, Mr. Talbot. But you will have to let us in on some of your plans. Mr. Raines has filed an objection concerning the relevance of these witnesses' testimony."

"Not to mention their prejudicial nature," muttered Raines, having failed to be recognized by the bench. Judith raised a warning finger in his direction, but continued her questioning of Talbot.

"What do you say, Mr. Prosecutor? Do they really know something we need to hear? What precisely are these men going to tell us?"

58

She could see by Talbot's face he had provided the details in his written response to the motion, but he answered calmly, "We understand that the defense plans to make an issue of Mr. Whistler's mental health. These witnesses can speak to the defendant's state of mind, Your Honor."

"Several weeks after the alleged incident?" Raines inquired.

The *incident* had been a car bombing with an infamous fatality, but the attorney's tone suggested that the whole idea was ridiculous – that the charge and in fact the whole trial might be just as pointless as the witnesses subpoenaed to testify.

"I'll ask the questions for now, Mr. Raines," said Judith stiffly.

"Of course, Your Honor," he replied with a genteel flourish of courtesy. He sat back in his wooden chair, prepared to enjoy the show.

That was not what Judith had in mind. But she wasn't about to be manipulated by the attorneys, one way or the other. "Mr. Talbot, aside from their cocktail conversation, do these witnesses from the Pierrot have any first-hand knowledge of Mr. Whistler's state of mind on the night of the murder?"

"Not that night, Your Honor," Talbot said, "but they did have ample opportunity to speak with Mr. Whistler on another night of relevance: the evening before he surrendered himself for incarceration. We have reason to believe Mr. Whistler made incriminating comments to these witnesses."

"That's absurd," said Raines.

"It's understandable, Your Honor. Only natural. He had been accused by the State of California of a serious crime—the most serious, with a possible death penalty. Wouldn't most people feel compelled to talk about it then?"

"No, I would not," responded Raines, "nor would I allow my client to discuss it.

"Mr. Whistler was my guest at that party, Your Honor. I brought him there to distract him from the morning's proceedings, with instructions to turn his mind to something else. It was a trying evening for Mr. Whistler. The last thing he needed to hear was every guest's opinion of his guilt or innocence, and the legal strategy most likely to prove productive. He was under orders from me to talk about restaurants, music, movies, travel ... anything that crossed his mind except the charges against him."

Judith said, "It doesn't sound as if your client followed orders."

"On the contrary," said Raines, straightening his back. "I'm sure that he did. The man was a marine."

"Then why object to our witnesses?" demanded Talbot, raising his voice to get a word in between the judge and indignant Raines. "If Mr. Whistler followed your orders and talked about the weather, why not let the court hear about it?"

Judith touched her temple, where the vein throbbed in earnest. She could feel its pulse with her fingertips.

A frown deepened Raines's ruddy complexion. "You might as well ask why the D.A. wants them to testify," he said, as if she had posed the question herself. "I'll give you the only answer that occurs to me. Because the jury might have feelings of their own about the kind of people who attend that sort of party. Opposing counsel has shrewdly calculated that my client's attendance might accomplish what he cannot do with the plain facts—turn the jury's sympathies against us."

Talbot rolled his eyes.

Judith said, "What sort of party was this, exactly?"

The lawyers exchanged a glance. "You haven't had a chance to view the material," Raines declared.

View rather than *review*—an odd choice of words. There was a video disk in the materials from the defense, wasn't there? Judith had no chance to screen it. "I'd like to hear more about it," she added lamely.

"A fat cat's feast," said Talbot.

Now it was Raines's turn to shake his leonine head. "It was an intimate gathering. A few colleagues, in open collars."

"All hired guns of the American Enterprise Group," said Talbot. "Investment bankers at play. Of what they wasted every day I wish I had a millionth."

"Before the district attorney starts singing *Yankee Doodle*," Raines said, "let me provide an accurate picture. Mr. Whistler was in very low spirits after the indictment. His experience behind bars had shaken him, as you might imagine. I tried to assure him the facts were on our side, but words do not always suffice. So I invited him to join me in dropping by an informal gathering of another client."

"AEG?"

"They have indeed faced some challenges lately, and some unfortunate press, as a result of the downturn in the housing market. But they rallied and earned the support of the Treasury. Afterwards, some of the principals came together to discuss how to get the company back on track."

Judith turned to Talbot for a translation.

"They whooped it up, Your Honor. Celebrating receipt of federal bailout funds. In the hundreds of millions."

"Partying on bailout funds?"

"Of course not," bristled Raines. "It was a modest gesture of gratitude from the board, for the team who negotiated with Washington."

Walter used to complain about accounting for those events. Not-so-petty cash used to underwrite the perks, followed by bailout funds to replenish the kitty. The bank pays for the party, and the funds float back into the account.

"Do you know what they charge for the ballroom at the Pierrot?" Talbot asked, "where they held the press conference? For a couple of hours under the lights? What do you think they get for the penthouse?"

"As I said," continued Raines. "Perfectly legal, but unpopular in the public mind. My opponent and his colleagues believe that my client's presence on that occasion will convince the jury he must have done something disgraceful. Murder, even. As clear a case of guilt by association as I have ever encountered. Engineered by the People's counsel."

"Is that really what you're up to, Mr. Talbot?"

"Of course not, Your Honor," said the A.D.A. "Despite his eminent attorney's advice, Mr. Whistler couldn't help talking about the charge he was facing. No one forced him to drink or to confide in our witnesses. But they listened, and their testimony does have probative value in this case."

"Even if it proves prejudicial?"

Talbot hesitated. "People have mixed feelings about banks," he said finally. "I own my home thanks to the financial support of my banker. Most people trust that their money's safe in a savings or checking account. We may resent all the interest and fees, but where do we go when we need a loan to fix a leaky roof?"

"To a banker," said Judith.

She couldn't tell whether Talbot knew that Walter was a banker – that he *had been* a banker, now. Was he tip-toeing around the topic, because he knew? Or ignoring it, because he didn't? She peered at the man's watery blue eyes, which blinked back at her but revealed nothing.

"Exactly," he said. "So how prejudicial is it that Mr. Whistler has some friends who are bankers? Or that his attorney does?"

"I wouldn't call them *friends*," said Raines. "Clients. Although I do like to think I treat all my clients as if they were personal friends."

Judith focused on Talbot. "The fact that Mr. Whistler attended a party celebrating bailout funds? Is that the same thing in the public mind as having a lawyer who knows a banker?"

"It is dicier," the A.D.A. admitted, "but people feel ambivalently about bailouts too. We resent the recipients whose greedy behavior required them, but our pensions and retirement accounts are in their hands. We'd like to hold the bankers responsible, but they can't be allowed to fail and take our savings along."

"Most people want to see them hanged," Raines said flatly.

"Most of us don't know how we feel," Talbot said. "It changes with every news story. The biggest banks are paying back all the cash they borrowed, and our pension funds are returning to where we need them to be. Now, should that uncertainty make the testimony of bankers prejudicial in all cases? Should it preclude the People from calling to the stand witnesses whose testimony might prove germane to the guilt of a defendant – in this case, Mr. Whistler?"

"That's the question, all right," said Judith, running her index finger down the list of proposed witnesses. "There are a lot of names here, Mr. Talbot."

"Yes, there are, Your Honor."

"All at the Pierrot?"

"No. Those are from the bank's personnel files. I've marked all the party guests with asterisks."

Judith skimmed the names. "There are only six or seven so indicated."

Raines stood up. "How many bankers does it take, Your Honor? To convince a jury that my client was in a foul mood, the night he was indicted? While each one makes him look more like a criminal?"

Judith thought of Lieutenant Newman and the suspicion in her eyes. She glanced back at Raines, who nodded his white head in sympathy. He knew that she hadn't been through the written arguments. Talbot did too. They probably knew why she hadn't, and all the rest of it. Judith felt a migraine blossom in her skull like a rose under time-lapse photography. The pain stabbing her eyeballs made it difficult to speak.

"I'd like to hear what these witnesses have to say. Mr. Talbot will arrange a 402 hearing. You'll have my decision after that."

13

Lieutenant Patricia Newman approached a criminal investigation like any other large-scale investment of money, time, and manpower. The decisions you made early in the process would determine your outcome. Cases went cold even faster than restaurants in Beverly Hills. Given the public profile of the Frick family, the Captain had put some extra officers at her disposal, but the disposition of those resources at an early stage of the investigation probably made the crucial difference in success. Patricia Newman did not like to consider any other result.

Success in a criminal investigation meant the timely capture and conviction of the perpetrator. To accomplish that, a detective had to collect enough evidence to convince some skeptical people the job had been done correctly. Before a jury was seated, before a judge ruled on the admissibility of evidence, the District Attorney's office had to decide they had a case strong enough to win. Assistant District Attorneys never like to lose but especially dislike losing a case that draws as much attention as the in-home homicide of a jurist's spouse—especially when that jurist is a suspect like Her Honor Judith Frick.

The Lieutenant did not mind sharing her suspicions with Captain Phil D'Alessio. Nor did she mind using the word *manpower* to describe the personnel of both genders assigned to her by the Captain. Phil appreciated *straight talk*, by which he meant the sort of language men used with each other. Newman's ability to talk the talk and walk the walk, to switch back and forth from heels that clicked on the courtroom floor to soft-soles in the station house, had helped convince the brass she was their kind of gal.

Now she crossed her legs with a quiet *zip* as she sat on the edge of a tidy desk in her glass-walled office in Homicide. The *zip* told the officers assembled around her that she was wearing pantyhose, which meant she had either come from or was on her way to a meeting at the D.A.'s office or Police HQ. Four of them sat in a broken semi-circle of hard chairs. Detective Sergeant Emil Warneke was second in rank after Newman and the senior member of the team in age and years on the force. His full head of white hair was slicked back on the sides, where the teeth marks of his comb were clearly visible. He had served in uniform for quite some time before hanging it up for plainclothes, but it hadn't taken him long after that to earn his sergeant's badge. Like most of the older men in blue, Warneke had first noticed Newman when she took the stand for Hermie Hoeffler. Her testimony made him a fan. He was the first man to salute when Patty made lieutenant and the first she asked to be assigned to her team.

The three other detectives included one woman, Marilyn Montoya, who had been on the force for seven years. She was a short strawberry blonde in a sleeveless tee, who shifted around restlessly in her chair. She had been through four partners in three years, but Patricia thought she knew the problem. Lynn found it easier to do things herself than to negotiate who did what, especially if her partner patronized her, as male officers with a couple of years of seniority were inclined to do. Newman needed a woman on her team who could work on her own, and Montoya needed a chance to prove she could work with a team. Now, as she sat between Warneke and the other men, resting her elbows on the thighs of her Levis, Lynn Montoya seemed to occupy a space of her own, with one hand beneath her cardboard cup to make sure the coffee didn't leave a ring on Newman's wicker chair.

The last two men, Bruner and Yost, had worked as a team for eighteen months in one of those pairings that seem inevitable, the weekend after they're matched. Inside a year their wardrobes had merged – both wore cheap suits, shirts that needed ironing, and badly knotted ties. Newman had not asked for Brewer & Yeast, as the pair were called around the station house, but the Captain had said they were careful men who carried out orders as they were given. They debated the merits of green corn tamales and Dodger relief pitchers, and D'Alessio thought they might provide a double-thick sounding board, if she ever wanted to bounce around her theory of the case.

Patricia didn't feel she needed that kind of help, but the Captain liked to add an element of his own to the mix, and this was the parsley he was sprinkling on top. She knew Phil's face well enough to know when she could push him and when to let go. She shrugged as a man would have, raising and dropping her shoulders with a rueful shake of her head, and closed the door gently behind her.

Newman couldn't afford to ignore any promising lead, but she couldn't give equal attention to all possibilities either. She had to clear the rabbit tracks to follow the grizzly. She asked Sergeant Warneke to go over Frick's credit cards, visiting the spots where he lunched and wooed clients, to find out which of his friends and colleagues most wanted him dead.

She sent Brewer and Yeast to check statistics on burglaries in the neighborhood, and to canvas door-to-door, to learn what the neighbors heard. That might indicate a break-in interrupted, or suggest a clue they would need for any solution – *a motive*. Getting an A.D.A. to arrest a sitting judge would prove difficult, for sure, but without a convincing motive, Newman saw no chance at all to perp-walk Her Honor.

Why had Judith Frick killed her husband?

Patricia figured there were a thousand good reasons for homicide in any marriage. He hung the toilet paper inside out or outside in, when she told him over and over again that's not the way to do it. He chewed with his mouth open and left poppy seeds stuck between his teeth. Newman herself had never married; rather, she had put off wedding bells until her career could afford the hit. She had lived with a man for six months, when they both went through the Academy. That had taught her enough to realize the tabloid motives—infidelity or money—were just icing on the cake. Any wife had reason to want to kill her husband long before she got the chance.

Jealousy and money were the big two, but they did not by any means exhaust the list of motives for murder. Abuse was a good one—wives got off on that. More often than, say, the desire to be free, to run off with another man, or just to get away from the guy they liked at sixteen. How many other choices made in our teens are we stuck with for the rest of our lives? There's always divorce, if you have the money, time, and a decent attorney. Some women get up in the middle of the night for a pee or a glass of water, and then hold a pillow over their sleeping partners' heads. Who knows why they do it? Nobody. Except, if you're honest about it, everybody knows why.

Her old boyfriend, the blinded cop, said that Judith Frick liked ... what? To tie herself to the bedpost, while some man has his way with her? Having worked her way to the front of the courtroom—to the *bench*, for Chrissake—only to go home and submit herself to whatever Wally wanted? It was hard for Patricia to see a woman like that as a victim of circumstances. Newman had served on enough Internal Affairs hearings to know that you couldn't believe a thing was true just because you heard it from an officer. This Stryker had an interesting file, an impressive if checkered professional history, but he also had a personal history with Judith Frick. That always had a way of screwing up whatever a cop had to say.

But even if everything Stryker said was true, how did that change the situation?

What if he and Judith Frick once played those kinds of games? What if under her robes the judge still thrilled to the same old tricks?

Some dark impulse, some real or imagined guilt had compelled Frick to hog-tie herself and suffer whatever was inflicted ... until, when she could stand it no longer, she snapped. She tramped down the stairs, picked up a steak knife, and ran her dominator through. You could almost feel sorry for her, until you remembered the mess she made of the Mexican tiles on the floor. And then picture her, coolly climbing back up those stairs and retying herself to the bed-frame.

It was all the explanation Newman needed. It wasn't a Motive with a capital *M*, but it answered the *why* with greater clarity than a mistress or money fight would. But that wasn't going to work with the D.A.'s office in the case of Judith Frick, was it? Newman and her team would have to discover the local cause—the button— that had roused Her Honor from the typical state of wanting to murder her husband to actually sticking a knife in his chest.

The means and opportunity were perfectly clear and handy in every kitchen. Every wife had the chance and the wherewithal. So why had this woman done what so many other wives managed to resist? The D.A. would require a simple explanation. Walter did that, so Judy did this. She said *yes* and he said *no*. The Frick case would hang on motive, Patty felt sure. Once she had that, the A.D.A. would have no choice but to file a charge of premeditated homicide against Her Holiness Judith Frick.

Lieutenant Newman smiled at Detective Montoya, whose green eyes watched her every move. In her lap she tapped an empty cup. Patricia took the cup from Lynn and tossed it in the trash. "Now that we're alone," said the lieutenant cozily, "would you like to help me solve this case?"

14

The Frick house in Cheviot Hills is set back from the street by a lawn sloping up to an impregnable front door. As they parked, the sun seemed brighter in Jack's eyes. He blinked and discovered if he tilted down his head and raised his eyes, he could make out the Spanish arches of the porch at the end of the flagstone steps. The driveway wound around to the right, where the garage sat on the alley. From the backyard, Jack heard a lawnmower buzzing and a dog barking warily at it.

"Nice digs," said Aisha, climbing out of the Buick. She watched Jack work the passenger lock but opened the back for Jerry.

Schiller had a key to the big front door, all cedar wood and wrought black iron. The kitchen was in the back, past a formal dining room, with an everyday dining table between them. They found the gardener inside, drinking a glass of tap water. The pipes released a deep rumble of air when he shut the tap, and the dog started barking again in the back yard. The gardener went out that way, his shoes shuffling over the floor tiles, which had already been scrubbed clean of pudding and Walter Frick's puddled blood.

"So much for the integrity of the scene," said Schiller.

Aisha gave him half a smile and leaned against the pinewood island, between the built-in chopping block and the coal-filtered faucet. "Are you coming?"

She wasn't talking to Jerry.

As he entered the kitchen Jack knew he was crossing a line, stepping squarely onto Patricia Newman's toenails. *Do you have a problem with female officers, Sergeant?* Jack didn't think he did. He remembered Judith's drive to succeed in her career when they worked for the District Attorney, and how he felt about that, then. Jack pushed the memory out of his mind to concentrate on the job at hand. It probably wouldn't have worked out anyway. Judith made a judgment, even then, and acted upon it. Well, so had he. And Maggie was a professional woman too, wasn't she – in the oldest profession? Jack lived in a world of professional women. He liked women, admired them, and, yes, respected them, as much as he respected anybody else, holding them generally in the highest regard. It was just the individuals he happened to know who challenged his faith in their sex.

He didn't think better of men, as a rule, who didn't give a damn about anything, half the time. They could be slow to catch on, slower to act, quick to jump to violence when they did. If you pissed off a guy, he took a swing at you—but you could see it coming and duck under it. He didn't threaten your pension, as Patricia Newman did. He didn't care how you felt and didn't expect you to care how he felt about things, either. Not that Judith cared how he felt at the time, about marriage or anything else. When he thought about it, what he liked least about Judith Frick were all the things she had in common with a man.

But he was here to prove she hadn't murdered Walter. That wasn't his usual job. Jack found it harder to prove a suspect's innocence than her guilt. He followed the clues to the crime, wherever they led. The only good news on this investigation came in front of the liquor cabinet. When he lowered his head and looked up to the right, Jack discovered he could make out the label on Walter's whiskey. *Glenfiddich.* Some retina cells were remembering how to focus. Jack felt a stab of hope that his eyesight might be returning, and then a colder stroke of fear that this could be as good as it gets.

"Here's where we found the body," said Schiller, squatting beside a block of perfectly clean tiles. The criminalist made a face, but Jack had no trouble understanding why Judith would scrub away any trace of Walter's blood.

"You think he stood ... where?"

"Here," said Schiller, striking an awkward pose where Frick might have stood.

"And Judith just walked right up to him?"

"Awfully close for anybody else."

"With a knife she picked up from one of those drawers?"

"It could've been out on the counter. We found orange peels in the trash and seeds in the trap of the sink. Let's say she's cutting an orange, by the sink. They have words, she turns, and --"

Ugh! Schiller made a face and clutched his solar plexus. He tilted toward Aisha, who stood him upright again.

"Did you find a cutting board or a plate?"

"Plenty of plates in the cabinets. And a couple in the drain board."

"So you think she stabbed her husband in the gut, washed the plate, went upstairs, and tied herself to the bed—leaving the knife stuck in his belly? While he bled all over her Mexican tiles?"

"I never said she did. But it could'a gone down that way."

"Uh huh. What about the pudding?"

"What about it?"

"You found chocolate pudding on the floor, didn't you? How does that square with her peeling an orange?"

"Maybe he was having the pudding, while she had the orange."

"Judith says he went downstairs for pudding after he kicked a bowl of jello off the bed. Maybe he found somebody waiting down here, who picked up a knife still drying in the drain board."

"We found bits of orange still on the serrated edge."

"So? You ever clean a knife, Jerry? And do a less-than-perfect job?"

"Okay, maybe that's where she found it, Jack. Just because the knife was already in the drain board doesn't mean Her Honor didn't use it on her spouse."

"It doesn't mean she did."

Schiller pointed at the back door. "Nobody broke in, Jack. Check the lock for yourself."

"Maybe they didn't have to. Lots of folks leave their back doors unlocked. It's on their property, out of sight, so they think it's secure."

"This is a judge's house."

Jack tried the handle, and the back door opened. "The shoemaker's children go barefoot."

"That could've been unlocked any time since that night by half a dozen uniforms going in and out," said Schiller. "Not to mention the gardener, who's working today. We saw him."

They heard the lawnmower buzzing in the yard again, and the dog barking.

Jack lifted a finger. "Doesn't take much to get him excited, does it?"

Schiller shook his head. "He's a dog. Barking's what they do."

"So why not that night?"

"What do you mean? He barked. It was the dog barking in the backyard that got a neighbor to call the police."

"Frick was stabbed at eleven, wasn't he? The call came in to the precinct, when?"

"Around one. They had to send a uniform first."

"So a neighbor listened for three hours – and two of them after midnight – before making the call?"

Schiller said, "The dog didn't have to be barking the whole time."

"What was he doing instead?"

"The dog? I don't know. Chewing on a bone."

"While his master was getting stabbed in the kitchen? Maybe he was. What do you suppose was on that bone?"

"You mean ... rib-eye? Or somebody doped the dog?"

"That would explain why he didn't bark for a couple of hours, wouldn't it? Until he woke up and started howling?"

"We had a man out back, Jack, bagging whatever he found."

"Which would've worked just fine, if the dog left it sitting on the path outside the kitchen door like a dead robin. But you know what dogs do with their bones, don't you, Jerry?"

"You want us to dig up the whole backyard? For a bone that might be buried out there?"

"Don't bother," said Jack and went out through the backyard door. Schiller and Aisha found him standing on the back door step, with his chin down on his chest and his eyes peering up, searching the backyard.

The gardener turned off the lawnmower. "Can I help you?"

Jack didn't answer, but marched across the grass to a wooden doghouse standing in the shadow of the garage. He got down on his hands and knees and crawled inside it. The gardener looked over at the two others on the back door step. Schiller shrugged, but Aisha set her hands on her hips with confidence. A moment later, Jack emerged with a red plastic pork chop.

"He's gotta be kidding," said Schiller.

Jack waved the thing over his head. Victorious.

"I don't think so," said Aisha.

Jack dangled the chop with two fingers gripping the tip of its curved rib bone. "Go ahead, Jerry," he said. "Bag this and test it."

"For what? Canine saliva?"

"For a sedative. Or Lunesca. Something to put Fido to sleep, while a stranger breaks into the house."

Jack dropped the pork chop into Schiller's open palm. "We're not going to find anything on this," the criminalist said. "I can tell that already. See the edges? It's hardly been chewed."

"Why not?" said Jack. "I mean, why hasn't the dog been at it?"

"Because it's a bad-tasting toy?"

"It is, if it's covered in Seconal. That's got to tell you something, Jerry. Nobody dopes their own dog."

71

15

Palos Verdes Estates is the only one of three incorporated cities on the peninsula with its own police force. That was why Mrs. Edelson dialed their number, rather than the L.A. County sheriff, when she opened the checkered curtains over her breakfast nook and saw a surfboard floating outside Lunada Bay, dragging a man in a wetsuit by his ankle behind it. She had to stop talking, so the girl could rinse the dye from her hair, but the two other ladies in plastic smocks in the PeeVee Style Salon waited for her to resume. She thought it must be the latest violence between localist surfers and adventurers from down the coast, she told them, but it turned out to be that nice Mr. Fleischer, who helped her load groceries into the back of her Touareg last August, at the market.

That's what the Palos Verdes Estates Police Department said. He had a house further out on the peninsula, which he shared with his brother, a grip, who was away on location. In the movie business, she explained, working with lights. The grip, it turns out, was younger than Mr. Fleischer and was also a surfer. They liked to go out together in the early morning, before they had to head into town. The odd thing was, according to the doctor, Mr. Fleischer had been in the water overnight. The women agreed it was harder to see at night. That was probably why he had hurt his head— the words they used were "blunt force trauma"— though they couldn't find the rock with his blood on it, and couldn't find any flakes of rock in the wound.

The seawater had probably washed them off, Captain Krueger thought, with the body bobbing around in it all night. The two men were squatting beside Mr. Fleischer, but the doctor raised his voice and Mrs. Edelson could see he didn't seem so sure about it, when he said they would have to wait and see what conclusions they could draw once they got Mr. Fleischer back to the morgue.

Was there really a morgue on Palos Verdes peninsula?

Mrs. Edelson assured them there was. But what did they think of Mr. Fleischer sharing his house with a younger grip? Was that really his brother? There was certainly no way to tell, when he moved her groceries from the shopping cart to the back of her Volkswagen. Mr. Fleischer had been a perfect gentleman about it. Maybe there was no reason for him not to be a gentleman, one of the other two ladies said, crossing her arms inside her smock. Her nephew was a location manager, who had a lovely wife himself but worked for some people, and the conversation turned from poor Mr. Fleischer's accident on the rocks to the more interesting topic of who might be living with whom in Palos Verdes; whether you could tell from their paint jobs and landscaping; and what it did to real estate values, generally, on the peninsula.

16

When he wore the right tie and sports jacket, Sergeant Emil Warneke could pass for a member of most gentlemen's clubs in Southern California. He had a fine head of white hair and he knew the collegiate color code. Blue and gold in town means UCLA; cardinal and gold, USC. Stanford is cardinal; the university's home is Palo Alto, which means *tall tree* in Spanish, and their mascot wears the costume of a tree on the sidelines of football games. Berkeley's colors are also blue and gold, though you have to call the school *Cal* among alumni. Sergeant Warneke had gone to Loma Linda, a Seventh-day Adventist school whose colors are purple and gold, but that hardly mattered. It was a question of how you held your shoulders, how you crossed your legs on a barstool and ordered your drink. Sergeant Warneke thought he would learn very little from the club members, but the bartenders, caddies, and checkroom girls knew all he needed to know, if only they chose to share it.

The Condor Club had taken over the estate of an aircraft magnate from the forties, who built a splendid cottage with a view of the Pacific on a swath of coastline between Long Beach and Laguna. They had renovated, of course, designing the clubhouse around floor-to-ceiling windows that overlooked a garden landscape of rocks and waterfalls, cascading down to an Olympic-size swimming pool, dazzling in its undulations under the summer sun. To the left were the dining room, bar, and deck with its seafarer's blue-striped umbrellas; to the right was the pro shop, where one browsed for titanium drivers, awaiting the call to tee-time on the club's eighteen-hole course.

The manicured greens were practically empty on such a warm afternoon, but Sergeant Warneke found his way to the Masthead bar. It looked like all the members in the club had done the same thing. There weren't many of them: two gentlemen at one table in the corner, extending a business lunch into the afternoon, and three ladies sitting next to the picture window, murmuring behind their white gloves and occasionally screeching with laughter.

Sergeant Warneke ordered a Johnny black on the rocks and set a fresh fifty-dollar bill under his glass. He sipped the drink, and the fifty rose with it, drawing the eye of the bartender like a flag in the breeze. He was a beefy young man in a green jacket and black tie, who stepped over as soon as the empty glass hit the bar, with the bill still clinging to its wet bottom.

"Would you like a refill, sir?"

Sergeant Warneke liked that *refill*. Like a fountain pen out of ink. Of course, there was nothing to do but refill it. He tapped the fifty under the glass while the bartender poured a second shot more generous than the first. When the man finally raised the bottle, Warneke said, "Is it always this slow in the afternoon?"

The man nodded. "It fills up toward dinner—starts to, after five. We keep it open now for the convenience of the members."

"Big tippers?"

"Not really, sir," said the bartender, glancing at the wet fifty but unsure if he could reach out and touch it. "Around here they say they know the value of money. Which means the value of keeping it."

Sergeant Warneke allowed himself a brief smile in sympathy. "All of them?"

"Most. Not all."

"Was Walter Frick a big tipper?"

The bartender winced, as if he had said too much already. "I really can't talk about the members, sir."

"What's your name, son?"

"Hector."

"I swear, Hector—President Grant will pardon you, if you do."

Hector looked at the bill sadly and then back at Warneke. "You're not a member yourself, are you, sir? Thinking of joining? Or just a guest?"

Segeant Warneke tapped his breast pocket. "I'm with the LAPD," he confided, as if showing his badge might give away the secret between them.

"We run a pretty tight ship, sir. I mean, once in a while I might pour a drink for a kid to bring to his dad. But we check IDs, even when asking-to-see-one kisses your tip goodbye."

"I'm not after your license, Hector. Or a handout. I'm investigating the death of Walter Frick. He was a member here, wasn't he?"

"What a tragedy!" The bartender shook his head. "You see a person one day, alive and kicking …"

"And the next you don't."

"Or ever again." The bartender sighed at the futility of life. Then he looked up. "In that case, I don't really have a choice—do I?—but to answer your questions, as a matter of law?"

"I would say no."

Hector slipped the fifty into his back pocket. "Then I would have to say no, too, sir. Mr. Frick was not a generous tipper."

"Was he having money troubles?"

"The club secretary would know that better than I would, sir. But I wouldn't say so, from his ordering. Pinch and a sirloin, eating alone. When things get tight, you might see a member order Johnny black with company but red when he's alone. Mr. Frick was sirloin all the way."

"Except on the tips?"

"None of them are really decent tippers—with one or two exceptions."

"The new money? Not the gentry."

"Well, Seven-0, for one. I don't know what kind of money you would call him. Every kind, I guess."

"Is that a room number?"

"Pardon me, sir—that's what they called Mr. Hazlitt around the club. Colonel Hazlitt, I should say. He used to keep a house on the far side of the golf course. They say a Saudi prince has it now, who keeps his harem there. I don't believe it. He never stops in the Masthead for a whiskey, the way the Colonel did. But you know all about Hazlitt from the papers."

"He must've spread it around pretty good," Warneke said, "since it wasn't his money."

"It was, once they handed it over." The bartender lowered his voice. "Which they couldn't wait to do. Some of it came from the members of this club."

"Some of it came from everybody."

"Not everybody, sir. You had to be somebody for him to take it. But they were all after him. Producers, real estate lawyers, even movie stars. You should've seen them in here, popping Dom Perignon. Begging him to let them in on just one deal."

"And the more he said *no* —"

"The harder they chased him. That's why they called him *Seven-0*—because he wouldn't take an investment under ten million dollars. Except from the marines."

"Is that true?"

"He liked to say he had a soft spot for servicemen. If they served their country in uniform, the least he could do was help them to their reward. But it was good business, too. You know how many soldiers make a brigade?"

A man was standing just inside the kitchen, behind the swinging doors. He had a moustache and bowtie in a stiff white collar. The assistant manager, Warneke guessed, with an eagle eye on his domain, trying to decide if Hector was serving the club or some other, nefarious purpose.

Before the bartender noticed his boss, the Sergeant raised his tumbler for another scotch. "Was Mr. Frick an investor?"

"I never got that impression. He would sit on a stool at the end of the bar there, watching them flatter Colonel Hazlitt. You should've heard the things he mumbled under his breath."

"Maybe because he wanted in, and Seven-0 froze him out."

"I don't think so. Mr. Frick was a banker, sir. They like to see collateral before they reach into their pockets."

"Not collateral damage?"

Hector grinned, feeling the folded fifty in his pocket. "That's very well said, sir. I think Mr. Frick would've appreciated it."

The man in the bowtie started their way. Warneke said, "Did he also appreciate other things? Like Stud or Texas Hold-em?"

"I've served a lot of bankers, sir, but never met one who enjoyed taking a risk. They don't even like to try a single malt they haven't tasted before. Maybe Mr. Frick sat in on a friendly game, for social reasons. Schmoozing is a major occupation around here. They just call it *networking*. But gambling debts are not good for business. I can't see Mr. Frick putting too many chips on the line."

"Redheads?"

Hector found a towel and began cleaning the bar. "I haven't seen him with too many women. He brought a blonde in once, last week."

"Once last week? Or once ever?"

"I never saw her before. Maybe twenty-five, thirty. With curls."

"With a ring?" Warneke waggled a finger.

"Didn't notice. But she was in a skirt, to the knee, with a jacket. Greyish blue – let's say wool or linen. Over a silk blouse, open at the throat."

'Showing her bra."

"But tasteful, you know? Just the lace. They sat right here, at a table in the light, and didn't stay long."

"Did you happen to hear their conversation?"

"We never eavesdrop on the guests," said Hector quickly. "That would be cause for removal at the Condor."

"But you might've picked up a word or two. Pouring refills, say."

77

Hector hesitated. "I did hear one word," he said, lowering his voice. "*Break-up*. The blonde said it. A little loud."

"*Break-up*? As in a marriage?"

"Or a merger. Maybe it was *crack-up*. Something like that. But I wouldn't jump to conclusions. I'd bet nothing very adulterous was going on between them."

"Why not?"

"Would you cheat on a wife who could throw you in jail?"

Hector turned his back, and Sergeant Warneke heard the click of the assistant manager approaching with taps on the heels. He raised his glass in commercial salute and received a stiff-necked nod.

Ulysses S. Grant had worn out his welcome. But that was all right. Sergeant Warneke had caught a buzz and something to report.

17

"A blonde!" said Patricia Newman in the late afternoon, when Sergeant Warneke gave his report at an impromptu meeting of the investigative team. Marilyn Montoya sat on the edge of her chair, clutching a paper cup of coffee, while Bruner and Yost sat back into the couch pillows like a pair of greyback gorillas. The lieutenant ran a hand through her own hair, tucking a loose curl behind her ear as if she didn't remember its color. "I knew it."

Warneke wasn't sure she understood the subtext. In the interest of full disclosure he said, "The bartender didn't think there was anything between them."

The Lieutenant shrugged. "So Frick didn't screw her on a table in the bar. That's all your bartender got to see of them, wasn't it?"

"She was dressed in a suit and a white silk shirt."

"I heard," said Newman. "Leaning forward, showing off her bra."

"But not in an obvious way. Hector said *tasteful*."

"Another word for *pricey*, Sergeant."

"You think she's a pro?"

"It's a good bet with a man like Frick. Someone nice and presentable, who won't ring in the middle of the night or sit in her car outside the house. Walter makes a call, names the hotel, spends an hour, and goes home to Her Honor. That's how they do it, in the civilized classes."

Sergeant Warneke nodded, unwilling to contradict Newman when she had a horse in the race. "It's a theory, Lieutenant."

At the word *theory*, Bruner and Yost exchanged a glance, each looking to see if the other would object. Bruner leaned forward and set both palms flat on his knees, but before he could speak up, Newman said, "Did you find anything on your canvassing that would contradict it, officers?"

Bruner seemed to lose his thread, but Yost said, "Nothing that would disprove it. The crime rate in Cheviot Hills is low, even for the Westside. The local streets wind in and out among the houses with no wide thoroughfare to serve as an escape route. No sign of a spike in burglaries, in particular."

Newman gave Montoya a significant look.

"But nothing to confirm it, either," said Bruner, rediscovering his voice.

"Among the neighbors," added Yost, backing up his partner. The two men were senior to be going door to door. If they thought their assignment was intended to keep them from second-guessing the Lieutenant, they chose not to share that thought with anyone else on the team. Which was just the way she liked it.

"We rang all the doorbells," Bruner said, "but by the time we got to talk to them, the word had spread around the block. A couple of people heard the dog barking – that was all we learned. The rest of it was what they had heard, or thought they heard, or else wanted to hear from us. The judge killed her husband, didn't she? She must have done something, or the police wouldn't be asking about her. Some of them got the story wrong and thought he murdered her."

"They knew he was going to do it, too."

"Any suggestion of domestic violence?" Newman asked.

Both men shook their heads. "No police reports. No logged calls or home visits. The neighbors on three sides never heard raised voices from the Fricks."

"What about the fourth side?"

"A typesetter, living there less than a year. Who never heard of the Fricks."

"In a year," said Bruner, for emphasis.

"It's hard to miss a couple screaming," said Yost, "even if you work nights."

"Not if they're living next door," added Bruner.

"You," said Newman, with a finger pointed at Yost. "Worked Vice, didn't you?"

Yost shrugged, but his red face gave him away.

"I didn't know that," said Bruner.

"I don't like to talk about it. Not a happy time."

"You still know the landscape, don't you?" said Newman. "Why don't you give Brewer the tour? Drop by some high-end brothels and beat the bushes."

"For what?"

"For Walter Frick's blonde."

"What about our canvassing?" said Bruner, who never left a job unfinished if he could help it, no matter how much grunt work it entailed. "We've still got maybe a dozen neighbors to go."

"If you count the folks around the corner and down the block," said Yost. "We ought to go back to the Black Forest cottage. She knows more than she told us."

"No, she doesn't," said Bruner.

80

"She hesitated," insisted Yost. 'When I asked how well she knew them."

"She was drunk," said Bruner. "And she likes you."

Yost blushed. "She does not."

"No more canvassing," said Newman. "If there was anything more to hear, somebody would have heard it. The kitchen door wasn't forced. No one broke into the Frick house. If we find Walter's curly-haired blonde, we'll make our case."

"Against a hooker?" said the Sergeant.

She looked at him steadily. "A blonde is a motive, Sergeant Warneke."

18

There were two women behind the reception desk at Walter Frick's bank, and the younger one seemed the more experienced. She was a perky blonde in her late twenties, training a redhead ten years older how to forward incoming calls. That was a thing Jack always enjoyed about Los Angeles: its abundance of blondes. Something about the sun, they said, lightened hair that would have been some shade of brown in Topeka or Duluth. Jack had grown up in the Southland—his grandfather had come in the forties to work the aircraft plants—but Jack had done some traveling after the navy, and was always cheered to see the long tan legs in shorts and espadrilles gathered around the baggage carousel in the LA airport.

The clusters of blondes at LAX were part of a larger abundance of good-looking women who had found their way to the Golden State of California. It was as if somebody had picked up the country by the Midwest, so that the most beautiful women tumbled one way or the other. They weren't all starlets, either. The movies drew beauty queens from all over the country, who took their head-shots and acting lessons and, in between casting calls, squeezed cantaloupes in the grocery aisles or swiveled on barstools at night, flicking their cigarettes. That competition made other women in town shape up too – first the agents and execs in the business who had to rub knees with the starlets every day, then the women who lunched with those agents and execs, and then the rest of them. Jack felt a dutiful sympathy for the women forking salads, trying to keep up, but he had to admire the result. It was a pleasure he dearly missed, when he lost his eyesight: the silhouette of an average girl window-shopping on Melrose, who looked like a million bucks in Dayton, Ohio.

Jack tilted his head to the left and centered the perky blonde in the small square of retina cells that came into focus. She sat in a chair on wheels, with a low backrest that held her spine in the gentle curve of its fabric. No one had taught her much about make-up, which she had applied with a free hand, bright red on her lips, dark blue around her eyes, a cheerful pink on cheekbones that needed no brushed-on color. Her hair swung loose, but it wasn't hard to imagine her at the gym or the beach with her ponytail bobbing out of a baseball cap. She would envy the ladies in Italian labels, with red-leather accessories and break-your-neck shoes that went with only one outfit. Jack would have liked to slip behind the counter to whisper never-you-mind; there's beauty and beauty, and you have your own.

Instead, he said, "Good afternoon. Can you point us in the direction of Walter Frick's secretary?"

"His *assistant?*" asked the blonde, without dropping her smile.

"If you say so."

"Whom should I say is calling?" she inquired just like they do in the movies.

"Jack Stryker," said Aisha. "He may not look like much, but he's a hero cop. Really."

"You're a police officer?" The blonde asked Jack. She was growing less perky by the minute, unwilling to seem uncertain in front of her trainee but unwilling to take Aisha's word for it.

"Not at the moment," said Jack, "unless you believe the papers."

"Are you shaking your head? Or ogling me?"

"Neither," said Aisha with a sigh. "He's trying to get a clear picture."

"Of what, exactly?"

"Mr. Frick's … office," said Jack.

"Here you go, Emily," said the blonde to the redhead. "That's Jennifer, on 21. Push the button and let her know she has a visitor."

There were no buttons on the receptionist's phone—just a series of grey boxes in columns on the flat screen. Emily hit the square for 21 twice before the perky blonde took her finger and touched it to the screen. A red light on the far side of the phone started blinking. Emily held the receiver to her ear, but the light kept blinking, while the others watched it shine.

"No one's picking up."

"Let me try," said the perky blonde, taking the receiver. "I saw her go back with a couple of cartons half an hour ago."

She hit the grey button with a practiced snap and the red light blinked again. She propped the receiver under her ear, but no one picked up, and the perky blonde set the receiver back on his hook.

"Jen must be in his office," she announced.

"I can show them," said Emily, to escape the phone. "Mr. Frick's in the third office on the left?"

"Right," said the perky blonde, with a little pout of surprise.

"I do pay attention," said Emily. She gave the blonde a quick smile and led Jack and Aisha down a long corridor, past many more than three offices on the left. They turned right, right again, and continued down another long corridor to a glass door. Jack held it, following her into the executive suite.

As he watched her pass, Jack noticed how much more confident Emily seemed in the hall than she had behind the desk. It was in her stride, the crisp way she turned right and left without a moment's doubt. She might have been a woman returning to the workforce after her children were grown; the assurance in her step came only from competence and its recognition. Jack wondered idly about her first career and why she hadn't returned to it, when she turned abruptly and opened the third door on the left.

"Here we are," she announced.

Jack found himself in an empty office with a black glass desk, a metal file cabinet, and a wooden door ajar to the inner sanctum. Inside that room, a slender woman in a flower print dress was packing cardboard cartons with file folders.

As the threesome entered, she looked up and asked in a voice like the principal's of a private school, "Yes? Can I help you?"

Emily and Aisha turned to Jack, who explained, "My name is Stryker. With the police. I'm looking into Mr. Frick's passing."

"The police have already been through," said the slim woman.

"We're coming through again," said Aisha.

"This is my personal assistant, Ms. Adams," said Jack, and Aisha made a little curtsy. "I think you already know Emily."

"The new girl," said the redhead, raising her hand. "In reception."

The woman lowered a pair of bifocals from the top of her head. "Of course you are, dear." Her tone suggested a doubt about Emily's department. Or the questionable word might have been *girl*.

"Now you know all of us," Jack said. "Do you prefer Jennifer? Or Jenny?"

"I prefer *Mrs. Hellman*."

"All right," said Jack, "Mrs. Hellman. You are—or were—Mr. Frick's personal assistant?"

"Only since younger women started getting hired," said Mrs. Hellman. "Before then, we were called *executive secretaries*, which had more dignity to it, if you ask me. It's a perfectly respectable title, even honorable. Like the Secretary of State, of Defense, or the Secretary of the Treasury."

"Did you work closely with Mr. Frick?"

Mrs. Hellman hesitated over the word *closely*.

"Professionally," added Jack.

"Only since his transfer to the Westside office," she said. "This is the regional office. Most of his career was spent in San Bernardino and the Inland Empire. But when Corporate decided to promote him, they assigned him to me."

"For training."

"For *orientation*, we like to say."

"So he would know which is east and which is west? Where the sun rises, and where it sets."

The etymological answer seemed to please her. "Something like that. He knew the banking business already, of course, but he had to learn the local geography—whose shrines to pass up and where he needed to kneel."

"And you taught him. That should have made you invaluable."

"At least *valuable*," said Mrs. Hellman. "Strange, isn't it, how opposite words should have such similar meanings? But, yes, I suppose it did. Mr. Frick spent more time with me than he did with anyone else."

"Including his wife?"

"More *working* time. But that was sometimes more than any other time. Banking can be a very demanding occupation."

"Did Mr. Frick have any other close associates?"

"He had professional colleagues. Like any senior executive."

"Any particular rivals?"

"For promotions or bonuses? Not more than anyone else at his level in the bank. As one approaches the top jobs, the field of potential candidates narrows. But I can't think of a single person whose career might be advanced sufficiently to consider pushing Mr. Frick aside. That is what you're driving at, isn't it?"

"Yes."

"Then, as I said, no."

"No enemies? Or threats in anonymous envelopes?"

"With cut-out letters? Lord, no."

"Did he have any particular friends?"

"What do you mean?"

"What do you call them, in finance? Allies?"

"We all work together, here, Mr. Stryker," said Mrs. Hellman. "This is one bank. Our executives have no need for *alliances*."

"Did he have any of those?"

"What?"

"Alliances," Jack repeated, and suddenly it sounded different from *allies*.

85

"Are you asking me if Mr. Frick … ? "

"Had any special friendships among his colleagues here. Or among his clients. People do, Mrs. Hellman, especially people with power and money. Mr. Frick was a man with both of those things, wasn't he? So I am asking if there was anybody for whom he made special allowances, because they allowed him to do special things."

"That's disgusting."

"Maybe so. But was there?"

"Mr. Stryker," said Mrs. Hellman, "I am not about to discuss Mr. Frick's intimate affairs with you or anybody else. People have personal relationships with friends and families that are best left between them."

"I'm trying to solve his murder. Mr. Frick would want that."

"Maybe he would. But that doesn't mean he would want his dirty laundry hung out in public."

"There is some dirty laundry, then? To hang?"

She shook her head. "Tell me, Mr. Stryker—don't you have any family secrets you would want respected, after your untimely demise?"

She had a great vocabulary—Jack had to hand that to her – and a feel for the right question. Both were skills beyond what he expected from your average personal assistant. For a moment he thought of Judith, and Maggie, and the little café on Montana Avenue. How long could a dead man keep his secrets? Or were they all opened with his assets?

"Do you know his secrets, Mrs. Hellman? Or simply that he had them?"

She blinked at him in disappointment over the frame of her eyeglasses. "I won't dignify that question with an answer, Mr. Stryker."

She already had. Jack stood and offered his hand. "I respect that, Mrs. Hellman. I think we have what we came for and won't take up more of your time. Before we go, please let me say: If I ever get to hire an executive secretary, I hope she's as thoughtful and discreet as you."

"Thank you," said Mrs. Hellman. "I do hope you catch your man – discreetly. It was interesting to meet you too, Miss Adams."

Aisha shook just the tips of her fingers, as if she were meeting the Queen of England.

"If that's all you need, Mr. Stryker, Emily can show you out."

Emily certainly did. She escorted them back down the labyrinthine hallways to the reception desk and kept going to the elevator bay. She pushed the button, waited until their car arrived, and held the door until they had taken their places. She stood watching until the door closed between them.

Once it did, however, she did not immediately turn on her heel and head back into the office. Instead she opened her cell phone and touched a number in its memory. When a voice picked up, she said, "Patricia Newman, please." And a moment later, "Lieutenant? It's Detective Montoya. Yes, you could say I'm finding a place for myself here … learning to use the phone and keeping an eye on who comes and goes. As a matter of fact, you'll never guess who just dropped by, asking about Walter Frick."

19

"Did we get what we came for, Jack?" asked Aisha when the two of them had returned to their car. She could sense the excitement in him, but couldn't tell whether it had come from their interview with Mrs. Hellman or the glints of clarity Jack was getting through his healing retina cells. He was definitely seeing things—squinting at the light on the windshield, blinking as the sun bounced off the chrome on passing cars. When the streetlight changed from red to green, he leaned forward as if to lend his weight to the forward motion of the Buick.

"We did learn a few things," Jack said. "His secretary is still loyal—which means that she doesn't know of anything Walter might have done to embarrass the firm. Or at least she doesn't want to believe in anything. And Mrs. Hellman doesn't know a rival whose career might have profited from Walter's death."

"Or else she wouldn't tell us."

"Or, yes, wouldn't tell us about one. But if she's still loyal, and did know of one, wouldn't she want to tell us? Since we were asking explicitly? Ms. Hellman is obviously a woman of discretion, but I doubt she would lie outright to the police."

"If she believed we were the police," Aisha said doubtfully. "I wouldn't. Maybe she was covering for somebody."

"Maybe she was," said Jack. "But an executive secretary's career rises and falls with her boss. Whoever stuck that knife into Walter Frick struck a vein in Ms. Hellman's status at the bank. That's got to be important to her. We gave her a chance for payback, beyond reproach. She could've pointed at anyone who ever took her parking spot or held her up at the fax machine. She had to tell us the truth, didn't she? But she didn't drop a name. I'll bet that's on the level. She couldn't think of anybody at the bank with a motive to stab Mr. Frick in the back. Or the belly."

"Well, that's something, I guess," said Aisha.

"I'm just getting started," said Jack. "Frick hadn't been at the home office long enough to make enemies in the executive suite, but that doesn't mean he didn't have any someplace else. That's not where he made his rep at the bank, is it?"

"Wasn't he like ... the Vice President?"

"*A vice president*. Big difference. There could be lots of them, who don't take over if somebody shoots the president. They're hard to tell apart, when everybody's wearing a clean white collar. If you want to find dirty fingernails, you've got to look at the other end, where he earned his office in the first place."

"Where's that?"

"That's what we need to find out," said Jack. "He was a regional manager in the Inland Empire, according to Mrs. Hellman. Why don't we drive out to the branch in San Bernardino and see what we can find?"

Aisha slid the shift into gear with a jerk of the transmission. Doing was always her preference over talking.

The drive out on the Ten took almost three hours. That was hardly Aisha's fault, who drove the Buick like a motorcycle, slipping its big chrome nose into spaces a Mini would hesitate to tread. But the motley fleet of cars rolling west into downtown every morning and east to their garages each night made the armored vehicles on the shores of Normandy look like a used truck lot. By the time the Buick pulled into the lot behind the California First International office in San Bernardino, Jack felt as if every muscle in his legs had been squeezed into its smallest possible shape and then pressed into that awkward position by a steam cleaning machine. Still, if he tilted his head at just the right angle, Jack could read the business hours posted below the *Bank-Parking-Only* sign.

Unfortunately, they were late. The bank had closed its glass doors two hours before their arrival. The big counter was dark, and the private desks in front were unoccupied. But Jack saw a light in the back, reflecting off the computer screens and the steel door of the vault. Banks used to hide the money in the basement, where no one was tempted to try for it. Now the shiny vaults were displayed in the window, as if to convince a passing crowd they really had money inside. Or perhaps they didn't need much cash any more, since the real money was just a blip on a chip of computer memory, crediting Jack with a deposit and Jill with a loan, which somehow seemed to multiply the value of actual cash beyond all reckoning.

Aisha tried the door, which was locked, of course. But she kept rattling it, as if she were planning to shatter the glass, making enough noise to rouse the dead—or at least the dead soul clicking away at his computer in the back office, after all of the tellers had gone home for the night.

It might have been a welcome distraction, a chance to get away from the numbers on his screen, when a gleaming head popped out of the inner office. At first Jack thought he might be a child, but as he drew near the plate glass door, a fringe of grey hair around his bald head and the worry lines on his forehead gave the man away for forty-something at least, in a job that kept him awake and out of the sun.

The banker couldn't have been taller than five-six or -seven. He stood just inside the plate glass and shook his head, pointing a crooked finger at the gold letters stenciled on the door. *We're closed,* he mouthed, in case they missed the point.

"We're police," Jack said aloud, showing the badge in his wallet. The gesture felt strange—he hadn't done that in a while.

The little man peered doubtfully at Aisha and then more carefully at the badge. It looked like a detective's gold shield, all right. He had seen them before, when the bank was held up, last Christmas. *Robbers had gifts to buy too, didn't they?* a San Berdoo cop said, while an officer from LA made a face but said nothing. Bank robbery is a federal offense, so neither one had jurisdiction, but the local cops turn up whenever the Feds come to town, in case there are any collateral crimes they can make their own. Or just to get their faces on the TV news.

"I'm not the law." Aisha pounded her chest. "But he is," thumbing Jack.

That confession reassured the banker, or his glance at her chest did the trick, because a moment later the little man unlocked the door.

"I'm not supposed to be doing this without authorization from the manager."

"Where is the manager?" asked Jack. "Home already?"

"We don't have one," said the little man, locking the door behind them with a key too large for his pocket. "We did have one, of course. We've had several. But it's not exactly the plum job it used to be. More of a raisin, these days, if you want to know the truth."

"You mean the manager's post?"

"Banking," said the little man. "The whole business—unless of course you've got one of those jobs where it doesn't matter if your borrowers make their payments. They call that *banking* too, but it's got as much resemblance to our regular business as a goat has to a goatee."

"What's your name?" asked Aisha.

"Carafiol," said the little man. "Gerald Carafiol."

Jack tried, "Assistant Manager?"

"God forbid," said Carafiol. "I'm the in-house auditor. The guy you bring in to go over your books before you turn them over to the pencils who can send you to jail. I used to be one of those pencils, myself, before I went over to the dark side."

"Got tired of sending folks to jail?" said Aisha.

Carafiol laughed. "That was the fun part. Couldn't have happened soon enough for some of those citizens. But the good guys never pay as well as the Evil Empire, do they?"

"Find anything?" asked Jack.

Carafiol eyed him slyly. "Who wants to know?"

"My name is Stryker. John J. I'm a Detective Sergeant in the LAPD."

"What does the J stand for?"

"Jay. This is my associate, Aisha Adams."

"Nice to meet you, Ms. Adams. But this is San Bernardino."

"We're not investigating a local crime, or a federal one, either. Did you happen to know a regional manager named Frick?"

"Walter? Of course. But what do you mean, *did*? He's at headquarters now. As a Vee Pee."

"He's not anything now. Somebody stabbed him in his kitchen in Cheviot Hills. We're trying to figure out who might have swung the knife."

Carafiol puffed his cheeks and blew out a stream of air. "Jesus. Walter? Well, you've come to the right place for that."

"We have."

"Did you happen to catch the *For Sale* signs on your drive out here?"

"Did Walter have something to do with that?"

"Was he a banker? Houses don't mortgage themselves."

"Were you doing internal audits then? When Frick was regional manager?"

"I've been at this job for six and a half years now. And counting."

"Find anything suspicious?"

Carafiol sat back against the edge of a desk and crossed his legs. The crease in his trousers was razor-sharp, but he plucked it anyway. "Is that why you're knocking after hours, John Jay Law? To learn what the sleepy old auditor blurts out, in gratitude for a little company?"

"We hit a lot of traffic," Aisha began to explain.

"Something like that," said Jack.

Carafiol nodded. He didn't say it wasn't going to work, just that he was aware of the plan. He looked at Aisha, as if she were a ploy

91

as well. "He wasn't handling loans himself, as regional manager. Just policy. Making sure our regional guidelines followed the lead of the mucky-mucks."

"Do you audit policies too?"

"I do. And did."

"You must've turned up something, after all these hours."

"Just what you'd expect." Carafiol shrugged. "Nothing outright illegal. Nobody goes to jail for what they don't say. *Caveat emptor,* right? That's the rule of the day. If it's too good to be true, it isn't. You can warn people even as you're picking their pockets, and they'll still believe whatever they want to be true. That's the beauty of it, they say—the people who find that kind of thing beautiful."

"But you don't."

"No."

Jack nodded. "What kind of thing, exactly?"

Carafiol hesitated—but he glanced at Aisha, who smiled at him. "Deception. Bait and switch. Promising what you know you can't deliver, but not quite promising it, either. Warning the buyers up front it might not happen, while you count on their hope and greed to convince them that you're just being overly cautious—that the law requires you to warn them of risks any businessman with balls would ignore."

"Isn't that illegal?" asked Aisha.

"To give people loans you know they can't repay? Of course not. No legislature would pass a law that prevented people from making fools of themselves."

"But why would a bank do that?" Aisha asked. "Lend money that can't be repaid? A pool-hall shark wouldn't. Do they want to lose money?"

"Banks don't lose money," Carafiol said, "unless it's stuffed in someone's pockets. Even then, they're insured against the loss. They *would* lose money, if they held onto a loan they knew couldn't be paid. But thanks to some innovations in the banking business, there's no reason to hold onto any. The loans themselves have value, if you can pile up enough of them. If a bank kept six loans that couldn't be repaid, it would lose a pile of cash, when the real estate those loans purchased had to be sold off. But if a bank can assemble stacks of bad loans, bundle them into a security and sell the kit-and-caboodle, that bank will make a killing before the first installment payment."

Aisha made a face. "Who's gonna buy that?"

"Another bank, of course," said Carafiol, as beads of sweat collected over his lip. "By which I mean a bigger bank, who can gather together six hundred or six thousand bad loans, with a few hundred good ones thrown into the mix. Now you've got a shit-pile you can sell for real money."

"To who?"

"Lot of people, here and overseas. Ultimately the Chinese. There's ten times more investment capital in the world today than there ever was before. Or I should say, there *was* ten times more capital. Some of it withered away in the crash. Not that the bankers got hurt—most of them. When the music ended and they got stuck with the last toxic assets they couldn't even sell to the Chinese, what happened?"

Aisha looked at Jack, who told her, "Their Uncle Sam stepped in and took it off their hands."

"Which is just what they knew would happen," the auditor said. "That's why they built those securities on home loans in the first place. They knew no elected official would let millions of American families lose their homes to China—not if they planned to get elected again. The bankers knew it, and the Chinese knew it too, when they were pitched those fancy new financial instruments. That's why they bought them."

Aisha said, "Is that what an *instrument* is?"

"Just a document with a signature at the bottom."

"I thought it was, like, a surgeon's knife."

"Or a cello? Nothing so precise. Basically they figured out a way to sell the real estate of the United States to the Chinese, parcel by parcel. Neat little scam, wasn't it? And as I said, perfectly legal."

Aisha whistled. "They toss us in the tank overnight for screwing one guy at a time."

Jack said, "The banks knew they'd be bailed out?"

"They *planned* on it," said Carafiol, "as a means of escape, when the game ran out." He patted the drops above his lip with a cotton handkerchief. "To cover their bets, they appointed the president of the biggest bank the Secretary of the Treasury."

Aisha was growing confused. "I always thought the President of the United States appointed people like that. Secretaries of things."

Carafiol looked surprised at the idea. "Right—so the big Wall Street banks make huge contributions to both candidates' campaigns. All they wanted in exchange for their checks was the key to the U.S. Treasury. Do you know any candidate who'd refuse them that? Not to keep the cash—just to tide them over, while they pass the house keys and the mortgages from one proud line of credit to the next."

"You mean the homeowners."

"You can call them that, if you want. They signed on the dotted line. Of course, once the banks were bailed out, they had zero interest in helping anybody who couldn't keep up his mortgage. The Feds were holding the paper by then. The banks couldn't wait to throw those deadbeat borrowers out on the street, so their houses would be empty and they could start the whole thing over again."

Jack squinted at the last daylight. "Don't they have independent agencies rating these things? Saying this is an A security and that's a B?"

"Oh, yeah," said Carafiol. "To help investors feel secure in buying paper they don't understand. Except the rating agencies are paid by the banks, who told them to rate these securities *only against each other.*"

"Isn't that the idea? Comparing deals?"

"Sounds like it," agreed Carafiol, "until you take a closer look. Let's say you have a thousand mortgages, and you rate each bunch A, B, or C. The banks sold off the A and B stuff. Then they repackaged whatever junk they had left and rehired the rating agencies to do it again. Now a bunch of mortgages that used to be rated C are suddenly backing an A-rated security, since they're marginally better than the rest of the junk. The banks then sold off those securities, and again repackaged what was left. It didn't take long before they had some very toxic assets on their hands."

"And no one complained?"

"Not so long as they could sell the paper to the next guy."

"You're talking about a national Ponzi scheme."

"No, this was much bigger than Charlie Ponzi ever dreamed. And nobody went to prison."

"Is that how Walter Frick did it?" Jack asked finally. "Is that how he made a name for himself in the Inland Empire?"

Carafiol shrugged. "I'd say Frick was riding the wave by then, like most regional managers. He'd made his name already on some really risky deals. But those were back in his salad days, as a wildcat branch manager. In El Monte."

20

It was too late to drive to El Monte with any hope of catching the California First International branch office still open, but Jack and Aisha were on the freeway by nine the next morning. They drove east, past downtown Los Angeles, where the sun bounced off the unremarkable slabs of a cluster of glass skyscrapers, the silver sails of the concert hall, and the golden curves of the Bonaventure Hotel. They followed the signs and found the Ten heading east again toward the Inland Empire, rolling through the neighborhoods of East Los Angeles.

Though neither of them knew El Monte, they found the branch office in record time. Business was off to a slow start: one teller was open, serving customers who refused to avail themselves of the ATMs. A man at the counter was counting rolls of quarters; an older woman waited patiently on line with her savings book clutched in her hand. There were three desks in the service area for home and auto loans, but only one was occupied, by a pleasant Latina in a light brown dress, who inquired if she could help them. She inspected Jack's badge and led them to the cubicle farthest from the door. There were pictures in a double frame of two smiling girls on a stone block at Machu Picchu, and a grim-faced man in a Dodgers cap.

Miranda had survived the staff reductions, cutbacks and furloughs. The name on her pin read *Ms. M. Lopez, Assistant Manager*, but she asked them to call her *Miranda*. "Yes, Walter Frick was the manager here, but that was before my time," she said, shaking her head. "We've had two managers since then, and it looks like we're due for our third. Business is not what it was in Mr. Frick's heyday."

That was true all over, Jack agreed. People had lost their faith in banks. But did she still have records of the time when Mr. Frick was manager?

"Not *records*," said Miranda, as if she wished she had thought of that. "We were running a different assessment regime for our loan officers, then. We have sales reports for the office as a whole and comparison figures with our sister branch in Gardena."

"Why Gardena?"

"It's a friendly little rivalry. They're just about the same size, and they opened right before us. Mr. Frick insisted we compete against them, to keep our adrenaline pumping."

"Did you win?"

"Walter Frick did, as you know. I'm not so sure about the rest of us."

"Do you have his sales reports?"

"We don't keep them back that far. But we must have the loans he signed. Are you really with the police department?"

"I'm not," said Aisha, meeting Miranda's doubtful eyes. "But he is."

"Then he can look through them."

It was the first time Jack tried to read any print since his accident at the meth lab. The letters swam a little before his eyes, but if he focused on a spot just above them, they took their places in line. Aisha sat beside him with pad and paper as he worked through the file cabinet Miranda said held the paperwork from loans at that time. Whenever Jack found a loan with Walter Frick's signature, they jotted down the name and address. All of the recent loans were done online, but they didn't use the same system in Walter Frick's day, and you couldn't sort by the manager's signature, anyway.

Jack had no patience for this sort of detective work. He could interview a suspect for eleven hours, but an hour and a half were his limit when it came to doing paperwork. Important cases were broken this way, involving tax evasion and securities fraud—they nailed Al Capone on his income tax, didn't they? But Jack could never have managed it.

By eleven he was going blind again, so they headed for the Buick to check out the homes on Aisha's notepad.

It made the filing cabinet feel like fun.

The first address on their list was a pink stucco house with a roof of broken tiles, squatting in a lawn of yellow grass. No one answered the door when they rang the bell. The front window was shuttered on the left side but open on the right. Jack tried to peer through the dusty glass but saw no lights inside. On the TV set was a clock that didn't move. The electricity had been turned off. He opened the screen door and knocked, but again, no one answered.

"Nobody's home, Jack," Aisha told him. "It looks like they took off a while ago. Let's try the next one on the list."

He turned to go, but as he did, something reddish caught his eye—the gingham skirt of a rag doll in the dandelions along the edge of the porch. Jack picked it up, smoothed the skirt, and propped it beside the door. When they went back to their car he heard the screen door open behind them. By the time he looked up, it had closed again, but the rag doll was gone.

The next two houses were pretty much the same.

They heard mariachi music from the second house as they crossed the lawn, but it cut off suddenly when they stepped onto the porch, and no one answered the bell. Jack thumped with the side of his fist on the splintered wooden door, until Aisha showed him a balled-up scrap of paper that had caught in the thorns of a bush. *FORECLOSURE*, it read, with the citation to the relevant section of the Municipal Code and a phone number for the office of the Federal Marshall.

At the third house they found a resident homeowner. She was a short, wrinkled woman in her late forties, wrapped in a head-shawl despite the heat of the day. She opened her front door but kept the screen between them. Jack told her they had come from the California First International on a routine check, to make sure she was satisfied with the service she had received.

"The bank?" she scowled at him.

Jack nodded. "California First International. That's where you got your loan, ma'am, isn't it?"

"No, no. He's not home. Out." The woman started closing the door.

Aisha checked her notepad. "Your name is on the mortgage, Senora. Luisa Inez Ramirez. That's not your husband's name, is it?"

The woman held the door. "My son," she said, "Angelito. He's not home." Then she shut the heavy door, leaving Jack and Aisha standing alone on another empty porch.

Jack said, "Luisa Inez is her son?"

Aisha checked off the address. "We're making progress. We met a borrower. And no one's shooting at us. Want to try Number Four?"

He squinted at the sun. "It must be noon already. I thought I saw a little *taqueria* on the way."

Aisha made a face at him. "You want to stop for lunch? Already?"

"Door-to-door detective work always makes me hungry."

The little *taqueria* was filled to capacity when Jack's Buick pulled up outside. They put their name on the list and went back to wait in their car. They hadn't waited five minutes when someone tapped on the passenger side window.

Jack said, "Let's go. They've got a table for us."

Aisha shook her head. "I don't think so."

She was right. When Jack climbed out of the car, he realized the young man who held the Buick's door was not about to lead him to a

97

table. He was small, no more than five-two or -three, but built like a fireplug under his white t-shirt. Jack hadn't noticed the tattoos when he tapped on the window, but now that he was out of the car he saw gang tats running up both arms, and two little tears inked at the edge of his droopy right eyelid. One for each kid he put underground.

Behind him were two more gangbangers, grinning at the blinking *gringo*. The big one had a shaved head, which he smoothed with a red hand, but Jack figured the little one for the immediate threat, who bounced up and down as if he couldn't wait to start pummeling somebody for something.

Aisha was still in the car. Jack hoped she knew about the forty-five in the glove compartment, but he couldn't tell her now.

The little guy stepped forward and bounced in Jack's face.

Jack turned and spoke to the muscular fireplug. "Something I can do for you?"

"*Si, Gabacho.* Or maybe you think a something I can do for you?"

"*Pegale,*" said the bouncy one. *Hit him.*

The fireplug laughed at his energetic *compa*. "Can't you see he's blind?"

Jack shook his head. "I can see you well enough."

"Is that what you told my mother?"

"Your mother?"

"She said you were asking for me. At her house."

A light began to dawn for Jack. "You mean one of the houses ..."

"*Quieres algo commigo?*" said the fireplug quietly. "*Pues aqui estoy.*"

Jack knew enough street Spanish to recognize a challenge when he heard one. *You want something with me? Well, here I am.*

"Angelito," he said. "That's you, isn't it? Angel Ramirez?"

'The fireplug looked surprised and wary. "So?'

"I asked your mother about her mortgage," Jack said. 'She must've thought I was asking about you."

"Because you're *jura*."

"Because I'm a cop? I guess," Jack said. "But I'm not with the bank, and I'm not here to foreclose on the house. I'm investigating a homicide."

"Not one of ours," said Angel flatly, meaning, *Why should we care?*

"No—not one of yours. A man named Walter Frick, who lived on the Westside."

Angel nodded, as if he cared after all.

"You knew him, didn't you? When he was the bank manager here?"

"Maybe," said Angel. "Or not. Maybe some of us did."

The other gangbangers seemed to be taking their cue from Angel. The *flaquillo* stopped bouncing up and down. The big *cholo* with the shaved head took his hand out of his pants pocket, where he must have had his *cuete*—Calo slang for firecracker, or gun. Jack started breathing normally again.

"He wrote you a mortgage, didn't he?"

Angel glanced at his *compadres*, who were shifting uneasily but looking to him for an answer. "That's right," he said finally. "Senor Frick was the first banker who ever wanted to talk to me. He said we could do business together—he could put our families into houses of our own. And you know what? He did."

The others were silent behind him. But it felt like a respectful silence.

Jack nodded, in pace with Angel. "Mr. Frick wrote mortgages ... for all of you?"

"And our families," said Angel. "*Mi madre*. And his. His girlfriend. And his. Grifalito has one house for himself and another for his *guerita* and son."

"*De verotas*," said the bouncing boy.

The truth.

"We didn't need to show we had *jales,* or anything. Just signatures on the line, you know? He said he could use the mortgages to make money for his bank, so we got a house and they got some action. A piece for everybody."

"So you signed."

"So? Wouldn't you?"

"A house for a signature? Maybe I would," said Jack. "But the market crashed, and you were suddenly facing foreclosures. Or your mothers and girlfriends were. Did you blame Mr. Frick for that?"

An impish grin stole across Angel's features, softening his face. "You mean, drop him a line? Or did we drive out to Beverly Hills and shoot him for scamming us?"

"Did you?"

"No, *vato*, we did not. He was the only thing that kept us in our houses, once the mortgage payments started piling up. And keeping us off the streets right now. *Hijole!* You might not like us ... *asi es,*

99

asi sera. We sometimes act like *locos*. But we're the last people who'd want to see Mr. Frick dead."

Jack looked from one of them to the next, dropping and shaking their heads as they thought about the loss of Walter Frick. They couldn't have been responsible for his murder. They had too much to lose. And the Fricks lived in Cheviot Hills, not Beverly Hills— though both were a long way from El Monte. Jack passed a hand over his aching eyes.

"You want to know why?" asked Angel.

"Why what?"

"Why Mr. Frick did it. Why he needed the money."

"He told you that?"

"You know what he liked best?" Angelito smiled. "Tequila with lime. And you know what people do when they drink?"

"They talk," said Jack.

"*Si*," said Angel Ramirez. "He told me all about the banking business, and his own home. A nice, big house on a hill. He had a wife in it, but no children. His wife, she wanted to be a judge."

Jack thought about that. Judith had always been ambitious. She must have needed money to finance her campaign. And where would she have turned to raise the cash but her banker husband?

"But the profits from your mortgages didn't go into Frick's own pocket. They went to his bank."

Angel translated their exchange into Spanish for the other bangers, who laughed. Grifalito murmured something, but Angel only shrugged and turned back to Jack with a straight face.

"That's what he told me, *Gaba*. 'My bank needs a friend in court.'"

"An *amicus*?"

"No, man – *amiga* – a friend on the court. They wanted to elect a judge. One a their own. And the way I hear it, they did."

21

Red-headed Emily was alone at the reception desk, but she happily abandoned it for a little while to lead Mr. Stryker and Ms. Adams to the President's office at the far end of the executive suite. She asked, "Remember how to get to Mr. Frick's office?" and when Jack shook his head, she wheeled out her chair, pressed a clipboard to her chest, and said, "Follow me, please."

Jack was glad that she did, because it seemed to him they were making turns into hallways he had never seen before. It was possible that she had decided on a different route, once she realized he couldn't retrace his steps, but every now and then Jack thought he recognized a water cooler, or a travel poster pinned above a cubicle, which must have meant they were passing over some of the same ground. They arrived at the double doors announcing the presidential suite without passing Walter Frick's office, or Ms. Hellman, so they must have used a shortcut or secret passage somewhere along the way. One thing Jack was sure of— he could never find his way back again without the assistance of the ever helpful Emily.

It must have been the president's name that had won her over. Jack had a theory that receptionists judged you by the people you came to see, and asking for a person by name set you yards ahead of asking for the same person by their title. *I need to talk to the President* will get you a half hour wait and a quick encounter with an aide, at best, whose job it will be to explain why the president is much too busy to see you today. *I have an appointment with Harold Spinnaker*, however, will stir a little commotion among staffers, who do not find your name on the daily schedule but rarely risk asking if you should be there. Add Emily's whisper to Mr. Spinnaker's executive secretary, including the word *police*, and the big door to the inner sanctum magically opens. An affable man in woolen pin-stripes and silver cufflinks offered them a smile of confident security and ushered them into his office.

"Please," said Harold Spinnaker, waving toward two chairs in burgundy leather with matching studs. "Make yourselves comfortable."

Comfortable was the last thing Jack felt in a room of such deliberate opulence. Every surface that could have been paneled in dark mahogany had been. A huge table on one side of the room was surrounded by a dozen chairs of maple and plush red leather. The opposite side of the room was occupied by a desk that looked like a hunk of granite hewn with a pick-axe out of the ribs of a mountain.

Aisha, however, seemed to have no trouble making herself at home. She moved right to the sideboard of the conference table, where a collection of family photos were mounted on the wall, and inspected a woman who had to be Spinnaker's wife on a racing bike in Italy; his son astride a bull-pen in Pamplona; and largest of all a glass-framed photograph of Harold Spinnaker himself, with racing goggles raised on his forehead, looking ten years younger and foolishly proud of the cherry-red California Spyder at his hip.

"Nice car," said Aisha, tapping it.

"The spirit of my youth," sighed Spinnaker." I loved that Ferrari. Sacrificed on the altar of marriage and fatherhood."

"Too bad," she replied, running her finger along the fender and then putting the tip in her mouth as if she had cut herself on the glass.

He held the back of one chair until Aisha has settled into it, folding her bare legs between the shiny leather and her bottom.

Jack was left to fend for himself, as he sank into a chair that felt too big for him. By gripping the armrests on either side, he balanced himself on the front edge of the seat cushion.

"Thank you, Mr. Spinnaker," he said. "I'm Jack Stryker, and this is Aisha Adams. We realize you're a busy man and won't take too much of your time. We're conducting an investigation into the death of Walter Frick."

"Are you?" said Spinnaker, with a glance at Emily, who had followed them into the room and now stood silently beside the door. "You must be working with Lieutenant Newman, then."

"I've met with Pat Newman," Jack said, "of course. But ours is a separate inquiry. We're chasing down some leads she won't have time to pursue."

Spinnaker sat against the front edge of his desk and seemed for a moment to be distracted by some papers there.

"We're cooperating fully with the police," he said. "We want Walter's killer to be caught as quickly as anybody does. He was a reliable employee, and a good friend—as I've explained already to the Lieutenant. It must be in her notes. Is there anything in particular you've come here to pursue?"

"We're exploring all angles," Jack said. "There are plenty of them in this case. Financial angles. Personal angles. Political angles."

Spinnaker listened silently, pausing long enough for Jack to hear the clock ticking on his walnut bookshelf. But the world *political* must have registered, because he said, "Wasn't it a burglary? Or a crime of passion?"

"We're working another theory."

"Are you thinking that Walter was *assassinated*?" When he said the last word Spinnaker smiled at Aisha, who looked down shyly at her ankles.

Jack had never seen her do that before. "Is there any reason to suspect he might have been?"

Spinnaker looked surprised to be taken seriously. "Assassinated? Certainly not. Walter was not a political animal, except around the office. I'm not sure if he even voted in the last election."

Jack let the last word hang in the air before asking, "Does your bank invest in political campaigns?"

"I wouldn't say we *invest*, no," Spinnaker said, forming each syllable with care. "We have a right to express our opinions about policy choices and the best candidates to implement policy. The Supreme Court has backed us on that and recognized our use of campaign contributions as a form of free expression. We have no mouth, so we use our money. But what does that have to do with Walter?"

"Did you bankroll the campaign to elect his wife to the judiciary?"

"Did we *bankroll* it? No. We may have contributed to it—you'll have to check with our accountants. We do things like that for our employees. Buy Girl Scout cookies, donate to the Y, sponsor blood drives and toy drives at Christmastime. But I wouldn't say we *bankroll* political campaigns, in the sense that the winning candidate owes us any special consideration. Is that what you're driving at?"

"How much?"

"Pardon?"

"How much do you think you contributed? To Judge Frick's campaign?"

"As I said, you'll have to get the details from our accountants. A few thousand dollars, at most."

"That's a lot of Girl Scout cookies."

"Would you like some thin mints? We have a freezer full on the fourth floor. Somebody in Purchasing adores them."

"No thank you," said Jack, and Aisha sat back in her chair, disappointed. "Have your attorneys argued a case before her?"

103

"No," said Spinnaker emphatically. "She would have to recuse herself, wouldn't she? From a case involving her husband's bank?"

"That would be the ethical move."

"Well, we haven't. I would've heard about that. I know Judith, of course; we've met socially, and I think the world of her. She's a thoughtful, intelligent woman. But we made our contribution as anyone does—as concerned citizens."

"Concerned about what?"

"Good government is important for our business," Spinnaker declared. "We do our part, as a role model for our borrowers and a challenge to our business partners. As neighbors in the community. We're renovating a playground in the Slauson-Crenshaw district, funding a reading drive in the Culver City libraries, and picking up garbage on a section of the freeway." As he spoke, a door opened in the paneled wall, through which a blonde appeared in a beige linen skirt suit. "My assistant Wendy Moore can give you the rundown on our public service programs."

Wendy Moore gave them an encouraging smile. Under her elbow she had a file full of public service announcements.

Those were not the details Jack was after, but Spinnaker stood up from his desk, presenting his assistant with an open palm, as if he had just sawed her in half. His hand looked larger than a normal human hand, and he used it as a warning. They could follow where it led, or face its backside.

Jack hoisted himself out of his chair, and Aisha rose faithfully beside him. Only Emily stood motionless, blocking the door.

"Excuse us, dear," said Ms. Moore, in a voice that suggested she was too kind to laugh at Emily's confusion.

But Emily did not seem to Jack to be confused. She peered at Wendy Moore as if studying every detail of her fashion choices—from her big, bouncy curls to the hint of lace peeping out through the folds of her white silk blouse. And when she finally moved, Emily ran back to Reception without waiting for Jack.

22

Since Sergeant Warneke became a patrol officer much of his time had been spent sorting through garbage. His first assignment, in the Hollenbeck Division of the Central Bureau, had him on the streets in Ramona Gardens and Boyle Heights, in Pico Gardens and Rose Hills Courts—places with pretty names where every sort of predatory criminal lurked in the stairwells and alleys.

When he made detective, he found himself even deeper in the garbage, searching through trashcans and garbage bins for evidence after the fact, for Saturday night specials and switchblades, empty purses and wallet sleeves, bloody clothes, body parts, or any of ten thousand items that held a finger or palm print.

Now as a sergeant he was still sorting through garbage of a wholly different kind.

He could sit at his desk and tap-tap his way through pictures and postings, photographs of old office parties and newspaper stories that included some mention of Wendy Moore—who had not always had big curls, or blonde hair either. As soon as Lieutenant Newman gave him her name, Sergeant Warneke began to search for any footprints she had left on the web. She was not the only Wendy Moore on Facebook or LinkedIn, but it didn't take him long to figure out which one she was, given her position at the bank and the physical descriptions supplied by Montoya and the bartender at the Condor Club.

She wasn't hard to look at—no surprise, in the personal assistant to the president of a bank, but it put her on the Sergeant's list of possible Other Women. Beauty may be in the eye of the beholder, but he had never seen a man stabbed by his wife for sleeping with a skinny-legged troll. Cheating was not always more likely when the Other Woman was younger, slimmer, and prettier than the spouse. Sergeant Warneke had seen men cheat with older, fatter, and uglier partners, when the Other Woman was kinder, more willing to listen, or sexually more responsive than the spouse. But wives didn't respond with equal enmity. They seemed to find some consolation in the discovery that the Other Woman was less attractive than they imagined themselves to be. When they found their husbands in the arms of a younger, more beautiful girl, her charms seemed to drive them to a double dose of violence.

Wendy Moore stayed on the list for her looks. Of course the photo posted on her homepage could be several years old. Many were, once a woman turned the corner of thirty-five. But you could still see the confidence of an attractive woman in the tilt of her head and her smile. She had been quite pretty, and kept herself well, and from the few exchanges on her Facebook wall, she seemed like a fun-loving forty-something. Sergeant Warneke searched through her friends, but didn't find Walter Frick among them. That could mean they had never exchanged an online poke, or she had left him off as a gesture of discretion toward his marriage. There was no choice but to go through all the postings, and the photos of Harold Spinnaker in which her face appeared, looking for a sidelong glance at Walter Frick.

Mostly he found trash—chats with girlfriends, photos of her nephews, gossip about new hires, fires, and retirees at the bank. But her postings definitely fell into a higher class of garbage than some he had sifted, and Sergeant Warneke tapped patiently through her photos and comments, invitations and gifts. At least he wouldn't have to wash the grime from his fingernails, once he was done with this search.

Warneke had access to Mr. Frick's office email account, but there was nothing damning in that—a few exchanges with Wendy Moore but nothing that suggested a more personal relationship than a Vice President ought to have with his President's assistant. The Sergeant thought he detected a lighter, flirtier tone that seemed to grow over the first few months and then suddenly vanish—but was he simply reading into their messages what he hoped to find?

The clue was a significant lack of personal email of any kind in Walter Frick's office account. Nothing to a buddy, to his mother, or even to Her Honor, and who never shoots off an email to his wife? Frick had to have another, more private email account, away from the prying eyes of the bank's technical staff—something on Gmail, or Yahoo, or MSN, accessible from anywhere but hosted on a server far from his colleagues at the bank. Sergeant Warneke began sending text messages, writing to *wfrick@* each of those three, to *WalterFrick@*, *frickw@*, and any other combination he could think of, waiting for the error message to respond: *Undeliverable.*

Sergeant Warneke knew he would need a warrant to access the account once he found it, and probable cause to get the warrant. But he remembered the catfight in which Judy Frick had won the nomination of her party to the bench—and old resentments die slowly, once they're robed in black.

Judicial elections are nonpartisan in California. But most Superior Court judges are first appointed by the Governor, as interims, and the political parties decide which candidates they want to endorse. The Governor can solicit whatever opinion he likes, from the state Bar Association, sitting Justices, or the heavy lifters of his party.

There were two possible candidates for the Superior Court judgeship at the time: Judith Frick in the District Attorney's office, and George Mendoza, who had served as a mediator and traffic court judge before throwing his hat in the ring for the Superior Court. Mendoza had looked like a shoe-in, with a strong rating from the Bar Association and the appointment in the bag, until Judith Frick appeared on the scene with a war-chest full of contributions from the financial sector. The party bosses read George Mendoza's resume, and Judith Frick's bank statement, and swung their support behind the funded campaign. It was the practical thing to do, the smart political move, setting the wheels in motion for a handy re-election. They promised Mendoza a shot the following year and made good on it. But he never forgot that Judith Frick had bounced him out of the running that first time around. They were colleagues on the bench, nodding in the halls, but the buzz around the courthouse was that George Mendoza never forgave Judith Frick for making him her junior.

Sergeant Warneke thought he could get a warrant from Judge Mendoza to dig into the emails of Judith Frick's husband, if he provided a fig leaf of legal cover—just enough probable cause to justify Mendoza's judgment. With Walter dead on his kitchen floor, a knife stuck in his belly, and the wife upstairs tied to her bedposts by her own hand ... how much more could Mendoza need to cover his judicial ass?

Sergeant Warneke just had to find a credible motive, which would reside no doubt on the server hosting Frick's personal emails. So he sent emails to *waltfrick@yahoo* and *frickbank@msn*, with *Very Important* in the subject line and a text asking, "Judith Frick, please call me. Detective Sergeant Emil Warneke, LAPD Homicide," with his phone number at the station. And watched for the message that never came back as undeliverable.

23

Judith Frick needed a place to do her homework. When she sat up in her usual spot in bed, propped on pillows against the headboard, she found she could no longer focus on the legal documents resting against her knees. Every branch striking a window in the evening breeze, every squeak of the timbers framing the house, made her look up and stare at the entrance to her bedroom, where Walter had entered in his ski mask and then that other had appeared as a child's cartoon. Walter was often home late, closing on a property in El Monte or San Bernardino, but never had the silence of his absence from the house felt so thick and permanent. When she looked down at the papers in her lap, something in the corner of her eye seemed to sneak out of the shadows, or slip into them. Judith felt vulnerable, exposed to the random violence of the night outside as she never had before—which was bad news for a judge. She saw the plastic grin with the bobbing head-feather and shuddered to imagine the face breathing through its molded plastic. It was ridiculous, Judith thought, but no less chilling for its Sunday morning absurdity. She put the Whistler file back into her briefcase and went downstairs to find a place where she could read through the motions in peace.

She and Walter each had an office in the house. His was on the second floor, hers on the first. But in the silence of the darkened house, without the occasional thump of Walter's weight overhead, Judith's office seemed cold and forbidding, despite the rows of comforting books and the soft brown leather of her chair. She called Clarence into the room—who trotted in gingerly, unsure of his place in the changed house—and closed the door behind him. That was a little better. But Clarence lay down just inside the door, dropped his jaw on his outstretched paws, and waited for it to open again. They were awkward companions, who only made each other more intensely aware of the absence of Walter between them.

Judith tried to focus on the Whistler case. Bernard Whistler was to be tried for the murder of Philip Hazlitt, who had earned the rank of colonel chasing Saddam Hussein's Revolutionary Guards across the Iraqi desert—and then retired from the Marines at the height of their success. When President Bush declared their *mission accomplished* from the deck of a battleship, Colonel Hazlitt was in New York, talking to the contacts at Haliburton and Blackwater who would become the first clients of his financial investment firm.

He had already acquired an impressive if sinister personal mythology. An article in the *New Yorker* reported that Hazlitt began his career as a commando, dropping into Granada with an advance team in Operation Urgent Fury. Six years later he led the team that bagged Noriega in Panama. Hazlitt got a Purple Heart for that one. A rumor in the corps had him diving from the deck of the USS Cole into the flotsam at Aden, swimming after the terrorist mastermind who sent his suicides into the destroyer. They said he almost snagged the gunwale of the powerboat. If Hazlitt had caught Khalid Sheik Mohamed then, the World Trade Center might still be standing tall.

That's what they said, in any case. It made good copy in the *Wall Street Journal*, and CPH was soon the hottest investment firm on the Street. Hazlitt was said to show the same strategic skill in buying and selling derivatives he had used in deploying technology on the battlefield. He used the language of the war zone, the *theater* as he called it, sending out *drones* rather than trial balloons, avoiding *IEDs* among the *IPOs*—all of which made the traders and investors feel like two-fisted heroes. And it seemed to work: those who were lucky enough to be managed by CPH received regular earnings of ten, eleven, even twelve percent on their investments, check after check. They called Hazlitt a genius. They said he did more than predict the market; his reputation was strong enough to influence his colleagues, so that a buy by CPH in the tens of millions could induce hedge fund managers to do the same. Hazlitt had taken the risk out of wealth management. Non-profit groups and movie stars vied to be his clients, and CHP had its pick of blue chips and blue noses. Its yuletide holiday party drew the *crème de la crème* of Wall Street and Washington, where bankers banged elbows with campaign finance staffers, securities regulators, and the chairmen whose committees oversaw them all.

Yet he never forgot the grunts on the line, the men and women alongside whom he had served. That was the word among Marines shipping out for Iraq and Afghanistan. If you left what you had in the hands of the Colonel, you would have something to show for it by the end of your tour. And it did work out just that way for hundreds of Marines, in combat and support positions, enlisted and officers. He famously treated a homeless vet to a four-course meal at 21. Philip Hazlitt was good as his word, rain or shine, upturn or downturn in the Dow Jones industrial average.

Which should have made somebody suspect something. *A high tide lifts all boats,* runs the maritime adage, but Warren Buffet added, *When the tide goes out, you can see who's not wearing a bathing suit.* With the sudden collapse of the investment banks and the freefall on Wall Street, Colonel Hazlitt and CPH were revealed for what they were: managers of a Ponzi scheme, in which the funds coming in from new investors were used to pay dividends for existing clients. So long as the rush of new money was constantly growing, CPH could maintain a return on investment unmatched on the Street. Once the dollars stopped flowing, the bottom fell out of their racket. The checks stopped coming, and the individuals and organizations throwing their money at Hazlitt discovered there were no invested funds to recover. The early investors had seen their money double and triple, drawing off interest with confidence, assured that their principal was still intact. The last investors suffered the most, losing whatever they entrusted to the Colonel's sure-bet management firm.

Bernard Whistler was one such individual, who sent half of his pay from Iraq to his dad and half to CPH. He lost three fingers off his right hand, dismantling an IED a quarter mile from the Green Zone. When the chopper lifted him out of Baghdad, soaked to the elbow in blood, he rested his head on the stretcher secure in the knowledge he had put aside a nest egg. But when he stepped off the plane from Germany and learned from his mother what his father wouldn't tell him, that all of his savings were gone, Bernard Whistler took it hard. Everything he suffered in the desert, on the road, peering through his goggles at the muddy ruts, had played a terrible joke on him, keeping him distracted while they robbed his life savings back home.

Judging by his testimony before the grand jury, Whistler had not been particularly stable since his return from Afghanistan. Defusing IEDs can do that to you. The *I* in *IED* stood for *improvised,* but it could have just as easily stood for *innovative* or *imaginative.* Every time you figured out how to prevent one going off—blocking a cell phone transmission, say, so the device couldn't receive the incoming signal—the enemy found another way to blow away your buddies. Whistler had kept the nightmares at bay in country by dreaming about his investments and the little brick house in Rochester or Schenectady they would buy, if he made it home to claim them in one piece.

Whistler tried to see Hazlitt again and again, and finally tracked him down to his Malibu hideaway on the afternoon of December fourth. According to his housekeeper, the Colonel had found Mr.

Whistler sitting in the catamaran he kept by the beachside porch. When the housekeeper left the house, Whistler was inside by the picture window, talking to Hazlitt and waving his tattooed arms. By his own account, Mr. Whistler received no satisfaction in that exchange; the lion's share of the money was gone, and the bankruptcy court would have to decide whose claims to honor first at how many cents on the dollar. Bernard Whistler's stake was so small, Hazlitt could have paid it off from the office petty cash, but the Colonel insisted that wouldn't be right. He would have to stand in line and wait his turn, like everybody else.

The following Friday, Hazlitt's Mercedes exploded in his garage. The Colonel's teeth, still in their jaw, were matched to x-rays in the dental records from his military file. Whistler was spotted in the alley by a neighbor on the intervening Wednesday, and the explosive device was a common design in the muddy ruts of Kandahar. The Malibu cops had written a parking ticket for a white Taurus rented in the name of Bernard Whistler, whose alibi, an old comrade-in-arms, couldn't confirm certain details, then contradicted his own account of their evening of beer and dominoes. Whistler was arrested, jailed, and bailed out by the firm of Bennett and Raines, who took the case *pro bono*, no doubt aware that the death of Colonel Hazlitt would keep their name in the media for several difficult months.

Two days before Whistler's indictment, the federal government announced its second bailout of the American Enterprise Group, the conglomerate widely believed to be too big to fail. The collapse of AEG would reportedly have set off a chain reaction of failing investment banks and financial institutions that would plunge the world economy into a prolonged depression. The high-risk investments of AEG's managers had played a central role in creating the crisis, but the stakes were too high to risk. If the Fed let them fail, there would be bread lines in the cities. Main Street would fall behind Wall Street. The Congress had no choice but to cover the check.

Bernard Whistler was released on bond the same day as a press conference at the Pierrot Hotel, where AEG's negotiating team announced the bail-out. A private party followed to celebrate the rescue, and Randolph Raines had friends among the AEG brass. Raines brought Bernie Whistler as his personal guest, to take the poor boy's mind off his legal troubles. Whistler spent a miserable few hours drinking champagne with the AEG boys, who asked if he had killed Hazlitt and lost all interest in him when at first he denied

111

it. But what had he said after that, to win their grudging respect? Had he actually said something relevant to the murder case— something they might repeat on the stand? The defense was clearly interested in his psychological condition. Would it really speak to his state of mind? Or was the AEG testimony just a ploy by the prosecution to make Mr. Whistler seem even less sympathetic, the kind of man who rubbed shoulders with the finaglers of Wall Street? That seemed to be the main points of the matter before Judith Frick, as she read the briefs filed by Lester Talbot and Randy Raines: relevance, state of mind, and the extent to which his presence at the party might prove prejudicial to a jury. There was supposed to be a video of their carryings-on that night, but Judith couldn't find the disk in her briefcase.

She looked over the names on Talbot's potential witness list: Henry Cordesman, William Fleischer, Everett Halloran ... bankers and financial managers. She had heard Walter mention a few of them but couldn't remember what he might have said to suggest how germane and reliable their testimony might be. Judith felt like running upstairs to ask his opinion. But that was impossible now.

That was when she noticed Clarence standing in front of the door, his ears back and teeth ready to snarl. Judith put down her papers and listened to the doorbell ring, an endless peal, as if someone on the porch outside was keeping his thumb on the button. For a moment she imagined it was Walter's killer come back to finish the job. The smell of cotton pillowcase filled her nostrils. Then she put her hand on Clarence's collar to reassure both of them.

"It's only Jack," she said out loud and got up to let him in.

24

When Judith Frick opened the door, Jack saw her for the first time: older than he remembered but still restless with energetic intelligence. She hadn't put her public face on. No makeup, her hair disheveled, wearing a quilted robe over a floral print nightgown of faded cotton. She probably thought she looked terrible. But to Jack she looked like a woman at home, unpinned, unhooked, unafraid to be seen for what she was—which was the sexiest kind of intimacy he could imagine.

"You left a message," he said. "You wanted to see me."

She stepped out of his way and let him into the foyer. He peeked into the living room to their right. White linen sofas, cherry wood tables, Mexican tiles around the fireplace, Navajo rugs.

"Nice," he said, as they passed it by.

She led him down the hall, back to her office, with its button-tufted leather couch and big mahogany desk— an upscale version of her old office in the Inglewood D.A.'s office, with better pieces in the same seating configuration. Judith sat against the front of her desk and gripped its edge, just as she used to do, confronting a defendant. A sharp, surprising question should have followed, but Judith sighed. "Did you talk to Harold Spinnaker?"

Jack nodded. "Yes."

"About me?"

"Your name came up," he conceded.

"How could it not? When you grilled him about contributions to my campaign?"

"I was trying to find someone who might have wanted Walter dead."

"And did you? Does Harold have a motive?"

"I haven't found it yet, but I will, if he has one. If he tried to pressure Walter into influencing you. If Walter refused and threatened to expose him. If he panicked—"

"And dropped by in the middle of the night to stab his Vice President?"

"Or sent somebody else to do it."

"Jack ... he didn't. If Harold Spinnaker wanted something from me, he would've asked me himself. I would have told him exactly what he'd expect me to—that I can't discuss any case before me, in or out of the courthouse."

"He certainly called you quickly enough, didn't he? To complain? Or to ask if you put me onto him?"

"He called to touch base. There's nothing to put you onto, Jack. No secrets to uncover, or reason to disturb Harold with all of this."

"You asked me to look into this. I'm looking."

"No," she said firmly, "I did not. You were half blind, remember? Though you seem to be seeing a little better now."

"I guess I am."

"Don't be snide. I didn't ask you to look into anything. I only asked you to tell Lieutenant Newman what kind of sex we had. What we enjoyed doing. So she'd believe me when I said that Walter had tied me to our headboard. Or rather that I tied myself before he went down to the kitchen, instead of following him down, stabbing him in the belly, and tying myself up, afterwards."

"You knew I couldn't leave it at that."

"No, Jack—I actually thought you could. We haven't talked in how many years? As I recall, we weren't saying such nice things to each other, when we did talk."

"That wasn't my fault, Judith."

"Judith, is it now?" She smiled bitterly. "That's more like what I expected—a grudging acknowledgement that we once meant something to each other, a long time ago. I didn't mean to draw you into a criminal investigation, for heaven's sake. Number one, there was already a competent homicide cop on the case. Lieutenant Newman focused on the wrong suspect for reasons of her own, but she could find the right one, if you turned her around."

"She'd be surprised to hear how much you respect her."

"Don't be an ass, Jack. I know a good cop when I see one. I knew you for a sharp eye, the first time I saw you in Inglewood."

Was she really playing that card?

Jack said, "I didn't know quite how sharp you were. Not at first."

Her hand fell on his shoulder. "Still sulking? After all these years?" She made a soft clucking. "Then let me say … I'm sorry, truly and deeply. Don't you think it's time we forgave each other?"

He drew a breath. "Sure." But there was no relenting in the line of his mouth or the glare in his eyes.

"It wouldn't have worked," Judith said. "The timing wasn't right. We were both so young, just starting our careers. You never would have asked me, otherwise. And that's the worst reason in the world to say *yes*. You know it is."

"But I did ask. And you did say *yes*."

"Then I thought about it and changed my mind. About how I felt and how you felt and what we should do about it. One of us had to think clearly."

"Is that what you did?"

"Yes. I don't know if I loved you, Jack. Really, I don't remember."

"I do."

"All right, maybe you loved me. Or believed you did. Maybe I loved you. But you're a full-grown man, now. Was that really enough? To throw over everything, all our plans, and run off into the sunset?"

"I thought it was."

"That was sweet of you. I thought so then and still appreciate it. But one of us had to make the rational decision, and it looked like it had to be me."

"Is that how you worked it out? Rationally?"

"We both had careers, Jack. You could have kept yours, if we settled down, but what about mine? Do you really think I could have kept going, stayed focused on my professional goals, if we started playing house together? If you thought about it calmly, even now, you'd have to admit there was little chance of that. No chance at all. You may have been too much in love to consider the actual consequences, but I wasn't. I couldn't afford to be."

"You didn't want me. That's all. You don't need to make it sound like a profile in courage."

She shook her head patiently. "It wasn't about what I wanted. That didn't matter. I was sorry to lose you— really I was. You were such a cutie-pie. But you must know, as a wise old man, we would both have been sorry in the end if I hadn't given you up."

It was the same line she had given him all those years ago. Jack couldn't stand to hear it again. He rose from the button-tufted leather couch, just as he stood up from the sagging, plaid, olefin in her A.D.A. office—and once again he walked out without a word.

Aisha wasn't waiting in the car outside. Jack had sent her home and taken a cab to Cheviot Hills. He told himself she didn't need to sit in the car all the time he was in with Judith. He wasn't sure how long that might prove to be. But another motive floated around the back of his skull, which Jack didn't want to acknowledge. He didn't want to answer why he was going to Judith's house, what he expected to find there, and what he hoped might happen.

So Jack had to walk down the long hillside, until he found his way to an avenue with streetlights on the corners. He could have stopped into a fast-food place and called a cab from there. But he chose to walk, as he had walked that night, ignoring the traffic that rumbled down the street, passing windows displays of mattresses and Persian rugs, pharmacies, thrift shops, bookstores, nail salons. He stopped into the first bar he noticed, with a neon Mexican beer in its window. He found the same half dozen men who are always at the bar, who look up surprised when you enter the place, as if they shouldn't really be squinting in the light.

He ordered a boilermaker, bourbon with a beer back, a drink for a sailor with no time to waste. It was the same one-two punch that laid him out years before, when first he learned she had changed her mind—would not marry him—and the life they imagined in the first flush of news would not be theirs, after all. It was only after he had put away two strong shots that Jack allowed himself to remember the rest of it. He wasn't about to be a father, either. She had gone ahead and done it, even though they had talked it through and decided to have it, to make a life together stable enough to add one plus one and come out three. He and she had discussed it, very seriously at first, and then with something like joy, so that when he left her, Jack was filled with a pleasant sense of accomplishment. He knew what he wanted, what they wanted together, and it would be a good thing they had begun.

But the next time he saw her, it was all gone. She had changed not only her mind but everything about her. It was all different then, what he hoped for and what they planned, swept away in an instant with surgical precision. She thought it the only rational thing to do, the sane choice for both careers at that point in their lives. There would be other times for other choices. It was the only thing she could've done. Jack had repeated that part to himself, looser and sloppier with every boilermaker, until he set down one glass and didn't order another but tossed a crumple of bills onto the hardwood bar and stumbled into the street.

The night he first encountered Maggie Malloy.

25

Everett Halloran liked to jump in his pool as soon as he pulled off the freeway, especially when Celia went to her yoga class and took Sven along. Two years before, she got the idea in her head to take in a foreign exchange student. Her gynecologist thought it medically unwise for Celia to get pregnant, and Ev was reluctant to adopt instead. But he had to hand it to Celia—she leveraged his guilt like a buyout, working on him each time they went to an Italian film or a French restaurant. Hell, if he buttered an English muffin, he got a lecture on London.

Still, he had stood his ground, mostly in silence, until she told him they could agree to accept a student from a particular country. Say, Sweden. Everett had imagined a svelte blonde sunning on a towel alongside his pool with the straps of her bikini bra open in back. Instead, they got Sven, a gap-toothed seventeen-year-old who wore striped bowling shirts and seemed to be studying nothing but the Belgian inspired beers of American micro-breweries.

Halloran bought his house in Encino before the real estate boom, so its value even after the crash was still more than he paid for it. It was located in the Valley, a demerit in the office, but the square footage and private back yard were way beyond what he could have afforded anywhere on the Westside. Encino was a status address, just down the 405 from Santa Monica and Brentwood. Clark Gable had a ranch there, in the grand old days of Hollywood. When Celia and Sven were out of the house, Everett could strip off his bathing trunks and swim laps in the nude, since the six-foot-high oleander kept the prying eyes of his neighbors off his bottom.

The sun was just starting to set, casting fluttery shadows from the top of his neighbor's eucalyptus tree. How many laps was he up to now? Eighteen, round trip—thirty-six lengths in all. Everett was feeling pretty good tonight, and the air smelled cleaner than it sometimes did after the rush hour. He thought he could make twenty laps, forty lengths in all, if he just held his head down, made racing turns, and kept stroking. He kicked off from the poolside, launched into a crawl, and cupped his hands to pull for the opposite wall.

One length and back. Lap one. Another length, turn, and back again. Got to make those turns tighter. What did the kid say? Sven—reach across his chest with each stroke of his arms, twisting his torso left and right, one two three strokes with his head under water and then tilt his face upward for breath. They didn't call it a crawl anymore. Freestyle. Was that the name of the stroke? Or was it simply that a racing swimmer, free to choose any style he liked, always chose to crawl, since that was the fastest stroke? Keeping his legs nearly straight, with his knees unlocked. Another couple of lengths and he felt it in his muscles, in his shoulders first, his thighs, and the muscles of his back. When his lungs began to ache, he started making deals. Just one more length, half a lap, just to the edge of the pool.

He knew he would have to stop and rest at the end of fifteen laps. He had flipped over onto his back for a couple of lengths of backstroke, then sidestroke, then a kind of submerged breaststroke, where his face hardly ever broke the waterline. He saw the blue pool wall and focused on that, keeping his head down, pulling the water out of his way, pushing it behind him.

When he struggled through the second length of the fifteenth lap, he had to come up for air. He touched the concrete side and reached up for the edge. With a single pull of both arms he lifted himself from the water, opened his mouth for a gulp of air—and felt a rush of chlorine fill it up again.

Something was pushing him down again. A hand on the top of his head, gripping his hair. Holding his mouth hardly a foot under the waterline.

For an instant he thought, Was it Sven? Pulling some kind of joke? Had Celia come home early, caught him swimming in the buff, and had the boy teach him a lesson? If so, he would be angry. He would let them know how angry he was. This was a pool, for crying out loud. This was no place for a joke. But the hand on his head, the fingers in his hair, were no teenager's digits. Too much strength in them, firmness in the grip. When he felt the second hand on his shoulder, pushing him down, he knew it wasn't Sven on the deck. And his anger turned to panic.

Was he really going to die like this? Would he ever see Celia again? Whatever would they think when they found him floating face down like an idiot penguin with his pink ass in the air?

Everett tried to struggle, to force his way to the surface. But the laps, the thirty lengths, had worn him out. He could feel the fatigue in his muscles, the weariness in his bones trying to rise against gravity, the weight of the water pulling him down, under the surface. While the hands above wouldn't let him fill his lungs. He looked up and saw through the splashing, through his own bubbles of air, the strangest face —

a stiff yellow cowlick bobbing over the goofy, grinning beak of a bird.

26

Jack found Maggie in the downstairs drawing room, playing *Casablanca* on the plasma screen for half a dozen girls in lingerie. As he entered, a black-haired beauty with a twenty-inch head was telling Humphrey Bogart, *The devil has the people by the throat.* Bogie looked unmoved.

Maggie pointed to the seat of a Queen Anne chair in a jacquard matching her own.

A platinum blonde sat on its ottoman, with her long legs folded beneath her. A brunette was stretched out on the floor, with her head resting on the ottoman. When the blonde stood up, the ottoman rolled, and the brunette's head slipped off. She smacked the blonde on her dimpled knee, who released a string of obscenities she could only have learned from a sailor with his sack caught in his fly.

Jack knelt down to fix the lever on the ottoman's wheel, but it kept rolling away. When he finally snagged it, he announced, "There you go," eliciting a round of *shushes* for his trouble. The working girls didn't mind bickering, but three words in a male voice were too distracting.

"Women drive me crazy," he said aloud, provoking another *shush*.

Maggie smelled his breath when he sighed. She took his arm and led him from the parlor to the kitchen, where she set two unmatched coffee mugs on the table.

"They're kids, Jack. That's all."

"*Young* women drive me craziest," he said. "Who have no idea what they want. But expect you to deliver it. When you don't—when you can't figure out what they want, because they don't know themselves—who do they blame for it?"

"All of them?"

"You ever hear a young lady say, *I guess it's my fault*?"

Maggie laughed and poured him a cup. "Have a little sympathy," she said, filling her own. "After being ignored for their entire lives, one day these girls wake up and everybody's interested. Not just the teenage boys— the bus driver and the dentist, even Daddy's friends are suddenly noticing everything she says or does. It's the same dumb shit she was saying the day before, but all of a sudden, every guy is paying attention. If she can draw his stare above her neckline.

"It's a power she never had before. You know how people do without practice. But she also senses *why* she has it, and how long it

120

lasts, once she says *yes*. She has to fuck someone – she knows that – but who should it be? Should she do it for love? For money? For the hell of it, when she's bored? Or just for a little edge in her otherwise honest career?"

"At least she has a choice," said Jack. "Guys never know what hit us."

"It only looks like a choice when it's behind her," said Maggie. "You know the choices my gals made, and the report you hope to hear from your bride. Most women settle for something in between—say, a few times with that beautiful boy, and once with Daddy's poker pal, just to blow his mind. Then how much of a leap is it from Uncle Bud to the guy in the corner office?"

"Not much, I guess. If he's moving out of it."

"It's as good a reason as any. Better, if he's got a view. She picks somebody, anybody, so she can stop thinking about it—when a pimple-faced kid whispers in her ear and something biological happens. Those hormones bubble up, her panties get wet, and she doesn't feel like talking. God forbid she actually comes, and that clinches the deal. She's got to love this wonderful guy."

"That's a beautiful story," Jack said, burning his tongue on the coffee. He stuck it out to cool it and Maggie shook her head.

"It's not just the orgasm," she insisted, "it's what she tells herself after all the stroking and kissing. The build-up is the tender part, what they call *foreplay*. But it's not *fore*-anything to her, and it sure ain't *play*. If she can slow him down enough to go gentle into the night, it can be very sweet. A screw involves lots of pushing and shoving, grunting and gasping for air. But a cuddle and a whisper can spark emotions that rev a girl's engine and start it humming, no matter what she had in mind when she first said *yes*."

"Isn't it romantic," Jack said, "at sixteen? But your girls don't react that way."

"Don't they? You should see them with their boyfriends—as goo-goo-eyed stupid as anybody else. The johns are a different story, of course. That's about money. There's nothing else these girls can do to earn as much with their time. They have to think differently about what they're doing, but it comes to the same thing in the end. In a house like this, most of their attention goes to the early show, to make the clients feel desirable, potent, and satisfying."

"You mean satisfied, don't you?"

"I mean satisfying. Women may show a little vanity, but there's no way we can compare to men, when it comes to preening pride."

Maggie fell silent for a moment while the beauty on the screen finished speaking. Jack heard Bogie say, *You want my advice? Go back to Bulgaria.*

"So your advice would be—"

"Try a little tenderness," said Maggie. "You always do, don't you, Jack? That's what I hear from the girls."

"You don't have to take their word for it."

She shook her head. "You know how I feel about that."

"Not really," he said. "At least, I don't know why. I'm not Jack the Ripper. I listen to your troubles at the end of the day, and play two-handed pinochle when you're in the mood for a game. I'm not a bad kisser, given the chance. We did spend a night together, once upon a time."

"I remember," Maggie said. "Do you?"

"Sure – "

"I doubt it. You were three sheets to the wind that night. And it didn't work out better in the morning. Let's not forget that part. As Rick says, *I wouldn't bring it up. It's poor salesmanship.*"

For a moment Jack thought he heard schoolgirls laughing in the playground on Montana Avenue. Then he realized it was coming from the other room, where Maggie's gals were watching *Casablanca*. Who could they be laughing at – the German couple? *What watch is it, liebchen? Such watch?*

Maggie was watching him closely, with her palms on the table. Jack thought her elbows might be trembling. He felt like reaching out and taking them, to buck her up and steady her. But she might take a swing at him, if he tried. Instead, he cupped his hands around his coffee mug and waited.

"Can I ask you something?" she said at last.

"A question?"

"A favor." She tried to make it sound matter-of-fact, but her face turned a shade he would have called a *blush*, if Maggie Malloy were capable of blushing.

"Sure," he said, trying to sound just as casual.

"You know Janie Mae Olsen, don't you?" Maggie said. "Of course you do! You asked for her the other night, after your bath."

"*You* suggested her," he said, "since I couldn't have my first choice."

"Jack, I'm serious," Maggie said. "She wasn't here the other night, remember? When you went off with Rosalind? Janie Mae never showed that night, and hasn't, since. That's not like her."

122

"Maybe she found a boyfriend."

"She has plenty of boyfriends," Maggie said, "and a number of regulars who will pass up the other girls to wait until she's free. One of those johns sat on the sofa, waiting half the night. That is absolutely not like Janie Mae."

"You tried calling her?"

"And texting her. She spends a lot of time on her laptop. She keeps a website, you know, where guys email, asking her to crawl around on her elbows."

"And she does?"

"For a charge on their MasterCard. But she hasn't been online either, and that's a real worry. She makes a nice income from her condo on that site and never has to wash up afterwards."

"Does Janie Mae live alone?"

"No. She lives with another girl. Suziko Mori."

"Another pro?"

"A part-timer. Suziko might work a weekend party or a double with Janie Mae. She went to Vegas Thursday for an auto parts convention and tried to talk Janie Mae into going along."

"There you go. Janie Mae must have changed her mind."

"She couldn't. She had a paper due."

"You're telling me … she's working her way through college?"

"I don't recruit in high schools, Jack. That's where she was coming from, when she never showed."

Jack knew what Maggie wanted. He thought of the woman who begged him to free her son from a crack house. He thought of Judith at the table on Montana, and saw her standing in her office with both fists on her hips. He shook his bleary head.

"F'Chrissake, Maggie. I was just thrown off one cranky case, and you want me to take on another? What kind of a sucker do you think I am?"

"What kinds are there?" Maggie said. "The kind you can take for all he's worth, if you press your knees together? Or the kind who falls for a broad who keeps a hammer in her purse?"

He peered over the lip of his mug at Maggie, whose face was drawn together at her wrinkled eyes.

A tingling spread across the back of Jack's skull, headed for a crash between his eyebrows. There were younger women in the house, hardly a whistle away, but Jack would rather have crawled under a quilt with Maggie and pulled it over both of them.

"All right," he said. "I'm good for a favor."

"You'll find Janie Mae?"

Jack shrugged. "I'll look. I'll stop by her school, first thing in the morning, and learn what I can. I'm sure I'll turn up something to set your mind at rest … if someone does the same for me tonight."

"Thank you." Maggie kissed him sweetly on his cheek. He felt the damp grizzle left by her mouth and his hope stiffened, until she called, "Rosalind! Honey— you're on, tonight."

27

Aisha was a big girl and she drove like one, making wide turns with sweeping motions of her muscular shoulders and elbows. Sitting beside her in the front seat of the Buick, Jack felt there was hardly enough room for their front bumper to squeeze down the aisle between Explorers and Suburbans, Escalades and Land Cruisers, whose oversize rears jutted out from spots marked for compact cars. He might have expected more in a parking structure on the corner of the downtown state campus. But this was Los Angeles, where people drove minis and smart-cars but never compacts, and traffic signs read as friendly suggestions rather than rules of the road.

They had stopped by Janie Mae Olson's apartment in Brentwood, where no one answered the door. Maggie had said that Janie Mae's roommate Suziko was out of town, on a trip to Vegas that should keep her busy for the next couple of days. But Janie Mae had been expected at the house in Hancock Park, and had answered neither her cell phone nor the land-line at her apartment for long enough to worry Maggie Malloy. You never wanted to worry Maggie, who switched from mother hen to a ruthless businesswoman at the drop of a straw hat. But she switched back just as quickly, for the most unexpected baby chicks.

Jack had expected to find Janie Mae holed up in her apartment, sleeping one off, or recovering after a night with a john. He had pumped the bell and watched Aisha bang on the door until a neighbor poked out her head. She had little squares of aluminum foil stuck in her hair, as if a radio exploded on her nightstand. A check of Janie Mae's spot in the garage confirmed that her Beamer was not at home. Jack got the plate from Maggie, who kept complete personal records on all her employees. Jack convinced the campus cops to run it through their server, which said her parking permit had privileges in certain lots and structures. He and Aisha began driving up and down those aisles, looking for a Beamer with Janie Mae's plates.

They found it in the back on the fourth floor of their second parking structure. Aisha spotted the plate between the bumpers through which she had to steer Jack's Buick. Her vision was better than his, when it came to making out digits low to the ground, half of them in shadow.

The Beamer looked like a lease—late model, low end, no personal items except a permit hanging from the rear-view mirror, so a cop in a cruiser could check the expiration without climbing out of his vehicle. Jack didn't like what he found. The driver's door was locked, but the left side door to the back was not. Most luxury cars use electronic keys that lock all the doors at once. Someone had to unlock the rear and lock the driver's door individually, by hand. Janie Mae Olsen would not have done that, with her arms full of books. She might have pushed the button to lock them all, but if she did, who unlocked the rear door? Or else, who locked Janie Mae's driver-side door?

Jack did not share this question with Aisha, who peered through the windshield enviously at the leather seats and Harman-Karman sound system. When she saw Jack open the back door, she slid inside, bouncing a bit to test the padding, running her fingers along the stitching.

"This is the life, huh?" Aisha stretched out her arms in both directions, spanning the whole back seat.

Jack hoped it turned out to be.

There was a piece of paper under the gas pedal. Jack held it up to the clearest patch of his vision. It was a lined index card with only two words, scrawled in black pencil. *Count Finckenstein.* Jack stuck it in his pocket and said, "Let's find her."

Janie Mae was a part-time student registered for only one course, an early evening class in philosophy. In the library Jack found a computer, and a scornful work-study helped him find the right seminar in the schedule of classes for the semester. Continental Philosophy met on Thursday nights in a building not far from the parking structure in which they had found the Beamer. The instructor was listed as Carla Crewell, an Associate Professor with an office in the Philosophy building, a short hike from the library. Jack tried the phone number on her website, but got only the briefest recording on her voicemail.

"You've reached Professor Crewell's line. You know what to do. And, yes, I've heard that one already. Beep."

She pronounced the word *beep* in her recorded message, which was not followed by an actual beep, so Jack wasn't sure when to leave his call-back number. He decided to walk over to the Philosophy building instead, in case she stepped out for some reason or somebody else down the hall could tell him anything useful about her hours or her class. He might even run into Janie Mae Olsen, laboring over a late paper or sitting in a chair in the hall, waiting for a conference.

Jack and Aisha did not find Janie Mae in the hall, but they did find Carla Crewell in her office, staring at a Kindle with a second book open in her lap, while the telephone at her elbow burred softly.

"Don't you want to get that?" Aisha asked through the door. "You never know. It could be important."

"I doubt that," said Professor Crewell, looking up when she realized Aisha was not alone in the hall. "That is, not important to *me*. It might be important to the junior logician begging for an extension on her deadline. But she should have thought of that last night, when she chose to do another shooter instead of reading Hegel. What's the point of free will without consequence? Let History take its toll."

There were two empty chairs in front of her desk, but she did not invite them to sit down.

The phone kept ringing until Jack said, "Do you know who that is?"

"Not individually," said the Professor. "But I know what day this is, and I know my thesis deadline, and those two facts are more than casually related to the desperate ringing of my phone."

Jack propped his shoe on a dowel between the legs of a chair. "And you know it's desperate—"

"Because it doesn't stop."

Just then it did. The three of them listened to the silence for a moment, to see if the ringing resumed.

It did not.

"On the other hand, you could be wrong."

"I could," agreed Crewell. "It was a probability based on certain assumptions, not a proof. It was probably a student, stressed by the deadline. It could have been a telemarketer, or my mother, for that matter. But the consequence to me of ignoring them all is just about the same."

"Unless it was a friend in need."

Crewell gave him a crooked smile. "I doubt that."

"Don't you have any?"

"Friends? Or friends in need?"

"Either."

"Of course I do. Friends and colleagues."

"But you wouldn't be the one they'd call," said Jack. "Is that it?"

"Probably not," she said, but whatever pleasure she took in their debate had evidently lapsed. She picked up the book in her lap and stared at its jacket.

127

Jack and Aisha exchanged a glance. She might have forgotten all about them, if Jack hadn't said, "You are Carla Crewell, aren't you? Who teaches a class in Continental Philosophy on Thursday nights?"

"I trust that's not all I am," the woman muttered, but she added automatically, "I'm sorry, but the class has already begun, and I couldn't possibly add another student now, after all you've missed. Besides, the room is full, isn't it?"

Jack dropped into one of the chairs. "I'm not here to wheedle a seat. I'm here to inquire about one of your students—Janie Mae Olsen, from your Thursday night class. A little older than most of them. An unusually pretty girl."

Crewell looked up sharply. She seemed to take it as a personal slight. She might have been attractive too, once upon a time. Auburn could have been her own color. But her hair was pulled back in a tight ponytail too bouncy for her complexion, and her mouth had set into lines of disapproval. Her gaze shifted away from Jack and settled on the light splash of acid on Aisha's neck and cheek. That seemed to provide some solace, and Crewell said, "I know who you mean."

"Janie Mae Olsen."

"She introduced herself to the class as Jane. But she sat in the first row, where she took copious notes on her laptop. She usually had questions after class, as well. But the truth is she was always more interested in my personal life than in anything I had to say about Heidegger."

"Is that who you're studying in class?"

"Last week. We were discussing Hannah Arendt on Thursday. But we had to consider their relationship in the context of her early career."

"Was Jane there? On Thursday?"

"Yes, she was."

"Are you sure? Don't you need to check your attendance records?"

"I recall our discussion. Arendt's ideas about the Third Reich were certainly different from Heidegger's, whose wife, you understand, was an ardent Nazi. But Jane was intrigued by their May-December romance. Convinced it had launched Arendt's career."

"Did she stay until the end?"

"Of class? At least. Jane usually stayed after, to ask questions. She had some place to go this week, an appointment she couldn't miss."

"She did miss it."

"Really? I'm surprised. Another student got to me first after class and peppered me with questions. Jane practically pushed him out of the way. When she finally had a chance to ask her own question, she scribbled down the answer with her eyebrow pencil and hurried out, shouting *thank-you* over her shoulder. That was not like Jane at all, who was usually so polite."

"What did she want to know?"

"If Arendt ever wrote about her love affair with Heidegger."

"Did she?"

"Not by name. But she wrote a study of Rahel Varnhagen, a Jewess in Berlin, who had an affair with a German nobleman. Hannah's treatment of their break-up is thought to reveal her own feelings about Martin."

"This German," Jack said, pulling a crushed index card out of his jacket pocket. "Rahel's nobleman. His name wasn't by any chance Count Finckenstein?"

Crewell examined the card. By her expression Jack knew he had found his Count.

"What does it mean?" she said.

"Janie Mae reached her car on Thursday night. But she got no further. You said she was in a hurry, didn't you? She left a client waiting on the other end. It means she lost control of where she traveled next."

"So ... you think she's dead? Or kidnapped?"

Jack scratched his head. "Her car was parked in the lot, and if this was inside it, so was Jane. That doesn't sound like a snatch to me. She either let somebody into her Beamer, or else they were there already, waiting for her. She's probably still around here someplace—because why not drive her off in the Beamer, if that's what you plan to do anyway?"

The Professor looked at Aisha, who offered no help. Then she screwed up her critical acumen and turned to challenge Jack. "That's a lot of meaning to read in two little words."

"We could put it to proof with a question," said Jack, slipping the index card into his shirt pocket. "It's been five days since your class. Where could you hide a pretty girl's body on a college campus?"

129

28

Cathy McConnell knew the mother of every girl on the Pink Panthers, the AYSO Division Four Soccer Team for which her daughter Melissa played center and scored the most goals of any girl, game after game.

Cathy organized the schedule of mothers who brought juice to the games every Saturday morning and Tuesday afternoon. She stepped in more than once to bring boxes of cranberry and apple when one of the others flaked out at the last minute. Some of the mothers brought Gatorade, which was just green or orange sugar water, with cookies or crackers or some such starch, but Cathy made it her business to bring actual juice with celery sticks or oranges cut into wedges small enough for a girl to take in her mouth. She used a rotating system, so that a mother who missed a Tuesday game was dropped down to the following Saturday morning, with just enough time to notify the mother who had originally been scheduled for that game.

It was a lot of work, but Cathy considered it worthwhile when she saw the smug grin on Lissa's face after a brutal victory. Mitchell was clearly proud of them too, *of both of his girls*, he liked to say when she drove the big Tacoma into the garage and told him about each goal Lissa had scored against the stone-faced goalie on the opposite team. To keep the whole thing going and her system on schedule, Cathy had to know all the team mothers and what to expect from each of them. She collected names and phone numbers, emails, Facebook pages, and the kinds of snacks each one liked to serve. Which is how Cathy knew that the woman in heels with the trampy canvas chair was not the mother of any girl on the Panthers.

But she didn't seem to be the mother of any girl on the other team, either. Cathy believed in *integration* in AYSO soccer. There was no reason for parents of one team to stay on their side of the field, while her parents stayed on the other. But the woman in the canvas chair turned up late on Tuesday afternoons, when the Panthers faced a slew of different teams. She always clapped when their goalie, Annabeth, made a save. But she never sat with the Farleighs, never spoke a word to either Ted or Marion, and didn't seem to know them when they passed in the parking lot.

So what was she doing on their side of the field?

And why did she show up dressed as she did? Most of the moms wore workout clothes—if not sweats, then Nike shorts or pants with a white line down the side. Maybe a matching dark blue t-sheet with a wick-away fabric on top. But the woman in the canvas chair wore tight skirts with stiletto heels that sank into the grass, nylons and a stretchy top cut low enough in front, so that all the fathers looked away conspicuously whenever you caught their eyes. She wobbled when she walked from her Jaguar to the sidelines, and when she set up her chair, she bent over in a distracting way. She was ten years older than most of the wives, but her red hair curled into striking waves, and they took a step closer to their husbands when she wiggled by. And what kind of seat did she bring for herself? Not one of the usual lawn chairs, with crisscross straps for a seat, or even a regular camping chair that folded into a sack you could carry across your shoulder. It folded all right, but the woven fabric had a pattern that looked like it had come from the boudoir of a courtesan, or a San Francisco brothel— although Cathy had been to San Francisco only twice, and never to a brothel.

And of course people talked. Cathy had heard rumors about the lady's *profession*, if that really was the word for the oldest. She didn't look like girls on the cable channel. She was overdressed for the soccer field, and underdressed for a dinner party or anyplace else Cathy and Mitchell might go. Not underdressed, exactly, because her clothes weren't skimpy or cheap, but *wrongly* dressed. Most women choose their outfits to win the approval of their girlfriends, but the woman in the canvas chair did not seem to care at all what other women thought of her.

To be fair, she didn't seem to care what the men thought either. You couldn't say she was there to steal anybody away. Cathy would have pegged her for a divorcee, if she ever batted an eyelash or asked a man for help. But she ignored them all, walking to the same spot on the midline, one or two Tuesdays a month, opening her chair and folding her legs discreetly at the ankles. She kept her attention on the girls on the field, until she felt the hostile eyes of the team mothers on her. Then she stood, folded her chair, and headed for her Jaguar, without a word to anybody. Like she was doing now – crossing the lawn to the parking lot. When she reached the gravel, Cathy knew, she would turn for one last glance over her shoulder.

Except this time she didn't. She stood, staring at the door of her car. She opened it, and Cathy could see that someone had broken the window. Shards of glass still clung to the frame, but the center had been smashed out, probably by a rock. Well, what did she expect, showing up at a soccer game in outfits like that, when she didn't have a daughter in the game? Cathy would never have thrown the rock, but she felt a certain satisfaction that somebody had taken the initiative to share their feelings about it.

The woman at the Jaguar did not seem to understand what had happened to her. She ducked her head into the front seat, so that only the rear of her tight skirt stuck out, and reached across the front seats. Then she crawled out again. She straightened and headed back toward the field, without her canvas chair. She marched over the grass in a beeline for Cathy, where she stopped in the middle of the team mothers, set both hands on her hips, and asked in a furious brogue:

"All right, so which one of you mothers stole my phone?"

29

A body is still a person, Marcus Dorfman believed, and frequently reminded the medical students when they came to check out the cadavers in his morgue. That was why they had to write to the families of the deceased, to thank them for their gift and promise to respect the dear departed. A person who donates his body to science imagines it might cure cancer or at least some infectious disease. They do not picture an awkward medical student groping around the torso like a teenager under a skirt.

There are always stories of pranks in anatomy labs, of body parts left in orifices for instructors to find, but Dorfman drew a hard line on his steel tables. *Picture yourself on the table*, he said. *Picture your dear old dad*. The students made fun of him—Marcus knew that—but they kept those remarks under their breath and showed their cadavers a proper respect whenever he passed their dissections.

Paperwork was an important part of showing respect. You have to know each one, the identity of each body, so it doesn't become a slab of meat beneath your knife. Dorfman kept careful records of each arrival from a mortuary or hospital morgue. He clipped a snapshot photo to the corner of each file, like a passport to the afterlife. So it posed a particular problem for him to open a steel drawer and find a cadaver without a toe tag or anything else to identify who she was or where she had come from.

She was young, in good shape—a pretty girl, alive. He didn't get a lot of those through the usual channels, let alone arriving on their own.

Marcus had already called around to all his sources, when a couple came into his lab, asking questions he did not feel like answering.

He called them a *couple* because there was one of each sex, though there didn't seem to be any family connection. She was a big black woman with a splotchy face, and he was an older white man who squinted under the fluorescent lights. They wanted to know about his bodies, where he got them, how he kept track. It was like they knew about the girl in the steel drawer and were waiting for Marcus to trip himself up. Baiting him for a slip-up—as if he shoveled the cadavers out of the ground himself.

Dorfman held out as long as he could. His bodies had nothing but privacy left, and he was determined to protect it. But they kept at him, with the size and approximate weight of the girl in the drawer,

133

her eye color and hair color and finally the date of her probable arrival at the anatomy lab. That was the detail that left him no choice but to let them take a peek at the girl in the drawer.

The white guy recognized her, or said that he did, and called the coroner's office, who sent over a man named Macauley with a van to take her away. That felt backwards, as if the poor thing had died twice. Dorfman had never lost a cadaver before. Macauley didn't say much … waiting him out … and in the end Marcus had to hand her over. It felt like he let her down, but what else could he do? At least he had a name and a source for her file. *Janie Mae Olsen. Philosophy.* The first corpse he ever got from that department.

30

"This place is a mess," said Aisha to Jack, as they stood in the living room of Janie Mae Olsen's condo in Brentwood.

The cushions were off the sofa, slashed open, and scattered across the rug. There had been a coffee table in front of the sofa, just a sheet of glass on a silvery metal base. The base was still there, three curves reaching up to support a slab that had been cracked off, split in half, and spider-webbed with a hammer.

What could anyone have been searching for, Jack wondered, to smash a sheet of clear glass to see what was inside it?

"You should see the bedrooms," said Aisha, calling from the hall. "Two of them. Totally trashed."

Janie Mae had a roommate, Jack recalled. Maggie had mentioned her. Susie Q, something like that. With Asian taste in room décor – a low mattress on a black wooden platform, matching dresser, and hanging silk scrolls decorated with Chinese or Japanese calligraphy. The dresser drawers were overturned and scattered across the room, underwear and nightgowns, spandex and lace, short shorts and short skirts and doll-size halter tops. Strips of bamboo wallpaper hung from the walls, which had gaping holes someone had punched through the plasterboard.

Aisha's face appeared in a hole. "Peekaboo, Jack."

"Clear through to the next room?"

"Somebody was pissed."

"Maybe. Or else looking for a safe in the wall."

"You should see this place. I'd say pissed."

Janie Mae's room was in no better shape. It looked like a library after a twister passed through it—the bookcase tipped forward with its shelves empty, loose pages and broken spines scattered over the carpet, which had been torn loose to expose the floorboards. Whatever someone had wanted here they wanted pretty badly and did a professional job, trying to find it.

Only it didn't look to Jack as if they ever found it, since they never stopped tearing the place to shreds. He picked up a kimono with the collar torn off, and a strip of wine-dark satin slipped between his fingers. That meant they would still be looking for it. Or anyone who knew where it was.

The kitchen was just as bad—plates thrown out of the cabinets, glasses shattered in the sink, food tossed out of the fridge all over the floor. Sixteen cups of single-serving yogurt in a variety of fruit flavors, souring on the tiles, a dozen boxes of Lean Cuisine in puddles of their own. No one had been here for days.

Jack picked up a soggy box and tossed it into the sink. "Any idea where Susie Q might have gone?"

"You mean Suziko?" Aisha picked up a sandal and set it down next to its partner. "No idea. But I know who would, if anybody does. And so do you."

"Vegas," said Maggie Malloy, when they returned to the house in Hancock Park. "For the weekend, with a client. She should be back by now."

Jack said, "Anybody you know?"

"One of her own recruits. She and Janie Mae were entrepreneurial, that way."

"She's in for some surprise when she gets back."

"You think she's in danger?"

"Maybe. Probably. You know where she's staying in Vegas?"

"No, but I have her cell phone. And we might've booked her ticket."

"A full service operation you're running here."

"When we arrange the trip, we usually cover the airfare. Some of the girls ask us to do the honors for private dates. We don't charge a fee, like a travel agent, but we do keep the miles."

Suziko's plane was due in the middle of rush hour. Aisha crept across the city, taking Highland to La Brea, the Santa Monica Freeway west to the San Diego Freeway, and Century Boulevard to the airport – where she crawled around the circle for forty-five minutes to the terminal. By the time they reached the lobby where passengers could be met, arrivals were already coming down an escalator, a stairway, and an elevator. Town car drivers held up signs, and reunited families embraced children and grandparents. Jack thought they might have missed Suziko, until Aisha spotted her not on the escalator but at the top of the stairs on their right, waiting for a flight attendant in front of her to bump a wheeled bag down the steps.

"There she goes," said Aisha, pointing.

Aisha's arm caught Suziko's attention, who stopped cold for a moment, frozen mid-step. She wore a scarlet jacket with braid over a tight black skirt and heels, with the leather strap of a computer case over her shoulder. She looked like a dominatrix fantasy of a stewardess. When Jack met her gaze, she backed up the stairs, pivoted, and clattered off in the opposite direction.

"Didn't Maggie call to tell her we'd be meeting her?"

"If she said she would, she did, Jack."

"Then where's she going? Didn't Maggie say I was a cop?"

"I guess she did," said Aisha.

Jack bolted up the steps, two at a time. At the foot of the stairs, a short, round woman in a TSA windbreaker shouted, "Hey!" When Jack ignored her, she picked up her walkie-talkie.

At the top of the staircase Jack spotted Suziko's scarlet jacket moving through a crowd of weary passengers headed from the gates to the baggage claim. To his right, on the far side of a plastic wall, were security checkpoints staffed by the Transportation Safety Administration. One officer ran a hand-held scanner under the outstretched limbs of a Pakistani traveler, while lines of departing passengers waited to pass through x-ray machines. A cop with a walkie-talkie turned his head to the staircase, but Jack was already making his way to the gates before the TSA officer could open his mouth and call for backup.

Suziko flew past the shops and newspaper stalls, the fast food counters and chain restaurants, and hesitated, looking back to see if she was still being followed. Her pause allowed Jack to close the distance between them, but when she saw him again, she made a sharp turn to her left and disappeared into a recess for a phone, fountain, and restrooms. Jack didn't bother with the men's room, but threw open the door to the ladies' and called, "Man coming in!"

Then he followed his warning into the room.

He was met by the disapproval of a businesswoman at a sink. Her briefcase was open on the tiles alongside hers, with a plastic pouch of cosmetics propped between the taps. Most of the stalls were unoccupied, and the shoes beneath the last door had clunky, low heels. He mumbled, "Scuse me, ladies," and fled from the room. The scorn of the businesswoman never relented, but she waited for his exit before returning to her face in the mirror.

Jack opened the door to the men's room and called, "Suziko?"

No answer, until a deep voice replied, "Not in here."

That left one door. Instead of a knob it had a lever to open it, like the mechanism on the back of a truck. Above the lever was a sign that read:

NO ENTRY. AUTHORIZED PERSONNEL ONLY

Jack lifted the lever and pushed open the door. A red light overhead started to flash and emit a constant stream of low-frequency *beeps*.

Jack found himself standing on a metal platform with steps down to the landing field. A plane was sitting not far away with its luggage bays open, where two handlers unloaded luggage onto the flatbed of a vehicle. The handlers were not looking at Jack, however, but watching the calves of the fleeing Suziko, as she headed around the nose. Jack tramped down the metal steps and went after her, only dimly aware of the door that flung open on the tarmac to his right, or the trio of uniformed officers who burst through it, waving side-arms.

He tried calling after her, "Suzy Q! Hold up!" But found he needed the breath to keep running. He thought he might have had her when she tried to re-enter the building at an open bay where bags were stopped, waiting for space on the conveyor belt. But she kicked off her heels and jumped on, crouching on the belt where it passed into a narrow, rectangular entrance, through hanging rubber straps.

Jack tried to follow on his knees but found he was still too high and rolled onto his back, clinging to a suitcase for protection. The conveyor belt suddenly dropped beneath him and Jack tumbled down a pitched ramp with an army duffle on top of him. When he sat up again, he was circling through the baggage claim area, while a mob of passengers eyed him sullenly. No one offered to help him to his feet.

He saw Suziko at the exit door, scuttling past a security guard casually checking packages. All she had was her computer case, which he didn't bother to open. Jack tried to follow her through the door, but felt his elbows suddenly seized by two officers on the street, as a voice in his left ear snarled: "We got you, Jack."

And in his right: "Motherfucker."

Did they know him? No, it was a *Jack* of indifference, of disrespect, a name like *Bud* or *Pal*, with no friendliness to it. It stung more than the traditional insult that followed.

At the curb Suziko hailed a cab, ahead of the line. A gypsy was standing a little further down the road, after dropping off a fare. The driver roared alongside her, Suziko slipped into the back, and they rattled off before anyone on line could complain.

"I'm a cop," said Jack to the security team.

"Like hell you are," said the officer on his left, gripping Jack's arm more tightly. The TSA had averted another disaster.

In the cab, Suziko watched the terminal slide away behind them and disappear in a swarm of yellow taxis. She sat back and felt something under her seat. She thought she heard a noise, too.

Thump! Thump!

Suziko leaned toward the cabbie. "Is something in the trunk?"

He didn't seem to hear her. At any rate, he didn't answer. The back of his head was covered with silvery hair, so she thought the problem might have been his hearing. But he seemed so focused on the traffic in the windshield, Suziko didn't dare to distract him. She climbed up on the seat, resting on her knees so she could see the taxi's trunk, and found something curious on the rear window ledge.

Plastic, with a rubber string.

Suziko loved masks. She put it over her face. *Cheep cheep*, she said.

But the cabbie never turned his head.

31

"We hate to interrupt your dinner, Ms. Moore," Patricia Newman said, "but we're trying to make an arrest in the homicide of Walter Frick."

The two women were seated in what Newman called an *interview room* at the Westside precinct house. The Lieutenant's back was to a large mirror, and Wendy Moore couldn't help wondering who else might be watching from the other side.

"You don't think I killed him?"

Newman shook her head. "No, we don't think you killed him. We don't think you *killed* him."

The shift in emphasis made the repetition deliberately significant. Wendy felt her ears grow warm, but she said, "I'm glad to hear that."

The two women faced each other across a green wooden table into which legions of suspects had scratched their names and features while waiting to be interrogated. The custodial staff had done their best to efface the more obscene engravings, so the table-top was no longer even, but scooped out where the most accurate artwork had been etched.

Wendy noticed a crude *Y* and lifted her hand from the table, running it through her hair to complete the gesture.

Both of the women were blondes, but there the similarity ended. Each was in her own way professionally coifed and dressed, but Newman had done everything possible to make her gender irrelevant, while Moore had played up hers, emphasizing softness in the style of her jacket, the silk of her blouse, the abundance of curls spilling over her collar. Patricia was strapped down severely, no nonsense; Wendy could be flirty, if the occasion required it. Both of them were accustomed to dealing with men who had strong ideas about women, and each understood the strategies adopted by the other to escape those expectations.

That didn't mean they liked one another. When Wendy tucked her hair into place, Patricia frowned and shook her head, ponytail bobbing behind her.

"We think you *fucked* him."

Wendy knew that shock was part of the Lieutenant's strategy and tried to ignore the blood rushing to her face. "That's ridiculous."

A second cop entered the room with some papers in his hand. Wendy had been brought in by two bulldog cops, but this was an older officer with stripes on his sleeve. His name-pin read: *Warneke*.

"What? That you would fuck him? Or that he would want you?"

Newman delivered the question with the same matter-of-face tone, but the fact that Sergeant Warneke was now in the room made hearing it aloud more embarrassing. Wendy shook her curls and said clearly, "Either one."

The Sergeant bent his head to the Lieutenant, who said, "Right. You were seen together, Ms. Moore—you and Walter Frick, at a private table at the Condor Club. We can bring in the bartender, if necessary."

Wendy seemed relieved. "We had a drink. So what? Several of the Vee-Pees are members. The view is the ocean, the greens are beautifully kept, and Walter liked to kid around, about our handicaps. Mine is five, or was, when I played in college."

"And his?"

"His wife, he used to say. That was the joke."

"Did he ever promise to leave her?"

"Not to me."

"The bartender heard you talking. Something about a *break-up*."

"A break-up? No, it wasn't like that." Wendy shook her curls vigorously. "We were talking about a *crack*-up. Hal's son, Bud Spinnaker, wrecked his father's Ferrari in a skid on PCH. That kid is a major screw-up, if you really want to know. Hal gave me the assignment of finding a replacement."

"Ferrari? Or Bud?"

"Is that a joke?"

"Is that the job of a bank president's aide?"

"Whatever he wants it to be," said Wendy. "I've gone for worse. That car meant something to Hal I never cared to explore."

"So you're saying ... what? You asked Walter Frick for help?"

"Do you know how hard it is to find a 1961 250GT California Spyder for sale? Walt was good at that kind of thing. Quick to laugh at a joke, or to reach for his wallet. He seemed to know everyone the day he arrived. Hal liked that about him."

"Did you?"

"Like Walter? I guess. No more than most people. He was a capable exec, who could hold his liquor. When Hal asked to see him, Walter showed up. He was always polite to the girls at reception. But he never helped me find a Ferrari."

Wendy thought that might have ended the interview, but Newman didn't seem to be releasing her. Instead, she turned to

Sergeant Warneke, lifting the top sheet off a stack of pages in front of her. Wendy felt like standing, but the Lieutenant's indifference kept her in her chair. "Is there something else?"

Newman studied the page in her hand for a moment, then turned it around to face Wendy.

"We found your emails," the Lieutenant said.

"Were they lost?"

"It took us a while to find his personal account. Frickazee@mymail.net. Slick for a banker, I suppose. People invent these names online to conceal their identities, then give themselves away with their cleverness."

Wendy glanced at the page with the transcript of an exchange between herself and Walter, which could have been any one of several similar online conversations. Her eye caught the words *sweetie-pie* and *darling* and she quickly looked away. It was one thing for the police to read her intimate chit-chat, making nasty jokes among themselves. They didn't have to watch her blush while reading it.

"So there was something more between the two of you," said Newman. It wasn't a question, but a statement of fact. "More than you've admitted. Something personal."

"We had sex, if that's what you're asking," Wendy said. "I don't know how *personal* it was."

Newman didn't press that point. "Then I'll ask you again. Did he ever promise to leave her? So you and he could be together?"

"I'll tell you again—it wasn't like that between us. Yes, Walter was fun to be around. He knew how to treat a lady. But he seemed perfectly content to keep the wife at home, hook up outside, and be candid about it. At least with me."

"Though not with Mrs. Frick?"

"I don't know what he told Judith. He told me they had an *understanding*, but husbands often say that and understand their understandings differently than their wives do. I don't know how candid he was with her, or the other girls."

"There were others?"

"I said everyone liked him. Walter was a charmer."

"And that was fine with you?"

"It was one of the things I liked best about him. After his sense of humor, I mean. I have a career at the bank, Lieutenant. Probably like your own. It may not be *brilliant*, yet, but it has potential. Walter's arrangement suited me, for this time in my life. I guess I'll want something more, when I have the time for it. I'll miss Walter, truly. But I didn't kill him out of jealousy, disappointment, or anything else."

"I believe you," said Newman, without the slightest sign of sincerity.

"You do?"

"Absolutely. Thanks for coming in."

Wendy stood uncertainly. "That's all you wanted? Or do I need to keep an eye out for squad cars every breakfast, lunch, and dinner?"

"We'll need your testimony, when the time comes. But we'll give you due notice for that." It was meant for a dismissal, but Wendy hesitated, and Newman added, "There's no need to worry, Ms. Moore. You haven't given away any secrets. There are several women involved in this case, not all as open-minded as you."

32

"Walter and I did not have an *understanding*," Her Honor Judith Frick insisted. "He did not feel free to engage in adulterous behavior."

"Without punishment," clarified Newman.

"I would never have stabbed him in the belly, Lieutenant, whatever he did," said Judith. "If that's what you're driving at."

The two women sat in Her Honor's chambers in the Stanley Mosk Courthouse in downtown Los Angeles. The day's proceedings were over. Judith was finishing up the paperwork for the cases she had heard and gathering up materials on the cases she would read overnight, when the phone rang and the Lieutenant offered to bring her up to speed on the case. To fill her in on their progress. Not to interrogate her, not to imply once again that Judith had murdered her husband with a steak knife in their kitchen—which is just what Newman did, when she got there.

"We know that he *was*," she said, "fooling around. Whether or not he felt free to engage. We have eyewitness testimony on that point."

Judith knew when somebody was trying to provoke her and resisted the impulse to react as she would have liked. She was a judge in her chambers, but Newman was an officer conducting a police investigation. The lines of authority were not entirely clear, and Judith could wait until the case was resolved before holding Newman accountable. It was the smart move, the calculated choice, and Judith would always choose to act smart over any more emotional alternative.

"It sounds like you think you have more."

"We have most of it, yes," confirmed Newman. "Your husband's philandering provides a motive for his murder."

"You mean jealous girlfriends … that kind of thing?"

"That kind of thing," echoed Newman. "We have no evidence of any person in the house except for you and Mr. Frick."

"Which doesn't mean that there wasn't anybody else in the house."

"It does mean you were there."

"So—I had an opportunity to stab my husband. The means was in its drawer. And now you believe you've found a motive for my doing so, as well?"

"That is the conclusion we would normally draw, on cases like this. I'm sure you know that most domestic homicides are spousal."

"That's inadmissible."

"In the courtroom, maybe, but we're just talking, here. You were tied up, when we found you. But you told us at the time that you tied the knots yourself. And there's a gap between the time you last remember and the time we found you. Is there anything you'd like to tell me now?"

Judith took a moment to collect her thoughts.

"I'd like to point out that my husband's *philandering*, as you call it, could only be construed as a motive if I knew about it, which I didn't. The testimony of some woman who claims to have seduced him does not establish the fact that I knew about it or reacted to that news very badly."

"Are we arguing legalities already?"

"I'm not arguing at all, Lieutenant. Merely pointing out the weak points in your theory of the crime."

"It's more than a theory already," said Newman, "though we might not have the last details nailed down. I thought you might want to save yourself the embarrassment of a public trial. Was it a crime of passion, Mrs. Frick? The District Attorney's office might allow some consideration if you spared the legal system that kind of a circus.

"Your picture in the paper, grist for the mill of every comic in town. Not to mention any challenges to your prior decisions."

"If I happen to be guilty of murder."

"If you are, we'll prove it. We'll find the missing bread crumbs in the trail that led from Mr. Frick's adultery to his homicide. Did you find his email to another woman? What was the straw exactly, that made you snap? I'm not calling it a premeditated act—at least not yet. Something must have tipped you off, and we will find it, in your mail, or online, or wherever your husband might have seen coming. A homicide has no secrets. If that's what you're depending on, I'd make your deal now."

"I'm depending on my innocence."

"Lots of convicted felons say that," said Newman, "usually in appeals from their prison cells. You know how few of those get heard? The choice is yours, but you might want to talk it over with a good criminal attorney before making any decisions."

"I'll take it under advisement," replied Judith. "Is this how you always do your job, Lieutenant? By threatening and coercing your suspects?"

"Not really," said Newman. "This is a special case and it gets special handling. If it was up to me, I'd have made the arrest already. My sergeant has an awesome respect for your office and keeps urging me to hold off until we have the whole story. And the D.A. seems to be listing that way too."

"My thanks to them," said Judith.

"You can thank them yourself when the time comes, if you still feel like it. But if you have nothing further to say, Your Honor, I'd better get back to my desk. I need to write up our conversation while it's still fresh in my memory. For notes, when I'm called to testify."

Judith let Newman show herself out. There were several things Judith would have liked to tell the Lieutenant, but again she restrained herself from acting on impulse. She considered calling a defense attorney, to talk it over, but the call itself would comprise a signal to anyone listening, and who knew the ins and outs of the system better than Judith herself?

She was going over the roster of talent in her mind, when she heard a tap on her chamber door and Lester Talbot opened it.

"Do you have a moment, Your Honor? Something's come up."

Judith waved him in. She poked Raines' number on her phone and hit the icon for the speaker. Together they listened to the soft buzz, to the click when it picked up, and to the defense attorney's deep baritone recording. Judith left a terse instruction for Mr. Raines to call her chambers as soon as he heard the message. Then she looked up expectantly at the prosecutor.

Talbot entered uneasily, standing behind the chair across from Her Honor's desk as if it were occupied. He sidled around it, holding onto the arm-rest, and finally sat on its tufted leather cushion. But he seemed ill at ease, glancing at the papers on her desk, at the lights of the city in her window, at the gleam on his own pocket watch. Judith asked, "Are you all right, Lester? Do you need something?"

"We have been trying to do as you ordered," he said, "for the 402 hearing—bringing in a few of our witnesses from the AEG party to give you an idea of their testimony. But that has proved more difficult than we expected."

Judith waited. "Your witnesses are no longer cooperating?"

"Our witnesses are no longer alive!" he said. "One after another we've tracked them down and found that something terrible has happened."

He took a sheaf of photographs from his briefcase and dropped one on Judith's desk. A headshot of a man in a pinstripe suit.

"Everett Halloran was picked up for running a stop sign. They found an ounce of cocaine in a silver snuff box in his glove compartment. A junior partner in his firm was a law school buddy of mine, and Halloran made a deal. He gave us the party and agreed to testify about his talk with Whistler—who was more candid at the affair than Mr. Raines would have you believe. Unfortunately, Halloran drowned in his swimming pool, one night after work. In the same pool where he swam laps every evening."

He dropped two more photos on Judith's desk and stabbed each one with his finger.

"Henry Cordesman was hit by a commuter train— possibly a suicide. He stepped off the platform just before it rolled into the station. Alan Fleischer washed up in a bay on Palos Verdes—where he has been surfing for years. One, two, three. The same discovery. Dead men all."

"And you think ... what? That Bernard Whistler killed them?"

"Mr. Whistler is still in prison."

"An accomplice after the fact, then? Abetting the accused by silencing your witnesses?"

Talbot shook his head. "Our case against Whistler is very strong. We have the medical records, releasing him from service with a psychological disability. We can prove he invested his military pay with Phillip Hazlitt and lost it all when Mr. Hazlitt was exposed. We know why he needed the cash."

Judith knew it too—in fact, everyone who read the papers did. Whistler's wife needed a new heart, because, as he told the *Times*, "he broke her old one" by returning in the state he did from Iraq. The picture that ran over the quote fed the public sympathy. Half the jury pool wanted to award him a Medal of Honor.

Talbot resumed his summary with a shrug. "Whistler was desperate and furious when he learned his nest egg was gone. He knew explosives—he disarmed dozens of IEDs before he lost it in Iraq. He stalked and finally got to see Hazlitt, who blew him off, as his whole scam unraveled on the evening news. Later that week, Phillip Hazlitt was blown to bits in his garage. We have his skull and jaw, which match the dental records in his file at Bethesda."

Judith knew most of this already. Just the sort of evidence Newman would have spit to collect against her. "So – "

"A handful of party guests on the night of his indictment wouldn't be worth the risk. They'd hardly make a dent in our case against Whistler. Why go after these people, before you've even ruled whether they'll be allowed to testify?"

"Are you saying these are all accidents?"

"They could be accidents. Random events are like that. Do you know that in a hundred tosses of a coin, odds are you're going to get a run of heads or tails, all the same, eleven in a row? Heads. Heads. Heads. Try it some time."

"The police should investigate."

"They should. I mean, we are. But we're not sure who was there. We've talked to Room Service, to all the staff, but can't find one who remembers serving them. Big tippers, I imagine."

Judith was losing the point here and certainly her patience. The prosecutor was dancing around something and wouldn't say why he had come. "What can I do to help?"

Talbot drew a breath. "I understand Mr. Raines enclosed a video disk along with his motion to exclude the party guests. In support of his contention that their testimony would be prejudicial."

Judith remembered packing it into her briefcase with their motions at the end of the day, although she couldn't recall seeing it since.

"Didn't he send you a copy?"

Talbot shook his head. "It isn't explicitly referenced in the motion."

"Then we'll have to ask Mr. Raines to provide copies," Judith said, "for both of us. I'm not certain what became of my own."

He nodded. "I understand."

It took Judith a moment to realize she had missed something. "You understand? What exactly do you understand, Mr. Talbot?"

He did not look happy to explain. "I meant I could understand why Your Honor would rather keep that disk off the record."

"And why is that?"

He hesitated. "Because of who was present at the party."

Judith knew the answer without asking. She should have confirmed it but said nothing. Talbot took her silence as his cue to exit. He mumbled an excuse and slipped out the door, pulling it shut behind him.

Click.

As soon as Talbot left, her phone rang. She picked it up automatically and heard a familiar baritone. Randolph Raines. He listened as she explained that Mr. Talbot had come to see her, and what he wanted. When she finished, he asked, "Are you sure?"

"Of course," said Judith, though her voice broke.

"You *have* screened the disk?"

The phone did not allow him to see her blush. "I seem to have misplaced the copy you gave me."

There was a long pause on the other end of the line. "I am sorry, Your Honor," Raines replied, "but I'm not sure I still have my copy either."

Judith felt a chill. "What do you mean?"

"I believe it was erased. Accidentally. Those disks are delicate, aren't they? So easily ruined by heat or cold. Even by a magnet, they tell me, if it's left too close to the disk overnight."

"Who told you that, Mr. Raines?"

"I don't recall," he said, and his deep voice made it sound convincing. "But I do recall the result. The disk is gone, Your Honor."

"It's gone?"

"Rest assured," he said. "Our only copy. Erased. Unrecoverably."

That did not help Judith rest, and the confidence in his tone made her even less comfortable. What exactly was Raines promising so smugly? Guaranteeing that the disk disappeared?

Why should that reassure her?

"When?" she asked urgently. "When was the disk erased?"

Judith heard him draw a breath, as he might for a peroration. But he did not answer her question directly. "When it first arrived," he said, "it came in over the transom in an unmarked sleeve. I thought it had been sent by a friend of the defense. Then I saw the piece in the *Times* about your husband, with a photo of the man. That made me see it differently."

Judith pictured his leonine head shaking over the telephone. "How?"

"With profound sympathy. An awful shame."

"Thank you," said Judith automatically, before stopping to consider just what he was implying. She understood each sentence in careful isolation, but what did they have to do with one another?

"My husband's obituary? Or an article about his murder?"

"Both ran with photos."

149

"Mr. Raines, please, are you telling me ... Walter is on that disk?"

The plastic went dead in her hand.

He hadn't hung up the line—she would have heard it click, if he did. He was still on the other end, waiting. Judith dropped the receiver as if the coiled cable connecting her to Raines had turned into a wriggling swamp adder.

Judith heard the snap as Pat Newman fit together the final pieces of her puzzle. Her Honor viewed the disk among the pretrial motions of the Bernard Whistler homicide and saw Walter in a filthy embrace with a prostitute supplied by his buddies at the bank. That set her off in a jealous rage, which ended with a kitchen knife stuck in Walter's belly, when he went downstairs for a snack.

It was just the piece the Lieutenant needed to make an arrest. Judith felt a rising tide of panic in her stomach and did what she always did before Walter entered her life. She picked up the receiver and punched in an old number, winding the black cord around her finger as she listened to the hum and jangle on the line and waited to hear a familiar, vexing voice.

33

It took Jack over an hour and several phone calls to convince airport security that he was not the next underwear bomber, even though he ran up the down staircase. The watch commander at his precinct confirmed they had a detective named Jack Stryker who was on disability at the time. That didn't help as much as Jack hoped, but opened a line of rather pointed questions.

If he was an officer, what was he doing, violating TSA guidelines?

Refusing to answer another officer?

Planes were the weapons of terror on nine-eleven. Didn't he understand that might happen again? Did he realize he was screwing with the feds?

What was he doing at the airport in the first place?

Picking up a family member? A friend?

Why did she run from him then? Did he have her name and cell?

Who was he trying to fool?

It was only when he thought to call his union representative, and the man got on the horn with the officers, that his interrogators began to relax and ultimately to treat him as a brother in blue. They wanted an apology, something like that, recognition of the job they did checking people's loafers, but Jack could tell they had decided to release him. It took another twenty minutes to convince them of his respect, and by the time he joined Aisha at the curb outside the baggage claim, Suziko's taxi had long before disappeared into the evening.

He hadn't caught the plate. Each taxi had a number on the light on top, on the body somewhere, but this one was a gypsy without a medallion, fleet number, or telephone advertised on its door. It was a blue car, not ten years old, probably Japanese—though it could have been Korean, or even an American car modeled to look like an import. Jack had nothing to go on, no way to find her, and no idea where the frightened Suziko might run, if she thought the police were after her.

He called Maggie Malloy, but Suziko hadn't holed up in the house in Hancock Park. She wouldn't answer her cell phone, or call Maggie back when she left a message. He tried the condo Suziko shared with Janie Mae Olsen, without expecting an answer. And he didn't get one. Jack was about to call it quits, to bail out the Buick and head for home, when Aisha said, "You might as well send her a text, Jack. Since we know she's got her laptop."

Jack pictured the laptop strap over her shoulder. It left her hands free to work the lever on the terminal exit door, because she had nothing else in them.

Jack turned back to the terminal.

He walked back to the security desk he had been so anxious to escape not an hour before, and asked the same security officer to look up a passenger. The cop gave Jack a nasty look, but paged through his desktop computer until he found the listing for Suziko's flight and seat. Jack asked for the numbers of her baggage claim ticket.

They found her Vuitton at the side of the carousel among the lost luggage, bags loaded onto the wrong planes, oversized objects, and suitcases left behind by travelers who picked up somebody else's belongings. A medium-sized case with the distinctive V design, tagged with the corresponding ticket.

Jack thought they might be challenged carrying it out, but Aisha rolled her eyes, picked up the suitcase, and walked out of the baggage claim.

No one said a word.

They drove back to Jack's place on the beach in Venice. In his early thirties Jack came into some money, when his father's brother made him partial beneficiary of a life insurance policy. With no better plans for the money, he allowed Judith to talk him into buying two rooms and a kitchenette on the ground floor of what had been a private home, half a block from the boardwalk on Venice Beach. Jack later thanked or cursed her for that financial advice, depending on the noise level of the evening.

The upstairs of the house was rented out to a fluid succession of tenants. At the moment it quartered three sophomores from Uruguay enrolled in Santa Monica College. Jack always said *enrolled* rather than *attending,* because they never seemed to go to class but wobbled down the steps after noon, for breakfast, and cranked up the music or video games on either side of midnight. After a sleepless week, Jack sought refuge in Hancock Park, where the warmth of his welcome kept him coming back to Molly's.

Inside Jack's apartment were two square rooms and a kitchenette. The outer room was larger, divided by the back of a sofa into a dining area and a sitting area, with a coffee table in front of the sofa, an armchair and a stereo, with a CD player and turntable. On the coffee table was a chess set with a game in progress and a small red book: *Common Sense in Chess*, by Emanuel Lasker.

"Was somebody in here?" Aisha asked. "Who were you playing?"

"The book."

"That's so sad, Jack! Who plays against a book?"

"Just me and Phillip Marlowe."

"You could probably find someone on line, you know. If you tried."

"Let me see that suitcase," Jack said.

He led her into his bedroom and tossed the Vuitton on the mattress. Its zipper was sealed with a tiny golden lock. Jack snapped it off, using a bolt-cutter from a toolbox under his bed. In the suitcase they found the contents of Suziko's hotel drawer, in reverse order: the laundry from her bottom drawer on top, a sweater-dress and bikini, negligee and baby dolls, silk shorts and a matching top. At the bottom of the bag, still folded, her unused underwear. Along the sides were shoes—strappy sandals, flip-flops—and at the bottom her cosmetic case, stuffed with personal items and folded cash. There was also a box of DuMariers, half filled with cigarettes. The other half concealed an assortment of colored pills.   Jack tipped the box and spread the pills over his palm. Ativan, Ecstasy, Viagra, and Lunestra. Suziko left nothing to chance.

Aisha picked up the sweater-dress and held it against her body. Its skirt fell shorter than her own. She tugged down the hem, and a shiny object fell out.

Jack picked it off the floor. A disk. "What do you suppose this is?"

"Not her medical records." Aisha took it from him and turned it over. Unmarked on either side, with nothing to identify its contents. "She must've burned it herself."

"For a computer? Or a player?"

Aisha held it up, so it glinted in the window light. "Why don't you give it a try?"

Jack took it back from Aisha and cranked up a DVR on a shelf under the TV at the foot of his bed. The set sat on a cabinet, and a small one—Aisha guessed not more than twenty-four inches across. She was pretty good at guessing inches.

When a picture came up, they saw a comfortable room, viewed from a stationary camera. To the left was an unmade bed. Directly in front of the camera was an empty armchair of overstuffed leather, and behind the chair a picture window, in soft focus, filled with pale greens and glistening colors. A moment later the chair was occupied by a middle-aged man in black socks and suit-pants—his hand held by Suziko, who pushed him into the chair, and knelt down in front of him. The shot showed his face grimacing in agony or ecstasy. It was hard to tell which, since he seemed to be imitating both the movements and the nasal groans from late-night cable soft porn.

"It's a party," said Aisha.

Jack didn't need to watch a blow job. From that angle it was even less erotic than pornography, which he never found arousing. Watching strippers pretend to swoon was not his idea of seduction. Jack was turned on by the unfocused look in a woman's eyes, when her juices started to flow. He had no desire to watch a young girl gnaw the knob of a corporate john, and ejected the unmarked DVD.

"So what is this? A party favor?"

Aisha shrugged. "We'd have to watch it longer to find out. But I can't, tonight, Jack. I've got something else to do."

That caught his attention. "Wash your hair?"

"Nope. I got a date."

He gave her a reproving look. "I thought you gave those up."

"Not that kind!" Aisha laughed. "A *date*, you know? Unpaid. I mean, I hope he pays—for dinner. Not for me."

Jack would have said something kind and encouraging, but the phone rang on his bedside table. Jack did not receive many personal calls, and most of them came on his cell. The land-line next to his bed sat sullenly in its cradle, disturbed only occasionally by the disability benefits office or the woman who cooked and cleaned for his father.

He lifted the receiver and hesitated. "Hello?" Then repeated more confidently, "Hello, Judith." His tone of voice suggested he might have crossed his arms, if he didn't need his hand to hold the phone to his ear.

Aisha watched him closely as he nodded to the air.

"Of course," he said. "If you need me to. Just give me half an hour to get there. No, I remember." He hung up without saying good-bye.

"Remember what?"

"How to find her chambers."

"Uh huh," said Aisha. "No problem. I'll drive you."

Jack shook his head. "No, you won't. You have a date tonight, with a guy who doesn't know he's getting lucky—just scoring the date. I can get myself to Judith's house, if she really needs me."

"How?"

"I'll drive. I still have a license, you know, and a Buick. There's gas in the tank, isn't there? I didn't check."

"I did."

'Then it's settled. You're off tonight. You go your way and I'll go mine."

Aisha looked at him sideways, but he didn't waver, and she said, "You better drop me off, then, so I can shower and change."

"I better."

Aisha gave him a different look. "It's not just in case you want to stay there, is it? You're seeing pretty well these days, aren't you?"

"You mean, don't I need you anymore? No, I don't, Aisha … not tonight. I'll see you in the morning."

"That isn't what I meant, you know."

He ignored that, or didn't hear it, and waggled a finger at her. "Remember, young lady—just one kiss, when you say goodnight. He can call tomorrow, for a second chance."

34

When Jack entered Judith's judicial chambers, he thought his eyesight was going again. It turned out to be the lighting. The overhead fixture had been turned off and the room lit only by the brass lamp on Judith's desk and a standing lamp by the couch under the windows. The room had been done in a masculine décor, paneled in dark mahogany, furnished in the same wood with brass fittings, green leather on the couch, greener drapes, and the deepest green lampshades.

The only feminine touch in the room was a wilted rose on Judith's desk. Its silver vase stood out against the brass like a planted clue in a crime scene.

When Jack entered the dim chamber, Judith was on the couch in her stocking feet and reading glasses, with a big leather book propped on her raised knees. A glass of red wine stood on the rug alongside her. When she saw Jack, she closed the tome, not with a snap but gently. She wore a rumpled grey skirt and a burgundy blouse with two buttons open at the throat. When she swung her legs around to face him, she looked like a goblet of claret herself.

"Hello, Jack," she said.

"Time for a new rose, Judith. That one has seen its day."

She contemplated the sad flower on her desk. "I have a little trouble letting go, sometimes. You know that, don't you?"

Judith had a way of putting him on the spot, eliciting a confession of intimacy if he said anything at all. From long experience he had learned to keep his answers brief. "I remember."

"Are you still with that whore?"

"I was never *with* Maggie," Jack replied quickly, then heard the words differently. "Only once."

"Congratulations on your restraint."

"It wasn't mine."

"I'm glad that someone has a moral instinct."

"Judith … is that the emergency you called me to discuss?"

"I'm sorry to have dragged you away from your whorehouse," she said, though they both knew she had reached him at his own place in Venice. "But it *is* an emergency. You recall that little favor I asked you to do? It hasn't improved the situation. Patricia Newman is still knotting a noose for the wrong neck."

"Yours?"

She put her hand to her throat, which was less firm but still as long and white as he remembered it. "Whatever else you think of me, you must know, Jack, that I could never have murdered Walter."

She was playing on old strings again, Jack knew. But he also thought she meant what she said. "A kitchen knife isn't your style."

"Exactly."

"You prefer a scalpel."

"That isn't kind," said Judith, surprised perhaps that he went there so soon. "You know I didn't want to do it. But it wasn't the right time for either of us."

"I would've liked to make that judgment for myself. To have a voice in it, at least. Instead of finding out after the damage was done."

"You're right," she said. "I should have told you. We should have talked about it first. But I didn't want to risk changing my mind, Jack—to let you talk me out of it. You could have, you know. I was in love with you. You could've held me in your arms and promised everything would turn out right."

"Didn't I do that?"

"Yes, you did, and swept me right along. Until the cold light of morning, when I went in to the office and knew it had to be one way or the other. I could keep it and you, and write off my brilliant career. Or I could let it go, for a little while. I could set my nose to the grindstone, make a little progress, and try to hang on to you, somehow."

"I think I asked you to marry me."

"Assuming we would keep it. *Enabling* us to keep it. But it wouldn't have worked out as you promised. We both know what happens to sweet young things who step out for a couple of years of radiant motherhood."

"They become sweet older things."

"That wasn't what I wanted to become."

"You made your choice."

"I did." Judith stood and wobbled a bit, but caught her balance and drew close to him. "You could have stayed with me, Jack, even though. But you didn't. You didn't stay with me for an hour."

It had actually taken him longer than that to get drunk and find Maggie. But he didn't argue the point.

"No."

"You said you would. You said you would stay with me forever."

157

"I thought you were different."

"From what? You thought I was attractive, didn't you?" There was no denying that. But she didn't wait for his answer. "Don't you think I'm still attractive?"

She was close enough for him to smell a trace of sweet wine on her breath. She put her hand to her face and turned away. But she seemed to reconsider. She crossed to the front of her desk, put her palms on the edge, and leaned forward.

"What do you say, Jack? How do I look tonight?"

She spread her feet, so the grey silk skirt crept up her thighs.

"Judith—"

She turned halfway around. "Let's not talk about it, all right? I don't want to hear why we should or shouldn't, what it means or doesn't mean. It won't mean a thing, okay? I'm perfectly clear on that. Right now what I need is to forget everything for a while. And I'll bet you do too, if you're really not with anybody." She turned back and set her elbows on the desk.

She was wearing stockings, not pantyhose, with a band of dark lace at the top of each leg, constricting her white thighs. Jack found the contrast more compelling than the satin *bustiers* and baby-doll nighties of the girls at Maggie's place. She glanced back over her shoulder at him and wiggled.

"Exactly how long are you planning to keep a lady waiting?"

Jack had been brought up too well for that. What could it hurt, after all this time? If that's what she wanted. Wasn't it what he expected, even hoped for, when he heard her voice on the phone? He brushed aside that uncomfortable thought as he felt her body press against his in the old familiar places.

"Mm," she said, "that's the Stryker I remember."

When it was over, Jack lay on his back on the green leather couch with a tufted button pressed against his spine. Through his eyelashes he saw Judith's silhouette moving against the window. She was gathering up clothing from wherever it landed around the room. Jack reached across the floor to recover his shorts, and Judith noticed him stirring.

"Want a drink?" She smiled. "Of water. To replenish your fluids."

His mouth was dry. He drank.

She sat on the couch alongside him, already back in her skirt and blouse. She crossed one bare leg over the other. "Don't look so worried, Jack. It still meant nothing but a healthy release. God knows we needed one. Right?"

What could he say to that? "It was nice."

"I've always been a nice girl. That's what you called me. Remember?"

Of course he did. "A nice, ambitious girl from the Valley."

She made a wry face. "Though I don't know I would call what we just did *nice*. Most people would call it *naughty*."

She was trying to engage him—Jack knew that—pleading her case for his help. She was in trouble. But she was awfully good at it.

He buttoned his shirt-sleeve and sighed. "What does Newman think she has, that she didn't have before?"

"A motive," Judith said calmly.

"Does she really? Did you have a reason to kill good old Walter?"

"Yes, but I didn't know it at the time. It seems Walter had fallen off the wagon, which in his case was never a question of beer but softer forms of welcome."

"Women? More than one?"

"One in particular has caught the Lieutenant's eye. But my homicidal rage was apparently provoked when I saw my husband cavorting with hookers at a party."

"You saw them?"

"On a video. Some yahoo taped the evening, no doubt for a souvenir. Working gals and guys in Brooks Brothers suits."

Jack felt a chill at his collar. "And someone sent you a copy?"

Judith said, "That was just dumb luck. We live in a world of cruel serendipity. The disk was evidence on an unrelated case that happened to fall in my courtroom. But that's not how she sees it. According to Newman, I was screening the disk in our bedroom, while Walter gobbled up chocolate pudding in the kitchen. The sight of my husband's open fly drove me mad, so I marched down and stabbed him with a knife from the drain-board. I bound myself to the headboard with a scarf for an alibi, then promptly told the investigating officer I had tied the knots myself. It would be laughable in a farce, if she weren't about to arrest me for manslaughter. Or worse. She didn't bother spelling out the charge."

Judith was close to hysterics. Jack saw them thumping below the surface of her skin, where the long veins ran up her neck.

"Don't worry about it. She can't prove what didn't happen."

"They don't teach that to all the detectives."

"Let me talk to her."

"It's too late, Jack! Newman won't hear anything except my confession. She dreams about snapping handcuffs on me. Now this damned disk has given her cause to hope."

"Is it really as bad as that?"

Judith clapped the top of her head. "Who knows?"

"You haven't seen it?"

"No. Not that night, or ever since."

"I thought you said it was evidence for a case in your court."

"I brought it home in my briefcase, with the written arguments. I was reading them that night, when Walter came in. He threw things around a bit. I must have left it somewhere, but I can't find it. The police went over the room with a fine tooth comb, and they didn't seem to turn it up. It's not in my briefcase. I've dumped the whole thing out more than once and torn apart every envelope and piece of paper inside. No disk. Anywhere. It's gone."

The chill tingled down his spine. Jack looked up, but the ceiling fan was perfectly still. For a moment he tried willing it to turn.

It stubbornly refused. He said, "Maybe not."

35

He left Judith for the first time trying to keep up with him, wondering if Jack was abandoning her or if he actually planned to return with something useful for her case. She hung onto his jacket sleeve and stood in the doorway behind him like a shade hovering over a grave. But he crossed town in half an hour and found the disk where Aisha left it, near the DVD player in his condo's living room.

The disk they found in Suziko Mori's luggage. How it got there Jack couldn't imagine. But could there really be two of those things?

Jack didn't stop to check but headed back to the car, driving downtown, where Judith was still waiting in her chambers. At that hour, he had to call up to gain entrance to the courthouse. Judith gave the guard permission to admit him, but when she opened her door, she looked surprised to see him. And when he held up the DVD, she stared as if she had never seen Jack Stryker before.

"Is that … my disk?"

"It's a party. I'm not sure it's yours."

"AEG's."

"The party that incited you to slice and dice Walter. Let's see what it does."

"Where on earth did you get it?"

"At my place. I was watching it when you called."

"You and Molly Molloy?"

"*Maggie*," he said. "But no, not with her."

He left Judith wondering who else had been at his place, when he slid the DVD in a player on her bookcase and started it rolling.

A young woman in a white towel moves away from the camera, into focus. Janie Mae Olsen. Behind her, a man in an open white shirt and boxer shorts is sitting in an armchair next to a bed. He looks up expectantly as Janie Mae draws near. She sits on the arm of his chair and strokes the grey hair peeking out of the top of his undershirt. His hands are folded across his belly, with his fingers interlaced. Janie Mae strokes the top of his leg, then inside his thigh. He unlocks his fingers and sets his elbows on the armrests. She sinks between his knees and pulls off his shorts.

"Do you know this guy?"

Judith peered at the screen, past Janie Mae's bobbing head. "He might be Harry Cordesman. Walter introduced him once at a dinner. Better dressed and combed than here, but it could be the same guy. Do you know *her*?"

161

"Janie Mae Olsen."

"Of course you do. She's a hooker. Do you know them all?"

"She's dead."

"She's looking pretty lively here."

Jack did not need to watch the blow job to its climax but hit the fast forward button. When the disk stopped, a different woman was squatting on her haunches in a thong and black lace bra.

Suziko.

In the armchair is another man, with his knobby knees jutting up, his thigh over her shoulder. The rhythm is different—a few slow strokes, a flurry of fast ones— and her head twists back and forth, as if she can't decide on an angle. But the faces and the noises coming from the man in the chair are remarkably like those of his predecessor.

Jack hit the button again.

This time it stops on a handsome man in the chair, still in his suit pants. Off to one side, someone mumbles, and his face creases in a smile.

Walter.

Jack hit the *fast forward*, but not soon enough. Judith hadn't uttered a sound, but her eyes welled up with tears.

That was enough to convince Jack all over again. Whatever his doubts about her, Judith hadn't murdered her husband.

The chair is empty. Behind it is a window through which they can see shifting shades of green, out of focus. An arc of rainbow colors sparkles through the green and falls below the sill of the window. In the foreground, dangling from an arm of the chair, is the white towel Janie Mae Olsen wore out of her shower.

A man picks it up, scrunches it into a ball, and tosses it offscreen. A moment later, a second man enters the picture. He pushes the first man into the chair and seats himself on an armrest.

Jack jumped the disk ahead.

Now a slender, older man is standing over the chair. He seems hesitant to sit, and when he does, he crosses his long legs. He picks a nit from his trouser crease and rocks his foot at the ankle. He looks like he's waiting for a tee time at the club.

"That's Ev," said Judith. "Everett Halloran."

"He's also dead?"

"A swimmer, drowned in his pool."

"Either these are the unluckiest partiers ever," Jack said, "or someone had a bone to pick with the lot of them."

"Maybe somebody didn't like the deal they negotiated."

"What deal?"

"What do you think they were celebrating, Jack? They called a press conference in the ballroom of the Pierrot to announce an agreement between the United States Treasury and the American Enterprise Group."

"Judith—the police might think you stuck Walter, but we know you didn't. And we can add another name to the casualty list: Janie Mae Olsen's. I found her body in the anatomy lab at USC."

"God ... how gruesome!"

"Someone has gone to a lot of trouble to keep this under wraps. I can't help thinking that man has something to hide. Anything announced at a press conference is probably not the secret these people were killed to conceal."

"Which was what?"

"I don't know yet. But it's on this disk. Who else was there?"

"At the party? For the deal-makers?"

"It's one place to start."

"We'll have to watch the whole thing to find out."

That was what they did. Together they watched one sex act after another, in the armchair or the bed beside it, Janie Mae and Suziko working through the guest list. Jack reached to fast forward through their coupling with Walter, but Judith placed her hand on his wrist to stop him, watching those encounters as soundlessly as she had watched the others. No gnashing teeth or foaming mouth. Just a clinical interest.

When the sex was over—when the camera held on the chair and bed for two minutes, three minutes, four— Jack reached for the control to shut it off, but Judith stopped his hand again. They watched the green window in the empty room for a few minutes more before finally tapping it off.

"So, who have we got?" asked Jack.

"Besides the dead men?"

"I don't suppose any of them have been murdering the others."

"We know Bernard Whistler was there," said Judith. "He doesn't show up on the disk, but the camera was in the bedroom. He could have dropped by and passed up his chance with the ladies. Randolph Raines brought him to the party—to cheer him up, Raines told me, after Whistler's indictment. Everett Halloran was willing to testify to Whistler's disposition."

"Whistler is still in prison," said Jack. "Isn't he?"

163

"There's no bail on a murder charge."

"So Raines was there too," said Jack. "If he brought Whistler."

"Another gentleman abstainer."

"Let's assume they dropped by together before the fun and games," Jack said. "If Whistler had just been charged, he might not have been in the mood."

"To stay."

"Let's say they didn't."

"Raines brought him to the party, but Whistler got restless. Uncomfortable around all those white collars." Judith was getting excited, picturing the scene. For the first time she seemed to imagine a scenario that did not lead inexorably to her arrest and conviction. Hope fueled her imagination.

Jack continued where she left off. "They schmoozed with the bankers and lawyers long enough to leave an impression of Whistler's state of mind."

Judith nodded, seeing it. "Then they moved on."

"So who else is left? Who else was hip-deep in hookers, but hasn't been killed for his knowledge of what happened there?"

"There are only two others on the disk," she said. "Both lawyers. One of them is Michael Bundy. He worked with Walter, negotiating the fine points of the complex financial instruments sold by AEG for Cal First International. The other one is Peter Wen, Michael's partner."

"In the firm?"

Judith hesitated. "Maybe there too. But definitely his partner."

"Since nobody else is still standing, they're elected," said Jack. "Bundy and Wen must have cleared the field, since they're the only suspects."

"In that case," Judith said, "one of them is the killer. And the other's in dreadful danger."

36

After a full day at the courthouse, Randolph Raines always returned to his office on the twenty-sixth floor of the Darrow Building on the Avenue of the Stars. His favorite chair was on his penthouse terrace, from where he could watch all the pollywogs below, clamoring into the shops and restaurants of Century City, or riding the escalators down to their cars, to join the tentacles inching down Olympic and Santa Monica Boulevard. It was a long way up from the street, a steep climb through the legal jungle of Los Angeles, and Randolph enjoyed his perch overlooking it all.

He opened the door to his opulent office, set his briefcase on the rosewood desk, and strolled out to his hard-earned chair.

Only to find it occupied by a black sweater, with steel-grey hair.

When the man turned to face him, Raines startled. "You! Christ, you scared me half to death. What are you doing here?"

"Waiting for you."

"Are you crazy? Someone will see you in the building."

"I doubt that very much. And I thought it necessary to meet again, face to face. To prevent any more accidents."

"It arrived in a brown paper package, without a return address," insisted Raines. "Naturally, I thought it came from you."

"A sex tape?"

"You said you would help get him off. Remember? It was just what we needed, once Halloran told Lester Talbot all about the party."

"Everett Halloran won't be telling anybody about anything again."

Raines wiped his face on a linen handkerchief. One thing about the penthouse—standing made him dizzy, especially if he got too close to the edge. He felt suddenly thirsty and fatigued by the day. "Can I get you a drink? No, of course, you don't touch the stuff. Do you mind if I get myself a drink?"

"If you need one."

"Must you put it that way?"

He poured himself a scotch from the sideboard in his office and returned to the terrace. The wind had picked up, but he found his visitor standing at the eastern edge with the sole of his shoe against a low wall that ran around the perimeter. "It's a long way down, isn't it?"

Raines rattled his ice. "It's been a long way up, I can tell you."

"Down must go faster."

Raines thought that it would. "As soon as I got the blackmail note, I knew I'd figured it wrong. But what could I do, at that point? Draw a lot of attention? No, sir. That wouldn't have helped. Now Judith Frick can't find hers, and you know what I say? No harm, no foul."

"No harm—is that what you say?"

"No harm to us, I mean," Raines added. "Those cunts who tried to blackmail us? Deserved whatever you did to them."

"And the rest?"

"The party guests? That's between you and them."

"As this is, between us."

"There's no reason to talk like that," said Raines, draining his drink. "Whatever you've needed, from the beginning—when have I ever refused? My guess is that you need something right now. Otherwise, why drop by to talk?"

The other man smiled. It was not a pretty sight. "You're worth every penny of your hourly rate. There is something." He sat on the wall and drew up one leg. His other went over the edge.

Raines imagined the loafer slipping off his dangling foot and couldn't draw the breath to say, *Just tell me what you need.*

"You would still like to be useful, wouldn't you, Randy?"

37

The problem with their slip in the marina, thought Mike Bundy, was the typical direction of the wind. It was too easy to catch in their sails on the way out, and too much trouble to overcome on their way back. He had to tack against it, which was work with Peter as his mate on the rigging, whose schooling at Penn had not included any time on the water. They usually made it back to the dock on the engine, puttering in, which made a pedestrian finale to a thrilling afternoon sail.

Peter's main emotional investment in the sailboat seemed to be furnishing the quarters below with marine-themed knickknacks. He bought a clock recovered from a Yankee schooner and hung it over the galley range. Michael thought it the loudest clock in creation. Peter's attraction was purely aesthetic, Mike understood that— in its brass bowl, the fine filigree marking the minutes, the elegant hands sweeping its face like the opera fan of a courtesan. But its constant tick tick tick rolled torturously back and forth over the boat from bow to stern, where he sat, guiding the tiller.

Peter came up from below with a silver tray on which he balanced two heavy pewter mugs. They were meant for ale, or grog, but neither of them needed the calories, so an icy bottle of Grey Goose stood between them. Condensation had soaked through the label, and the base of the bottle was wrapped in a towel, white with a blue anchor. It made a pretty presentation, and Peter was evidently pleased.

"I thought you might be thirsty, in this wind."

He stood for a moment in profile, so the breeze tousled his hair. Striking a pose, Michael knew, but Peter had the boyish looks to pull it off.

"Thank you. I am indeed."

He took a sip, and a twist of lemon floated against his teeth.

They were closing in on the mouth of the marina and had to come around to catch the channel back to their slip. Peter said, "Do we have to go in already? It's so lovely at this hour."

"I promised to meet that cop for a drink at the Pelican. That detective. Stryker."

"Stryker? What kind of name is Stryker?"

"I don't know. Teutonic? Nordic?"

"Probably changed from something like Strichartz."

"Do policemen change their names?"

"I suppose. Doesn't everybody? Let's say you've been raped. Would you want to tell your personal bio to Officer Strichartz?"

"Can you take the tiller, please? I need to fix the sail."

"Oh well." Peter moved to the edge of the deck and tossed something overboard, so that it spun away from the sloop. It flashed in the sun like a UFO, angled to dodge radar. It landed flat on the water, tipped, and sank under the surface.

"What was that?" said Mike.

"Just something that came to you in the mail. A nasty little sex tape."

"I didn't order any."

"It was a keepsake. From AEG. Did you actually go in the bedroom with one of those skanks?"

"Me? Of course not. You saw me the whole time. I was just on the guest list, that's all. They must've sent one to everybody."

"Not me. I didn't get one."

"Maybe they thought you wouldn't appreciate it. Or maybe they thought you might post it online, instead of keeping it under wraps. Was there a note?"

167

"Nothing. Just the disk."

"The note must be coming. Did you check all the mail, or just the packages?"

"Are you saying they didn't send me one because I'm not as butch as big, broad Mikey? That I'm not manly enough to be blackmailed by a couple of whores? Is that really what you want to say?"

Michael sighed. He had to go trim the jib.

"Peter, I'm wild about you. You know that only too well. I want you to feel this sloop is yours as much as mine. But isn't there anything you can do to shut up that damn clock? It's ticking is driving me mad."

Peter gave him a curious look. "You've told me that before."

"Don't you hear it?"

"Impossible. I let it wind all the way down, 'til the hands stopped completely. And haven't wound it again." He lifted his head and listened.

Tick. Tick.

*   *   *

The *boom* crossed the water to the dock where Jack was waiting, watching the sloop come in. When he heard it, he stood up from the post that had been his seat and squinted through the sunlight on the water.

At a slip below him was a sunfish with two brothers on deck, who looked to be twelve and fourteen years old. Both had sun-bleached blond hair, wore white cutoffs with white t-shirts, and were tugging the lateen sail in different directions. They ignored the explosion until Jack stood up, when they peered out to see what had raised him.

The younger boy was the first to declare, "I see smoke."

His brother said, "From the mainsail or the jib?"

"Aft."

"Then it's the mainsail. Probably the gas tank underneath. That's bad news for them. Is that your boat, Mister?"

Jack shook his head and watched the forward sail catch fire. The flames ran along the lower edge first, and up the central mast. Then it attacked the cloth. In minutes, the whole thing was ablaze. "Is there anyone to call?" he asked the boys.

"They see it," said the older boy.

"But it's not gonna make any difference," piped in the twelve-year-old. "They're scrape-away toast."

"Shut up, Sheldon," his brother said, raising his hand. But Sheldon was too fast for him, jumping under the slap into oily water.

38

Jack was stirred from his dumbfounded stupor by a lick of trumpet—Miles Davis, from *Kind of Blue*—and a buzz against his thigh. He answered his cell phone and heard Maggie's voice, upset.

"Are you holding onto a DVD that's really overdue?"

"What?"

"Somebody wants you to return their disk."

"Who?"

"How should I know?" Her voice dropped. "Jack, this is serious. And scary. You'd better hear it for yourself."

By the time he reached Hancock Park, the girls had all been shuffled off to their bedrooms upstairs. Jack heard Chevy – the auto-dubbed Knight of Pleasure – on the phone in what Maggie called *the office*, which was the former pantry of the house, a tiny room with a desk and plenty of shelving.

"I'm sorry, sir," he was saying into a mike wired to his ear, "I understand you'll be in town for only a couple of days. And you'll need discreet companionship. But Maggie is not allowing any of the girls out of the house. You can stop by … of course. Security is an issue for all of us in this day and age, and I'm sorry to say it's taking its toll on our industry as well."

Jack mouthed *Where is she?* Chevy motioned toward the front parlor.

"I can take your number, if you like, and ask Maggie to give you a jingle. Yes, I understand what it means. Do you?"

In the front parlor, Maggie was not alone. She sat in the Queen Anne armchair near the fire. Across from her, a couple in their thirties sat on the edge of a sofa upholstered in floral brocade. They sat close together, holding hands, and their faces were whiter than the background of the fabric.

"Here he is," announced Maggie, as he entered the room. "Jack, you remember the Farleighs, don't you? Ted and Marion?"

They were certainly polite – he'd say that for them. The Farleighs gave him the weakest smiles Jack had ever seen.

"Of course." He sat on the ottoman. "It's been some time, hasn't it? How's Annie?"

"Missing," said Ted, without losing a beat.

Jack looked at Maggie, who said, "She never came out of school today. Marion waited at the curb for half an hour, then went inside to look for her."

"According to her homeroom teacher," Ted said, "Annabeth was called to the office around one-thirty. And never came back to class. Marion went to the office, looking for her, but they said they never called her."

"Have you called the police?"

"You're the police, aren't you? That's what Maggie said." Marion blushed. "I mean, Miss Malloy."

"Maggie will do," said Miss Malloy. "They thought you might care more than a stranger cop. As if there *is* a stranger cop."

"Could Annie have taken off? You know – decided to cut school?" Jack had done enough of that in his own school days.

Marion shook her head. "She never did anything like that before."

"There's always a first time, isn't there?" Jack directed the question to Ted and Marion, but Maggie shook her head.

"You haven't heard the worst of it," she told him quietly.

Jack said, "What?"

"We got a call," Ted said, "about an hour ago. I think it was a man's voice, but I can't be sure. It was disguised by one of those machines that make people sound like they're speaking in a tunnel."

Jack nodded. "Disguised."

"Right," said Ted. "A voice disguiser." He looked at Marion as if to say, *We're getting through to him.*

She put her hand on his knee. "He told us he had Annabeth. She's safe—or she was safe—but he wants something in return for her."

"A ransom."

"Not exactly. That's what we expected. I said we didn't have a lot of money but would give him what we could. He said he had enough money, thank you. More than us. What he needed was a *disk.*"

Jack waited. "Do you have the disk he wants?"

"That's just it," said Ted. "We don't."

"He knew we didn't," said Marion. "But he said we could get it."

"Did he tell you how?"

"From you." Marion flushed. "We hate to impose like this, after all you've done already. But he didn't even tell us the name of the disk. He just said, *Tell Jack Stryker I want my disk back.* When I told him I had no idea where you were or how to find you, he said, *Go ask Maggie Malloy.*"

"Which brought them here," said Maggie, "where I could call you."

"That was it?" asked Jack. "The whole conversation?"

"He gave us a number. You're supposed to call and arrange to return the disk. I wrote it down. Here." Marion fished a torn piece of paper from her bag. It had a little heart in the corner and a phone number printed in a feminine hand.

"Fuck me with a spoon," said Maggie.

Marion blanched an even whiter shade of pale.

"I think *gag* me with a spoon was the expression," Jack murmured.

"*Gag me?* I didn't know that Valley Girls were so kinky."

"I don't think they whisper it in the sack. Are you trying to say this number has some special significance for you?"

"It's my own."

"That's not the house phone," Jack replied. He knew that number by heart.

Ted tried to be helpful. "Perhaps a call-in line?"

"My cell phone," said Maggie. "It was stolen out of my car."

"Where?"

"The front seat," she said, but couldn't avoid his eyes. "Which was parked at the side of a soccer field, all right?"

Jack guessed the goalie. When Judith told him what she decided, all those years ago, Jack went straight to a bar. He drank enough bourbon to blear his sight and found solace with Maggie. He didn't remember much about their one night together except the noisy mattress springs. His rubber must have burst under that furious strain, and Annie Malloy was the result. Maggie couldn't raise a kid the way a little girl deserved, so she signed the papers to rename her a Farleigh, and she made Jack promise to stay away. But once in a while, she needed to see that Annie was all right. Those were the nights she went to watch soccer.

Jack understood, because he had days when nothing would do but a certain café table on Montana Avenue, where he shut his eyes and listened for the voice of a little girl as she ran from Roosevelt Elementary School to the Farleigh minivan at the curb. But someone must have made the connection, and Annie was in danger because of it.

You had her in your phone?"

"I keep a couple of baby shots, for when I need them," Maggie said.

172

"I'd rather hear her laugh," he said.

She took the note from Marion and smoothed it on Jack's knee. "You know what this is about?"

He nodded. "Blackmail."

She held it, as if it might flutter away. "Do you have the disk he wants?"

"Maybe," he replied.

"Jack—it's Annie. She's a prisoner!"

"Maggie, do you know where I found it? Hidden in Suziko's bag. She and Janie Mae kept a laptop going while they entertained a suite of bankers. They made DVDs of the file and used them to blackmail all the johns at the party."

"I don't believe it," Maggie said.

"They did. They sent each man a disk in a brown paper package, followed by a note, demanding five thousand dollars to keep them from posting the video online. I spoke to Gloria Cordesman, who told me her husband Harry took that much cash out of the bank. A few days after a package arrived in the mail."

Maggie shook her head. "Maybe Suziko would—she never worked in this house. But Janie Mae wouldn't do that."

"Oh yes she would," said Chevy. "Uh hum."

The bouncer was standing in the doorway to the parlor. He might have been standing there for a while.

"She talked about it all the time," Chevy said. "Janie Mae had a prof who made her whole career by screwing a French philosopher. Then there was Hannah For-Rent, who got her start, up-close and personal with a German. She once asked the other girls if they ever thought about calling up their regulars at home. I'd like to be on a party line when they make those calls."

Maggie was weakening. "Why wouldn't my clients have told me?"

"All right," said Jack, "maybe she wouldn't with your regulars in the house. But that's what she did at the AEG party. What do you think is on the disk?"

Maggie said, "So you have it."

"Maybe."

"Come on, Jack. Spill. Do you have his disk or don't you?"

"I have a disk. But I don't know it's his. Even if it is the one he's after—I'm not sure the best thing to do is hand it over."

"Why on earth not?" declared Marion.

Jack understood her sense of urgency. But too much was at stake to act on that impulse. He tried to speak patiently, as kindly as he could, but not by concealing the danger. "What will he do, once he has the disk? Kiss her on the forehead and let her go? Or make sure Annie can't identify him?"

Marion clutched her husband's hand. "Don't even say that."

"We've got to consider it—"

Ted interrupted. "Can't you make a copy?"

"I tried. It just sat in the machine like a pancake. They must've done something to the disk to keep it from copying."

"They do that at Netflix," Ted confirmed, "and Blockbuster. They won't let you make a copy of a rented DVD."

"You'll just have to turn over the one you've got," said Maggie.

Jack hesitated. "It's the only clue we have to a possible killer. I'm not giving it up, unless we have no other choice."

"What killer?" Ted asked. "He hasn't killed anybody yet."

"He says he won't," added Marion, "if we hand the stupid thing over."

Jack said, "We *don't know* if he's killed anybody yet."

"You mean Walter Frick?" Maggie spat. "For Judith? You're still trying to protect her, aren't you? By finding another suspect. Jesu Christy, Jack! I can't believe you're putting her ahead of your own daughter, whose *life* is at stake."

He shook his head. "I'm trying to protect her. He can't risk hurting Annie so long as he doesn't have the disk. Once he does—"

Marion covered her ears and hummed.

"Are you going to make that call," Maggie asked over the noise, "or aren't you?"

Jack said, "I'd like another chance to screen the disk."

"Take your time," said Maggie. "When you're done—if our daughter is still alive—you can come back and make the call. Til then, you'd better find another place to lay your head. And every other part of you."

Jack looked from one face to the next and found no sign of sympathy. He went out the way he came in, through the back alley. He placed a call to Aisha, who didn't pick up her cell phone. So he walked over to Highland and taxied back to his two rooms at the beach, where the ceiling rattled all night long with Latin jazz.

40

There wasn't enough space in Jack's living room for a fifty-inch flat screen, and besides, you had to put one of those on top of something or mount it on the wall, and Jack needed the top of his set as a place to drop the mail. It was mostly bills and advertisements, but his name was on the envelopes, and emptying the mailbox always made him feel like he was home.

Next to the junk mail on top of the TV set sat his small silver DVD player, into which Jack fed Suziko's disk before he had his jacket off. He kicked off his shoes and plopped down on the couch, putting his feet up on the coffee table to air out his socks. The boys from Uruguay were playing games, not music, so the boards of the ceiling did not thump or vibrate until someone upstairs lost enough lives or ammunition to groan and stamp his feet.

Jack put up coffee, opened a fifth of whiskey, and prepared for a night of writhing and moaning.

He started the file at the very beginning, when Janie Mae set it on a flat surface, most likely a dresser in the bedroom. He watched her and Suziko do one middle-aged man after another, kneeling or straddling or settling backwards onto their laps. Most of the men sat passively, being done to rather than doing, though now and then someone would thrust, or reach for the working girl's hair. Suziko didn't seem to care, but Janie Mae reclaimed her pony tail, reaching up to slap or pry off a hand without losing a beat of her rhythm.

He let the disk run until the final gasp of release and the awkward exchange that followed. Several of the johns were uncertain whether AEG had covered the cost of their orgasm. Some decided that a gratuity was called for, on the spot. They were bankers and lawyers, who regularly viewed social interactions as a series of financial exchanges. The fact that human bodies were part of the equation did not affect their impulse to quantify the relationship in dollars. As they were being serviced, more than one of them calculated aloud the probable hourly rate of the girl in his lap and compared it to his own. The special thrill this afforded helped them reach a climax.

When the last client had sighed and cried and wiped himself off with a tissue, the file continued to record the empty chair. Janie Mae and Suziko couldn't tip their hand by crossing to the dresser to snap off the camera in the laptop. Jack watched the empty chair for

175

several long minutes, until he was sure no one else would follow. Then he pushed the rewind button and watched it all over again. There had to be something on the disk, if someone was willing to kill for it. Janie Mae was dead, and Suziko probably too. All of the men who had sex with those enterprising roommates had also died under questionable circumstances. No one survived who might have wanted to keep their names out of a scandal. Yet someone had gone through the trouble to locate and kidnap Jack's daughter.

He thought it might be his last chance to watch the file closely. Jack figured he could stall through the night, but time was running out. He would have to trade it away. He tried not to think of little Annie, where she might spend this night, because he didn't know how to keep her safe. This man was a killer—he had proven that. Jack thought he wouldn't hesitate to kill a child. She was probably frightened, with good cause to be. But Jack was a grown-up and her natural father. He couldn't afford to allow his fears to overwhelm his judgment. The best way to love Annie—the safest way for her—was to think and act with ruthless reason.

By the time he started the file for a third viewing, there was nothing at all erotic in what he saw. By the time he started his sixth viewing, every slurp and tickle seemed to mock excitement, as if the people on screen couldn't bear the boredom any more than he could, watching. He had to drink more Irish coffee as the night wore on, just to keep going, and finally gave up on the coffee and drank the whiskey straight.

He fell asleep at four to the noise of someone murmuring *ohyesbaby ohyeslikethat* who was far past the age of *baby*ing anyone but an infant. He snored for nearly an hour on the couch, still in his shirt and trousers, until something woke him. Maybe the silence from the college boys upstairs. He opened his eyes and saw the file was still playing on his TV set, long after the blow jobs had ended.

But something was moving, a great blurry mass, too close to the camera for him to see what it was. There was a loud scraping sound as the dresser drawer was dragged open below the laptop. Someone was fumbling inside it. They took out an orange cylinder with a white cap. Pills. Someone had come for pharmaceuticals.

The person moved off screen to the right. Jack never saw his face. He heard the bedroom door click shut. The rest was silence.

Jack rolled off the couch onto the floor and scrambled over to his TV set. Still on his knees, he reached for the DVD player on top of the set and jabbed the rewind button. He overshot the mark and had to watch a full minute of empty chair, but his patience was rewarded at last, when he saw for an instant the face of the man who opened the drawer for his pills. Jack froze the frame. And still could hardly believe it.

He had an old video camera at the top of his closet, which had been used to record a drug buy. It turned on, though it hardly had any juice left in its battery. Jack balanced it on the front edge of his sofa's seat cushion and turned on the DVD for one final screening.

By the time he had what he wanted, it was close to six o'clock in the morning. Jack was wide awake, but no one would be up for hours at the house in Hancock Park. His mouth felt like the floor of a taxi garage. He hadn't had any dinner the night before, and his stomach ached. From excitement, maybe, but he was definitely hungry. He thought of the Spanish omelet he saw Jerry Schiller eating at Rae's diner. The idea of two fried eggs in a pool of salsa made his mouth water. He might even catch Jerry there, who was always ready to talk. And Jack badly needed someone to listen.

It was too early to call Aisha. Those cab fares were piling up, from his place to Judith's, to Maggie, to home. Jack saw the Buick parked in his spot behind the house. His eyesight was recovering, not entirely clear, and bleared by a night of watching porn. But he thought he could make it to Pico without an accident, at this hour, when all of the roads would be empty.

It felt strange to crawl behind the wheel, the first time in weeks. But the ignition was just where he had left it. He turned the lights on, and turned them off again. Gave his windshield a wash with the wipers. Released the emergency brake, put the gear shift in reverse. Then he rolled backwards out of the spot as if he were anxious not to wake up the college boys upstairs.

There were more cars on the road at six than Jack expected, but he peered through the windshield and kept a light foot on the gas, and made it all right.

Rae's was open when he pulled into a spot, shut off the engine, and pocketed his key. The tables at the front were occupied already, and he considered taking a stool at the counter, when Jack spotted Four-One-One at his usual table, toward the back of the central aisle. Jack headed down to join him, only to find he wasn't alone. Sitting beside Jerry at the funny table for three was a tall, black woman.

Aisha. In a fuck-me dress.

"God morning, Jack," said Four brightly. Almost in sing-song.

"Morning, Jerry," mumbled Jack.

177

"You know Isha, of course. Care to join us?"

Jack sat across from the two of them. "If I'm not interrupting."

"Not at all. What brings you so early?"

"I came for a Spanish omelet."

"Good choice. I see Miranda is on her way over."

Aisha said, "You drove yourself?"

Jack nodded.

"We came together," announced Jerry, louder than necessary.

Jack murmured, "So much for just one kiss."

Aisha blushed. But Schiller put his hand over hers on the table, looking happy and rather proud.

41

"All right," said Jack from the doorway of Maggie's bedroom at the house in Hancock Park. "Let's give him the disk."

Maggie sat up against an overstuffed pillow at the head of her four-poster. It was a magnificent bed, with hand-carved wood and woven colonial hangings. Her hair was a mess and her eyes were red. She hadn't slept long. But she opened her eyes and seemed at once very pleased with herself.

"I thought you'd come around. A bed is a lonely place, isn't it?"

Jack sat on the edge of hers. "What do we have to do?"

"Call him," Maggie said. "You've got to make the call. I tried, but he wouldn't pick up. I've got you in my cell phone as a contact. I think he's waiting to see your name in the little box. He probably thinks you're still blind as a bat." She yawned and pulled on a frilly dressing gown.

Jack sat at the foot of the bed and hit the numbers for Maggie's stolen phone. Someone on the other end picked up, whose gravelly voice said, "Stryker?"

"You can have your damn disk."

"Have you tried to copy it?"

"Yes. But it wouldn't duplicate."

"That's right. If you had said *no*, I'd have known you were lying. Now I know I can deal with you."

"Good for you. What kind of deal did you have in mind?"

"I don't want to kill the girl. Will you work with me so I don't have to?"

Jack said, "I need some proof she's still alive."

"Just a moment," said the voice. Jack waited the longest moment of his life, then heard a scream through the receiver. Unmistakably female, and young.

"Stop!" he shouted into the line.

The shrieking ended. "She's alive," said the gravelly voice. "Now get a pen and write down what I tell you. There's too much at stake for any mistakes."

Maggie kept a Mark Cross on her dressing table. It looked suspiciously like a pen Jack had lost one night, waking up down the hall from her bedroom. It clicked the same when he opened it.

"Where do I go?"

Trastevere is a restaurant on a corner of the Third Street Promenade in Santa Monica. The name is Italian, referring to the neighborhood "across the Tevere" or Tiber, the river dividing Rome. Tables covered in white linen provide a view of the Promenade, where musicians perform, crowds collect, and a constant stream of pedestrians pass by. Mothers and daughter march briskly from shop to shop, their faces differentiated only by their years. Couples stroll hand in hand, while groups of teenagers chase one another from the Barnes & Noble on the north end to an indoor mall on the south end designed by local resident Frank Gehry.

The Promenade had been a run-down stretch of shops in the early eighties until the city of Santa Monica passed a zoning ordinance declaring it the only spot in town where new movie theatres could be opened. The Promenade became popular real estate overnight. A crafty designer heightened its appeal by decorating the central aisle with topiaries shaped like triceratops and brontosaurus, with water pouring from their mouths. The impression they created was a child-friendly space, although few of the shops and restaurants actually catered to children.

The gravelly voice on Maggie's phone instructed Jack to take a corner table on the terrace of Trastevere, order two portions of oysters, and wait. He was to place the disk on the low wall along Santa Monica Boulevard, so his guest could see he had brought it along. Any sign of a policeman, in uniform or plainclothes, would spell certain death for little Annie. The gravelly voice assured Jack that it could spot a cop, no matter how badly the officer was dressed.

Jack did not need to see that proved.

He had to dislodge an elderly couple from the table in the southeast corner of the terrace, but he simply drew up a chair and joined them at their lunch. That was enough to drive them away. He set the disk on the low wall and ordered two plates of oysters. He ordered a bottle of Chianti as well, poured a full glass, and watched the show. Four Latin American guitarists squatted on the curb of the closed street that divided the Promenade. They strummed feverishly, playing together and against one another. To his right, a lanky black woman leaned against the wall where it met the white stone building. She was dressed in a halter and short shorts, with the restlessness of a hooker on holiday. A shoeblack shined shoes at the foot of raised chair. A jogger passed by, in striped sports pants and a hooded sweatshirt, with an easy loping stride.

At that moment a woman at the next table cried out, standing so suddenly she knocked over her chair.

A waiter rushed to help her. "Is there a problem, Signora?"

"What is that thing in my *pasta fasole*? A spider, isn't it? I think it's a creeping black widow!"

The waiter picked up the bowl and peered at the thing crawling up the spoon onto the edge. It had a red hourglass on its back.

The bowl crashed to pieces on the cobblestones.

Jack turned back to the disk on the terrace wall, but it still peeped safely from its paper sleeve. He sat down to wait again, watching the people pass, until ten minutes after the appointed time. The oysters were getting warm. The Latin guitarists finished. And Jack felt that something had gone wrong.

He reached for the disk on the wall and it dropped out of its sleeve. Where he had written *Suziko's disk,* someone had erased his handwriting and scrawled instead a series of numbers: *12:00 314 26-8-11.*

"Aisha!"

The lanky black woman stood up and turned to face him over the wall.

"He's switched the disks." The new one flashed in the sun.

Aisha blinked and peered at the thing. "What the fuck do those numbers mean?"

Jack drew a breath to calm himself and concentrate on the sequence in black Sharpie. "Twelve o'clock—that's a time."

"Midnight or noon," said Aisha.

"There's a gym with a name like that on the Promenade. What do they call it? The Midnight Workout?"

"It's upstairs, near the hoity-toity hardware store." Aisha was bouncing on her toes, ready to take off. Jack tapped the disk, to focus her.

"This looks like a combination. They must have lockers there. Look for 314 and try 26-8-11. Twice around clockwise to twenty-six, once around the other way to eight, back again to eleven."

"You want me to look for the locker? Where are you going?"

"After the jogger. Remember—in the striped pants? Did you see anybody else?"

She hesitated.

"Get going," said Jack, giving her a little push. Aisha took off, and Jack pulled out his phone. He hit the contact *411,* who picked up on the first ring.

"Schiller."

"I need a jogger, slender, five-ten. Black running pants with a double white stripe down the leg, and a grey sweatshirt with a hood. Heading east on Santa Monica about five minutes ago."

Jerry was standing in the parking lot built into Frank Gehry's mall. From there he could see to the north the full three blocks of the Promenade, and west to the ocean. All the best views in Los Angeles are reserved for parked cars.

"Not anymore," said Schiller, holding his phone with his chin and shoulder while he adjusted his binoculars. "Your jogger is walking now, matching the pace of the crowd on the street. Heading west, toward the pier."

Jack turned the corner at Santa Monica Boulevard, running in the street to avoid meandering tourists. He turned south at Second and cut through the traffic to the corner of Broadway, where he paused to breathe and caught sight of a grey hood another block to the west. The flow had slowed at the corner of Ocean Avenue, a uniform directing traffic on and off the pier, and the jogger seemed to hang back to avoid drawing attention to himself. But he glanced over his shoulder and must have spotted Jack. Slowly he began to wind his way through the plaid shorts and sundresses.

When the light changed he bolted, a beat ahead of the cop's signal. He trotted through the intersection, onto the concrete walkway that led from the top of the bluffs to the wooden boards of the pier.

At one time Santa Monica Pier was a working dock. Elzie Segar, the creator of Popeye, kept a boat moored there. It was built by the city in 1909 to toss its garbage off. In the twenties, flappers flocked to the Whirlwind Dipper roller coaster and La Monica Ballroom. The pier burned, washed out, and they built it back again. In the seventies, the City Council decided to tear it down, but the people of Santa Monica didn't like that idea and a different City Council was put in charge.

On weekends, the boards groan under sandals and flip-flops, running shoes and plain bare feet. Jazz concerts in the salt air bring an extra load of visitors, and the concession stands and souvenir shops do a brisk trade in twice-fried snapper and undercooked steamers, overpriced T-shirts, and tacky seaside knickknacks. Windows sell *churros* and soft pretzels, cotton candy and potato chips dripping with oil. The Playland Arcade stays open until the morning, with rickety rides that rattle over Pacific Park for three or four tickets apiece. Bumper cars bump; steel wheels roll; a Sea

Serpent soars for the clouds. The West Coaster plunges past buzzing neon tubes with shrieks that travels from car to car like hiccups through a caterpillar.

Into the middle of this noise and confusion Jack followed the jogger. He zigged around stalls selling stones and seashells, zagged through tourists gathered around coin telescopes and cardboard celebrities. He was headed for the end of the pier, where the Harbor Master's station overlooked the ocean.

At the very tip of the pier and around its edge were platforms where fishermen sink lines into the bay, to catch whatever lurks among the steel poles below. When Jack broke through the last gaggle of tourists, the hooded sweatshirt was nowhere in sight. The jogger hadn't slipped past him, back toward the shore—Jack felt certain of that. He must have climbed down the steps to his left or his right, to hide among the fishermen and their tackle.

But which way did he go?

Jack tried his left, not climbing down the steps but keeping his footing on the pier and searching the platform below. No sign of the jogger. Jack tried the platform at the very end, where the pier looked out over the grey-green ocean. He did not spot the jogger there either. That left only the platform to his right, facing the sandy beach from above the restless Pacific.

Jack approached quickly but cautiously, crouching with his hand on the sidearm holstered at his belt. He peered over the edge of the stairs, where several men stood or sat among fishing lines propped on the guard rail. No jogger among them. Jack took the stairs one by one, his eyes fixed on the fishermen. None of them were in grey sweats or white-striped black running pants. Then Jack noticed some clothing crumpled in a ball at the corner of the platform.

He turned just in time to deflect something very hard that would have caught him on the back of his head but instead landed on his cheek. It hurt like hell, and he felt the warm rush of blood in his mouth. A silver-haired man was standing in front of him, with one foot in the mesh of the fence that marked the end of the fishing deck.

Jack lurched for the man's arm, but he was too late. A second foot went over the side and the silver-hair behind it.

Jack ran to the fence and looked over—saw no boat, but a silver head bobbing in the water, untying something strapped to a post of the pier. Jack kicked off his shoes, slipped off his jacket, and leaped over the fence.

He did not land as smoothly as his quarry had done, but made an awful splash in the water. It felt like falling onto a concrete slab that opened to swallow you whole. Jack had to struggle back to the surface, where his lungs exploded for air. He floundered, turned, and found himself facing a curious sea creature with a round, open mouth that flashed as it turned toward the sun.

A mask – the man was masked with a tube to his mouth and a tank hanging off his shoulder. He must have left it strapped to the post of the pier, just in case he needed an escape route. Or else he planned to make his exit that way all along.

Jack reached for him but could hardly keep himself afloat and hang onto the man's arm as the silver head dove beneath the waves. Jack was forced to let go—and felt his trouser leg pulled from below. Jack cried out and swallowed sea water, as his mouth dipped below the surface. He stopped struggling upward and doubled over to challenge his attacker face to face.

The man was pulling him down, watching grimly through the rush of his own bubbling air. Jack reached for his face mask and tried to pull it off. He couldn't, but managed to land a glancing punch on the glass. That was enough to shake the man off, who might have liked to drown Jack but not at the cost of his face mask. He kicked back with both legs and swam down into the murky water. Jack tried to follow, but his lungs were empty, forcing him to surface for oxygen.

There was no ripple in the waves around him, except where they struck the poles of the pier and broke into trickles of foam. The silver-haired diver was gone. Jack swam over to the nearest pole and wrapped his arms around it, calling for help. It felt like a scream when it rose up his throat, but when it came out through his chattering teeth, his voice sounded weak in his own ears and he doubted if he could be heard over the constant slapping of the waves.

42

Jack felt something cold and hard grab the back of his shirt and haul him out of Santa Monica Bay. It was a hook on a long pole, which dragged his backwards past the concrete posts holding up the pier. When he was dropped, soaked and shivering, on the wooden slats of the boardwalk, he saw Lieutenant Newman seated on the back of a green bench. Officers Bruner and Yost, who had evidently done the heavy lifting, were trying to swing around the grappling hook and lean it against the fence.

"You all right?" asked Newman.

Jack's teeth kept chattering. "F-i-ine."

"Sounds like it," she said. "You're lucky I like Four-One-One so much." She turned to Sergeant Warneke, as he squatted beside Jack. "We'd better dry him out first, I suppose."

"Don't b-bother with me. No t-time for that. He's got my daughter."

"No, he doesn't," Newman told Jack. "Your streetwalking driver—"

"Aisha?"

"Found her in a locker at the Midnight Gym. Drugged but alive, with no broken bones or signs of abuse. A bus took them both to St. John's. You ought to go there yourself."

Jack shook his head. "Did she say anything?"

"She had a black hood over her head and a rope around her neck – apparently from the time she was grabbed."

"His idea of mercy," said Jack. "So he wouldn't have to kill her."

"Did you get a look at his face?"

"D-didn't need to. I know who he is. But you won't believe it."

"Try me."

"You'll have to see it for yourself."

Newman wanted to drive him straight to the station to take down the story, but Jack insisted on stopping at his car, where he took a wind breaker from the trunk and a folded page of newsprint from the trunk. He pulled on the jacket and stuck the square of paper in his pocket. "All right," he said. "Get me a TV set."

They drove with the bubble flashing, issuing short bursts of siren when necessary. They led Jack to an interrogation room, where he took the paper out of his jacket pocket and unfolded it on the table. At its center was a shiny silver disk.

"Isn't that what you traded away?"

"This is a bootleg copy."

Bruner and Yost wheeled a monitor and DVD player into the interrogation room. Jack shoved his disk into the machine and hit the *play* button. His video filled the screen, eliciting a choir of groans.

"Porn?" said Newman. "That's what we needed to see?"

"It's not even *good* porn," said Bruner or Yost— Jack couldn't remember which one was which. "Look at that crappy image."

"Where did you copy this?" asked the other. "On a Xerox machine?"

"The original disk wouldn't copy," Jack said, "so I played it on my TV set and taped it with a camera."

"That's your TV? I didn't know they still made those classic consoles."

"No flat screen for the hero cop."

The picture broke up, reformed, and wavered. "Is that a bouncing ball? Or the back of a hard-working head?"

"That woman is in the morgue right now," Jack said, and the grins disappeared from the faces of Brewer and Yeast.

Jack hit the fast forward button and let the machine run. When he stopped it, they saw Suziko's thong settle into a banker's lap. Jack was about to hit the button again, when Newman caught his hand.

"Whoa. Freeze the picture, right there. Isn't that Walter Frick?"

"Could be."

"Stryker – was Frick at this little party of yours?"

"It wasn't mine. But, yes, he was there."

"Has *she* seen this show?"

"Judith? Not until after Frick was dead. Randolph Raines sent a copy to her, with a motion to exclude some testimony. But it disappeared from her briefcase."

"According to Her Honorable self."

"That's right."

"But you still don't think she killed her hubby— after watching him in the chair? Do you know any wife who wouldn't want to?"

"Maybe not. But she didn't do it. I told you, I know who did."

"Who?"

"Phillip Hazlitt."

She stared at him. "The Ponzi schemer? Who was blown up in his car?"

"I guess he wasn't."

"Weren't his remains identified by the military?"

"By the Medical Examiner."

"Using dental records from his marine corps file."

"We all make mistakes, Lieutenant. The M.E. got it wrong. See for yourself." He reached for the button, but she stopped him again.

"The only thing I see is a crucial piece of evidence in an ongoing investigation. Stryker … have you ever heard of Occam's Razor?"

He paused. "I use an electric."

"Not often enough. But here's the idea—when other things are equal, the simplest explanation is the best. You're telling me that Judith Frick watched Walter hump a hooker. But instead of stabbing him with a kitchen knife, you'd like me to believe … what, exactly? That Phillip Hazlitt, the biggest scam artist in the history of Wall Street, came back from the dead to party with the sharks at AEG, then turned up in the Frick house to stab his old friend Walter?"

Jack said, "Things are never equal."

"Why blame Phillip Hazlitt? Maybe Ponzi himself rose from the grave. Maybe Jack the Ripper did it, or Son of Sam."

"David Berkowitz is still alive—he's in prison, not a grave." Newman glared, and Jack said, "Just watch the damn video to the end."

The Lieutenant shook her head. "I don't give a rat's ass what's on your grainy screen. They have programs that can edit Adolph Hitler into the forest with Bambi. But I still don't think he lit the match that killed Mommy Deer."

"It's evidence. You can't ignore it."

"You better hope I ignore the fact that you withheld a piece of evidence that would have helped us arrest your girlfriend sooner."

"Judith Frick isn't my girlfriend. She hasn't been for years."

"Right." Newman pointed at Bruner and Yost, then crooked two fingers at them. "Come on, boys. Let's go for a walk."

She led them out with a look that dared Jack to follow her. As soon as the others were gone, Montoya stood up.

"I've seen enough porn for one day."

Sergeant Warneke didn't follow her out. His gaze was fixed on the frozen screen, where Walter Frick sprawled in an armchair with his eyes closed. The Sergeant moved right up to the screen and finally said, "That's not the Pierrot."

Jack didn't utter a word that might interrupt his thoughts.

"Did you notice the window? Green, with a rainbow across it?" His fingers made an arc through the air. "That's a sprinkler, over a golf course. The Hotel Pierrot is on Wilshire Boulevard, in Beverly Hills."

There should have been buildings out the window. Not shifting shades of foliage.

"And that wasn't a *P* in the terrycloth," Warneke added.

Jack scrolled back the disk to the beginning, where Janie Mae Olsen was wrapped in a towel, having showered, ready for business.

"You see the letters embossed there?" Warneke traced their curves on the screen.

"Not a *P*," said Jack.

"That's a *CC*," said Warneke, "with their little tails tangled."

"Do you know where that stands for?"

"I saw it the other day, on a cocktail napkin. The Condor Club. The bartender told me that Hazlitt had a house on the thirteenth hole. One of his creditors scarfed it up before the scam hit the fan."

"That wouldn't be, by any chance, the American Enterprise Group?"

Warneke nodded. "You guessed it."

43

Phillip Hazlitt did not like to hurt children and tried to avoid it when he could. There had been times overseas when it came down to a choice between some unfortunate child and the safety of his troops that left him no choice at all. His first duty was to the men under his command. But the mission that began with the bombing of his car was not overseas, and the circumstances morally ambiguous. Colonel Hazlitt did not like moral ambiguity any more than he liked hiding from the municipal police.

He hooded the girl so he wouldn't have to drown her. He wasn't a monster, after all. Drowning was always his first lethal choice: it required no implement that could be used to connect you, and left no marks or toxins in the body. People drowned themselves by their own ineptitude. He loved the feel of water, its taste in his mouth, its resistance as you thrust against it. And it made him nostalgic for the old days when he and his team would set out by moonlight with the weight of their tanks on their backs.

Drowning wasn't always an option, of course. Sometimes he had to use whatever was at hand—a fork or a knife in a kitchen, drying in the drain board. But Walter Frick never should have tried to get in his way. He could hardly have stopped the Colonel from going upstairs. And once he killed any of them, he had to kill them all.

In his thoughts, Hazlitt was always a commando first, an officer and a gentleman who loved his country and risked his life, defending her honor. *Stars and Stripes* called him a *hero soldier*, a goddamn *national treasure*, with all the trimmings but the gold stars on his shoulders and the pearly-butt pistols at his waist. And he was shopping around for a brace of those when he unpinned his eagles.

Hazlitt approached the financial jungle of Wall Street with the same resolution he carried into Panama. His mission there had been to make money, for himself and the investors who trusted in him. He would no more consider letting them down than leaving a wounded soldier on the beach in Granada.

This resolve created some difficulties, when the market succumbed to an attack of toxic derivatives. The bankers were quick to gobble up whatever securities they could, before the towers tumbled down. He was surprised when his buddies at AEG foreclosed on his house at the Condor Club. Hazlitt shouldn't have been, he supposed – survival of the fittest was the law of every

189

jungle. The Colonel had lived by its rule often enough and watched other species die by his hand.

Now he slid the last disk into the whore's laptop and watched the drive illuminate. When the picture came up—of a banker's fat ass—he poked the button to move it faster forward and waited for the video disk to reach its bitter end.

It wasn't out of malice, Hazlitt presumed, just their typical ignorance. They had no way to know where he went to ground after Bernard Whistler staged his death by car bomb. The front door had been padlocked on the evening news. The signage on the lawn made it clear that the bank would accept only private offers that could be approved in advance by the bankruptcy trustee. AEG was technically in possession of the property, but lawsuits were circling like buzzards over a battlefield. He had done his prep-work with care. No one should have set foot in the place.

But the team that negotiated the AEG bailout didn't respect such niceties. They were interested in a private hideaway and had access to the garage key. The Colonel had been forced to hide in his basement, in a secret room he built for his arsenal. When the music stopped thumping, and the party moved to the poolside, he had crept upstairs to his bedroom for a few blasted pills. How on earth could he have known that the laptop on the bureau was on and still recording?

Even worse, that the whores were blackmailing their customers with copies of the disk? The Colonel assumed that few of them would watch the file to the end and recognize his face. But he had no way to know who might—so he had no alternative but to recover every disk and silence any man who might have seen it. His plan had been simply to disappear in Bernard Whistler's fireball. Instead, through no fault of his own, he was forced to take innocent lives.

Not entirely innocent, by the video evidence.

There it was: the endless image of his empty bedroom, the vacant bed and chair. He stopped the file and started it again at twice normal viewing speed, letting it go go go, until he saw something loom into the picture frame. He stopped it again, rewound it a second, and let the disk play. He saw himself enter the room, draw near the camera, and open the bureau beneath it. He needed his medication. Without it, his face looked haggard and worn.

He ejected the incriminating disk from the DVD drive.

At last he could tie up the loose ends. No one was left who could identify him except a half-blind cop with no evidence. The hookers had write-protected each disk, so it could not be erased or recopied. That showed a native strategic understanding—they had taken control of their territory. What did he tell his men? Every black-ops strategy had to plan for the unexpected contingency, and those two whores were his. The Colonel had not seen them coming. Of course, they hadn't seen him coming, either.

He took a hammer from the pegs on which it hung in the garage, leaving behind an empty silhouette. He was a careful man, and his personal care had always paid off—in the service, on the Street, in his escape plan. A motor launch was waiting at a dock on Balboa Island. His course to Tuvalu had been charted. From the little island he could easily slip away to any destination he chose. There were always despots anxious to take in fabulously wealthy refugees.

The hammer claw fell on the Asian whore's laptop, once, twice, a third time. Bits of its interior flew with each upstroke. Hazlitt had done the same to the first computer, from the girl at school. She had been trying to improve herself – of that he approved. Blackmail was another thing. They didn't know they had caught his face at the end of their disk. They wouldn't have watched it that long. Nor would either of them have recognized him, with or without the mask. But that's what can happen when you practice to deceive. You never know whose ox you might gore by accident. Some oxen are capable of goring back.

When the second girl's laptop was a pile of scrap, he turned his attention to the last recorded disk. It had cost him more trouble than any of the others. He had nearly been forced to kill a child. He did not want to risk the smoke from a fire in his chimney. He smashed the disk to pieces, as he had done with the others, pounding the shards into tiny bits of silicate.

Hazlitt enjoyed the exercise, as he always did when an act of violence was personal, wrought by his own two hands. He was breathing hard when he was done. He sat and listened to his lungs pumping, his heart beating in harmony. And thought he heard something else stirring in the yard.

*   *   *

"Careful," whispered Warneke to Officer Montoya as she followed him and Jack around the corner of the garage. Under her feet the driveway was bordered in grey and white stones, smoothed in a river and trucked to the site to mediate the landscape between

191

the concrete driveway and short-cut grass of the lawn. Montoya's soft left sole had slipped off the pavement and crunched the paving stones. Her attention was divided between the shuttered windows and the sidearm clutched in her hand. Now the sergeant touched a finger to his lips and pointed to the space between her feet. She nodded and crept forward, placing each step with care, making softer, more deliberate crunches.

In the meantime, Jack advanced twenty feet ahead of them, crouching below the smaller kitchen window. He thought Hazlitt might have done the same thing, edging toward the Fricks' kitchen door. Their dog would have smelled him, of course, but Hazlitt had come prepared with a drugged doggie bone. He must have scoped the house out beforehand. Unlike Judith's backyard door, Hazlitt kept his own locked tight. He knew what could sneak in, if you trusted too much in your neighbor's good will, or even in your old friends.

Inside, the downstairs was dark. It had to be. If Hazlitt was around, he would keep an invisible profile. Jack knew the man was widely reviled as a Wall Street shark who gobbled up any little fish within reach of his jaws, but beneath the Bond Street suit and hand tailored shirts beat the heart of a Navy SEAL—or whatever the Marines were calling them lately. Phillip Hazlitt was trained to kill and had kept himself in practice. Jack did not like the idea that those eyes might be on him now. His only hope was surprise—to catch Hazlitt before he knew they were wise to him. Behind him, Jack heard the crunch of Officer Montoya's shoes.

He signaled to Warneke—Jack was going in the back door. The Sergeant nodded to show he understood what Jack was trying to communicate by pointing to himself, the rear door, to the Sergeant, his eyes, and the front yard. He would keep watch on the front. Montoya looked as if she were about to speak, until Warneke lifted a finger to silence her. She followed him around the corner of the garage.

Jack crept back to the kitchen but didn't try the knob. Locks on secondary doors are never works of mechanical art. A house may hold thousands of dollars in cash and jewels, protected by a Medeco on the big front door, but people rarely treat their side and rear entrances with equivalent caution—as if burglars could be relied on to come in the front. Jack took the key for the handcuffs at his belt and stuck it in the kitchen lock, which popped without complaint.

The kitchen was bright enough in the afternoon sun with no other source of light than the window. The room had been cleaned and straightened, the dishes stacked in the cabinet, the silverware in the drawer, but it did not have the feel of an abandoned place. Someone cooked something on the stove not long before. There were no stains on the steel burners, but no dust either. Jack could not identify what the last meal had been, but a faint savory aroma still floated in the air.

He passed from the kitchen into a hallway that led to a sitting room at the front of the house. On his right, toward the back of the house, was a wall of glass that overlooked the pool. Between them was the staircase that led upstairs to the bedrooms. Jack didn't bother with the sitting room on his left, with its big picture window over the thirteenth hole. There was too much chance of a hash golfer chasing his lost ball and stumbling onto a peek at the interior.

The back room was a solarium, with heavy white drapes that could close out the sunlight for media exhibitions. A ten-foot screen and Bose speakers had been built into the wall opposite the sliding door to the pool. The furnishings were soft, buttery leather and hand-woven fabrics from the equator. Jack pictured the Colonel stepping in after a swim to check the feed from Wall Street on his wide screen.

The room was empty now. No cigars in the ashtray. Which left only the upstairs of the house.

Jack did not like the look of the staircase at all. It wound around like a turret climbing to a castle chamber. Jack could not see above him unless he turned around backwards and picked his way by feel. The steps were made of pale wood polished to a high-gloss shine, and the risers taller than his feet expected. He stubbed his toes twice before adjusting to their height. He had to watch his footing when he made the turn at the landing, and that was when it hit him—something large and heavy that knocked him to his knees. A thin strip of leather caught him under the chin, and he could not draw breath through his throat. Jack heard a female cry, "Emil!" as the glistening steps under his shoes swam up to swallow him whole.

44

Marilyn Montoya was first on the stairs, three steps ahead of Emil Warneke. She found Jack Stryker dangling precariously, with his knees still on the landing, his butt hanging off, and the rest of him trailing down the steps. She pulled his slack body upright and checked the pulse at his neck before the Sergeant joined her on the landing.

"He's breathing," she announced, "but check out that welt." A dark red band was purpling around his throat.

"Someone's in the house," murmured Warneke, as if she hadn't realized it. He dragged Jack onto the landing and propped him up against the wallpaper. "I'll go up," said the Sergeant. "You—" He pointed toward the solarium.

Protecting me again, Montoya thought but didn't want to argue with the man. You had to pick your battles. She put a hand on Stryker's chest, which was rising and falling regularly now. She headed back down the stairs.

Warneke found three doors on the second floor. One was partially open. It must have been a library, with bookshelves to the ceiling. A lamp was lit on a table, luring him, but he knew it could be a trap. Someone might be anticipating which door he would choose. Any reasoned approach made him more predictable, so he had to trust to random chance. He trod heavily on the floorboards toward the door on his right, then burst through the door on his left.

It was a woman's bedroom, with inlaid headboard and a frilly spread. Ivory fittings, filigreed with gold, for the handles on a cream-colored nightstand. *The things rich people spent their money on.* Off the toilet, a dressing table filled with cosmetics, combs and brushes, under a beveled mirror surrounded by lights. It took a lot of confidence to see your face so plainly. The Sergeant saw his own reflection, lined, baggy, haggard and worn. No matter how much money Warneke made, he could never stand a thing like that staring at him every time he went to take a piss.

Something silvery flashed in the mirror behind him. He turned but never got to see what it was.

*   *   *

The drapes fluttered slightly when Marilyn Montoya entered the solarium. The sliding door was not entirely shut. Could a bank

194

employee have left it ajar? Or the cleaning crew? Montoya's cousin Elisa worked for a cleaning service, but she would never have been so careless about her job. Every girl wasn't so dedicated, but Marilyn didn't jump to any conclusions. She had to move carefully, picking her spot. She gripped her nine millimeter, but if she had to go hand-to-hand with a Marine commando, she wasn't so sure who would come out on top.

She kept two hands on the stock and swung her body around her weapon. She covered the room methodically, starting on her right, leaving no space behind her back. Nobody there. Nobody. Nobody. Then she canvassed the whole room in reverse order. Secured. But that door was definitely open, far enough for someone to slip through. She had to follow. It was her job, for one thing, and for a second, that was the kind of cop she was. Ballsy, *loco*, medal-of-honor brave. She took a deep breath and went through the fluttering drapes.

The pool was beautiful, glistening in the sun. Around it reclined wooden chaises. Did you lie on those cedar slats? No, of course not, somewhere nearby would be soft pads to spread on top. A raft floated against the deep end.

Montoya moved to the edge of the pool, where blue-and-gold Mexican tiles lined the circumference at the water line. Looking down, she saw clear to the bottom, clearer than her own bathtub. She watched the afternoon sunlight play on the surface and listened to the suck of the filter and the gentle buzz of a lawnmower someplace clean and green.

Suddenly, she was part of it.

Without a chance to catch her breath, she went face first into the turquoise water. It exploded into bubbles rushing past her cheeks with all the oxygen in her throat and lungs. She struggled up for air, reaching for the slippery surface undulating above her … but something held her back.

No, not something—*someone*.

She felt strong fingers on her forehead and scalp, pushing her down.

She tried to knock it away, but the hand was big and its grip hard as the wall of the pool. She tried to fight the fingers, the panic, and the force of gravity. She needed both hands to pull herself up, away from the depths beneath her feet where she felt nothing except gallons of water slipping away as fast as she kicked against them.

She was losing ground, sinking deeper, scraping her shoulder raw as she tried to brace her body against the rough concrete wall.

She tasted something bitter in her mouth and throat. Bile. In a desperate lunge, she reached up with both hands and sank her nails into his murderous wrist and forearm. Her nails weren't long but they were strong and she squeezed with all the force of muscles trained by thousands of reps with free weights in the gym. She drew blood—she felt it seep down her fingers—but his grip on her hairline did not relent and there was no air to suck inside her.

Marilyn gasped and swallowed chlorine. It was all around her, inside and out. The sunlight on the surface grew dim. Suddenly she was floating free, no longer pushed down, but without the strength of will to resist the weight of water. It turned to mud before her eyes, and then to ink.

*   *   *

On the squares of pavement alongside the pool Phillip Hazlitt sat on his ass, reeling from a blow to his head. In front of him stood Jack Stryker, trying to swing the skimmer around for a second whack at the Colonel. The first caught his cheekbone, a glancing blow that cut to the bone. The shock made him let go of Montoya's head but failed to knock him out. The man had a thick skull – Jack had to say that for him.

Under his arm Jack felt the wire mesh of a strainer. Someone used the pole to clear leaves from the pool—the Colonel himself or his pool boy. Jack had little practice with a thing like that. Both hands gripped the metal above the net, but he found its weight awkward to control, like a tournament lance wielded by a knight on the ground. When he swung it around the second time, Hazlitt saw it coming. He ducked under it and let its momentum carry Jack forward. Then he struck Jack in the shoulder, using his elbow. It felt like a sledge. Jack caught his balance and turned to face Hazlitt, balancing the long pole like a tightrope walker. The Colonel chose not to confront him, face to face, but fled to the fence and vaulted over.

Jack wanted to chase after him, but Montoya had not emerged from the pool. He jumped into the water, grabbed her under the armpits, and dragged her lifeless body to the surface of the pool. He had to carry them both up with his legs, frog-kicking through the heavy water. When he finally pushed her over the edge, she vomited

196

on the concrete and drew a raspy breath. Then she drew another one. When Jack was certain she could keep her lungs filled and heart pumping, he crossed to the fence on property line and bounded over.

He found himself on the grass surrounding the thirteenth putting green. Two men in golf shirts and Condor Club hats were squatting at the top, staring at a ball only inches from the hole. Their caddy held a flag in his right fist, a golf bag slung over his left shoulder. Down the slope behind them, their cart was parked, under a green-striped awning. At the wheel, Jack spotted Hazlitt trying to release the brake.

Jack raced across the green and snatched a nine iron from the bag on the caddy's shoulder. Raising the club over his head he stormed down the slope and smashed the glass windshield of the golf cart. It shattered just as Hazlitt shoved the gearshift into first. Lurching forward, the cart nearly ran Jack down. Side-stepping a tire, he lost the club but managed to grab onto one of the poles supporting the green-striped awning.

Jack was dragged over the grass as Hazlitt tried to shake him off, weaving back and forth over the ground. Jack clung to the pole, raising his feet over the highest grass, swinging them finally high enough to hook an ankle on the rear pole. Hazlitt floored the pedal, picking up speed as the cart bounded over the bumpy course. With one hand on the wheel, he pulled a titanium driver from the golf bag, swinging at Jack's head and the grip of his fingers on the pole.

Jack ducked the first swing, then a second. He couldn't keep it up for long. Using the pole as a fulcrum, he twisted his body around and then up, into the back seat, where he landed with a thud beside the golf bag. He ducked another strike and reached into the bag, blindly pulling out a five iron. Hazlitt swung his driver again, but Jack caught it in the middle of the five iron—which bent in half under the blow.

The Colonel was standing, facing Jack in the cart with his heel on the pedal and his two hands free to swing the driver. The steering wheel turned itself back and forth as the tires followed the contours of the earth beneath its tread. His aim was thrown off by the tilting of the cart as it bounced left and right. Faster and faster the car sped forward as it pitched into a depression and rose up a slope on the far side. Jack was thrown back, out of the reach of the titanium driver, as the cart began to climb a long incline that led to a water hazard at the fourteenth hole.

Hazlitt angled the driver behind him and swung at Jack's neck. Jack raised the five iron at the last moment, catching the head of the driver in the center of the iron's vee and turning the ends, so that both clubs twisted out of their hands and tumbled over the side of the cart. Hazlitt threw a punch, a big roundhouse, but Jack slipped inside its arc and hit Hazlitt in the face, twice, breaking his nose.

Blood gushed from the center of Hazlitt's nose and from the gash on his cheek. But he didn't seem to notice. He swung around his elbow and caught Jack outside his left eye. For a moment Jack went blind again on that side. Then his sight returned, in a burst of light. He swung for the Colonel's mouth, but missed, as the cart reached the top of the slope and leaped off ...

Sailing for a full minute with no tires on the ground. The front wheels spun as they lifted into the air, and the rear wheels tumbled forward as the cart toppled over and fell backwards on its awning—which crumpled under the weight of the carriage, when it landed in a water hazard beside the fourteenth hole.

As the cart flipped over, Jack was thrown in the air and landed with a splash in the man-made lake, a dozen feet from the crash. But Hazlitt's heel caught on the steering wheel, and when the cart struck ground, its engine fell on top of him, pinning him beneath it as it sank in muddy water.

Jack stood up, wobbly, blinking at the sunset. When at last his eyes refocused he saw the overturned cart, three-quarters submerged, with its tires still turning in the air. But no sign of Colonel Hazlitt. Jack dove into the shallow water and found his man trapped under the chassis of the golf cart, his eyes open and engorged, staring at the mud. His lips were parted, wavering as the brown water floated in and out. His spine was broken and an awning pole stuck awkwardly from his ribs.

45

"This isn't Phillip Hazlitt," said the Medical Examiner, gesturing toward the cadaver on his table with a rib-spreader. "I ought to know the Colonel when I see him, and that ain't the man."

Jack and Lieutenant Pat Newman were in the morgue, on one side of a steel table. On the other side stood the Medical Examiner, an overweight pathologist named Rudolph Dennison, who wore a stained apron over a cowboy shirt with pearl-snap cuffs. His bolo tie preserved a black scorpion in amber. Face up on the table in front of him was the man Jack had chased across the golf course. On a table behind Dennison lay a second corpse, under a sheet—Suziko, whose frost-bitten body was found in an ice chest in the basement of Hazlitt's hideaway.

Chevy de Plaisir had identified Suziko Mori, but Dennison balked at assigning a name to the body from the fourteenth hole at the Condor Club. It did not much resemble the infamous officer. Its nose and cheek were broken, the skin wrinkled, the eyeballs veined and bulging from their sockets.

Newman said, "It should be him. Right, Sergeant Stryker?"

"That's Hazlitt," said Jack. "He looked just like his pictures. Before."

"Before you beat his face to a bloody pulp?" asked the M.E.

"You had to be there," Jack said.

"I'm rather glad I wasn't," said Dennison. There was a pinkish bruise alongside Jack's left eyebrow, near the temple. His lip was split on the right, and a brown stripe ran under the skin halfway around his throat. Emil Warneke was in St. John's, recovering from a concussion. Marilyn Montoya had taken off a week to visit her grandmother in a fishing village outside Manzanillo.

"What makes you think it isn't Hazlitt?" asked Newman.

"Two things, really," said the doctor, adopting a professorial tone. "First of all, Phillip Hazlitt is already dead."

"Did you do the autopsy?" Jack asked.

"No, sir, I did not. That was done in Beverly Hills. But I know the man there, a classmate as a matter of fact. Desmond knows his pathology. If he says a thing is true, you can believe it a hundred percent. As if I did the work myself."

"How would he know?"

"The military keep records. They take DNA samples from every recruit. In case of an IED, you understand. Your jeep rolls over a can of Spam and kablooey! All over the road. Sometimes it's the only way to separate the pieces."

"Hazlitt joined the Marines—when? Thirty years ago?" said Jack. "They weren't taking DNA samples then."

"No, but they did have dental records. Desmond recovered a skull from the wreckage of Hazlitt's Porsche. He matched the teeth to the dental records from the Colonel's file. Same fillings in the same places. No chance that the skull in that car belonged to anyone other than Phillip Hazlitt."

"There had to be," said Jack.

"What was the second reason?" Newman asked. "You said *two things*."

The M.E. tapped the jaw on the body stretched before them.

"This mandible. I made the call myself, requesting Colonel Hazlitt's x-rays all over again. Just in case the clerk screwed up on the set he sent to Beverly Hills. I compared the Colonel's dental plates to the teeth in this very mouth. They do not match. Not close."

Newman turned to Jack. He stared at them both for a moment, then scanned the damaged face of the corpse. Had Hazlitt somehow escaped again?

Then a smile creased his face. It hurt his lip, but Jack couldn't keep from grinning. "Of course they don't," he said. "How could they?"

The M.E. waited. "You're not about to accuse the both of us, are you? Me and Desmond? Of misconduct or ineptitude?"

Jack shook his head. "Philip Hazlitt ran a Ponzi scheme that bilked thousands of people out of their life savings. He was a retired Marine, who accepted funds from other Marines going overseas. Some made it home. Some didn't. Sometimes he must have heard from the family of a dead Marine who mentioned Hazlitt in a letter. I'll bet he sent a check to all of them."

"We know he did," said Newman.

Jack shook his head. She didn't see the connection. "So long as recruits kept going overseas, the money kept coming in," he said, "and Hazlitt could return dividends on the pay invested with him. But the build-up in Iraq dropped off, and the economy crashed. So the bottom fell out of his financial plan. Hazlitt knew he would be held accountable by some Marine, for losing his battle pay. So he recruited an accomplice to help him escape his well-deserved come-uppance.

"Bernard Whistler was perfect for the job. He knew explosives and needed the money to pay for his wife's surgery. He found out that the pay he sent Hazlitt was all gone and went to confront him about it. But the Colonel had been waiting for a Whistler to come along. He offered to give Whistler all his money back, if Bernard helped him accomplish one final mission—arranging his own murder."

Newman held up her hand. "Why would Whistler go along with that? After what Hazlitt did to him?"

"What choice did he have?" asked Jack. "He could testify against the Colonel, of course, bring the scam to light and the crook to justice. But that wouldn't get his money back, or his wife her surgery. He was out of the service by then, with no coverage for his family. Hazlitt knew how to play on his loyalties. All he had to do was what he felt like doing anyway—blowing the Colonel sky high."

"And go to jail for it?"

"Maybe, maybe not," said Jack. "Hazlitt hired the best attorney in town, one he knew he could control. Whistler hadn't actually killed him, after all. There might be some wiggle room in that. Whistler hoped he might get off, but even if he didn't, he agreed take a bullet for his wife."

"That doesn't explain our autopsies," Dennison said. "The corpse that burned in the Porsche had a mouthful of Hazlitt's teeth. This one doesn't."

"Whistler could handle explosives," said Jack, "and his job at the green line made him perfect for the press. But Hazlitt had to prove that he was in the car when it blew. He knew how you would verify his identity. It's not exactly a secret. He had money and personal contacts all over the armed forces. He had somebody switch his dental records. There must be a system for updating those things. A clerk tossed out Hazlitt's old dental records and slipped in somebody else's. Then Hazlitt made sure that the skull you found in the wreck matched the records in his file."

"Whose?" asked Newman suddenly. "Whose skull? It's one thing to convince a sad sack like Bernard Whistler to take the rap for a homicide that never happened. It's another to find some other schnook to blow up in Hazlitt's car. Whose records are these, Jack? How did the Colonel get a hold of them? And shouldn't somebody miss whoever it was?"

"They might," said Jack, "if there was anyone to miss them. Didn't I read in his press release that the Colonel bought a gourmet

201

dinner for a hungry vet? I'll bet there's another homeless vet who never made it back to the streets."

Dr. Dennison was not a betting man. "You can make any wager you like," he said, "if you find a taker. But that's all conjecture, isn't it? Which doesn't count for much against forensic science. I have a body on my table with teeth that don't match the military's records."

"Are they loose?" asked Jack.

"Loose?"

"The teeth."

The M.E. shook his head. "No. They're still attached to the jaw, all right, which is still attached to the skull. Right here, in front of us."

Jack nodded. "Hazlitt was given the Purple Heart after the Noriega kidnapping. Don't they give that only when there's been a physical injury?"

"That's right."

"So, what was the Colonel's injury?"

"A fractured cranium."

"Take a good look. Does the body on your table have a cracked skull?"

46

It should have rained on the morning of Walter Frick's funeral, but it does not rain easily in Los Angeles. The sky was overcast, a lumpy grey, but the moisture in the air never came together with sufficient conviction to burst through the clouds. Instead, each drop hovered overhead, like day laborers on a corner or actors at a casting call. Down below, a somber group of mourners picked their way up a hillside and gathered around an open grave to hear a host of platitudes in the listless gloom.

Walter had relatives, colleagues and acquaintances, and all of those parties were represented. Judith sat in front with her sister from Milwaukee, in a black hat and widow's weeds out of *film noir*. There were men-folk who resembled Walter but for his age, his hairline, or his weight. There were faces Jack recognized from El Monte, with ink running out of their buttoned shirt cuffs. Harold Spinnaker was there with his aide Wendy Moore. Jennifer Hellman, Walter's *personal assistant*, was also there, sniffling. So was Gerald Carafiol, the auditor from San Bernardino. Jack had a weird sense of *déjà vu*, as if he were watching *This is your life, Walter Frick*, with the star unable to cry or give anyone a hug.

The service was short and drier than the air in which it was held. The minister did not seem to know Walter, but spoke as if he did. As it came to an end, Judith stood up from her folding chair as if taking an oath of office, witnessed by her sister. Along the edge of the assembly Jack spotted Lieutenant Newman, Sergeant Warneke, Officers Montoya, Bruner, and Yost. The cops didn't speak to anyone, but kept an eye on the deceased as if he might run for the gate.

When it was over, Jack felt a shaky hand in the crook of his elbow and looked up to see Judith beside him. "Thanks for coming," she whispered. Then, finding her voice, she added, "And for everything else you've done."

Jack nodded. "I couldn't let them put you away for Walter's death. You didn't kill him, did you?"

"Of course not. I'm innocent."

Jack hesitated an instant before agreeing, "You're no murderer."

She smiled thinly. "But not quite innocent either. Is that it?"

"Whistler is, I guess."

"Of Hazlitt's homicide? Yes. And it seems the vet was already dead when the Colonel propped him in the Porsche. But Whistler was involved in Hazlitt's scheme to fake his death by car bomb. Once Hazlitt was really dead, Bernard started talking. He came home from Iraq to find his wife in bad shape. She needed high-priced surgery. He went to see Hazlitt and demanded his life savings, only to be told all his money was gone. But the Colonel felt terrible about it and promised to cover out of his own pocket whatever care she needed, if Bernard would do this one little thing for him."

"Blow him to smithereens."

"His car at least. Hazlitt told Whistler he would step forward, if it ever came to the death penalty."

"You think he would? After all the trouble he took to disappear?"

"Maybe not, but who would've voted for the death penalty for a man like Whistler? A war hero with a sick wife, cheated out of everything while he defended his country? For blowing up maybe the most hated investor in America?"

"We should throw him a parade."

"By the time Randy Raines was through, we probably would have."

"Raines didn't know what was on the disk, did he? When he sent it to you with his motion?"

"He never screened it to the end himself. He thought it came from the Colonel, who had promised to help with Whistler's defense. But when Hazlitt learned I had a copy, he had to get that back, too."

"Like all the others."

"Poor Walter! He would've paid off the hookers, when they sent him the disk. They were working girls, after all. But he must have been surprised to see Hazlitt at the backyard door. He probably tried to pay him, too. But Hazlitt insisted on going upstairs, to get the disk Raines sent me, from my briefcase. Walter tried to stop him and got a knife in the belly for his loyalty."

"He was a good man, Judith."

"I've had two of them in my life, Jack," she said, wiping a tear with her fingertip to keep the mascara from running. "I hope you'll come back to the house with me. We have a lot to talk about—and not just the past but the future. I notice our friends from the LAPD are still keeping an eye on me."

"I think you're out of the woods, Judith. At least on the murder charge."

"But not on something else? That's the second time you've implied something … unseemly. What's on your mind, Jack? Your restless, suspicious mind?"

He shook his head. "This isn't the time or place to go into all of that."

"Into all of what?" Judith insisted, her voice rising. "No, tell me. I want to know. What do you think I've done?"

He sighed. "Somehow Hazlitt learned that Annie was my daughter."

"He was very knowledgeable. He stole a cell phone, didn't he? From one of the whores?"

"Maggie's. But she's always been careful with her records. She wouldn't have risked the most important secret of her life to a phone chip. She probably had the Farleighs in her contact list, but not what they meant to her. Not Annie."

"He must've learned it someplace else, then."

"The only place I can think of would be the court records."

"They would have it. Sure."

"But adoption file are sealed, aren't they? Annie's was – I know that much. Somebody opened it. Any idea who could've done that?"

"They keep those files pretty close."

"That's what I hear. But they wouldn't keep them from a judge, wouldn't they? If she requested them?"

"You think I opened it?"

"Did you?"

"Why? Why would I do a thing like that? To you, Jack? When you were the only one who believed I was innocent?"

"I never said you were *innocent*, Judith. I said you didn't stab Walter." He reached into his jacket pocket and fished out a slip of white paper. "You know what this is?"

She stared at the thing. "It's a routing slip."

"From the courthouse records office. You see what it's routing? Annie's file. In response to a call from your office."

She looked away. "After all we've been to each other, do you really think me capable of that?"

He didn't answer. Waiting.

"I didn't get Annie's file for Hazlitt, Jack. I got it for me. I was falling for you all over again, and that raised some troubling, tired old feelings. I wanted to see what happened to Annie for personal reasons."

"So you called for her file. And then handed it over to a kidnapper out of spite?"

She clutched his arm. "I didn't know about him, Jack. I wouldn't do that to you. I had no idea it was for Phillip Hazlitt, or how he planned to use it."

"No – you thought you were just doing another favor for an old friend. To whom you owed a great deal. Hal Spinnaker bankrolled your first judicial campaign, didn't he? And I'll bet he's already lined up to fund your re-election."

"I'll probably run unopposed."

"Will Spinnaker see to that? How generous. But he was pissed off after our talk, wasn't he? So you had to make it up to him."

"You were rude, Jack. You had no cause to make those accusations against him. Or these, against me, now."

"You didn't know that Raines asked Spinnaker to get that information for him. That he needed it for Hazlitt, who brought Blackwater and Haliburton to California First International. But those were just the details, why. It was all just a question of favors, owed and collected, wasn't it?"

Judith shook her head. "Harold Spinnaker never asked me to do anything illegal. You make it sound so tawdry."

"What do you call it when a judge sells her office to the company that puts her up for it? You gotta dance with them that brung ya?"

"That's not fair. Campaigns are expensive, yes. Everybody has to fundraise. But in my case there's no pattern of judicial abuse anybody could establish."

"We're back to legalities, are we? I can't match you on that. But I think there is a pattern of abuse, if anybody cares to establish it."

"What do you mean?"

"Something else I noticed in your court records. Hal Spinnaker has a son, doesn't he? Who cracked up a Ferrari on Pacific Coast Highway?"

"I don't know. He might. It wasn't one of my cases. I would've recused myself, if it came to me."

"That would've been unseemly, wouldn't it? But you didn't have to draw the case—because the arresting officer at the burning Spyder was Herman Hoeffler, testifying in your court against Scanlon. All you had to do was come down like a ton of bricks on the Sergeant and drive him off the force. Without his testimony, they had to drop the charges against Bud Spinnaker. You can look it up."

"You can speculate all you want, Jack, about legal issues you don't understand, and politics you can hardly imagine. But it makes no difference. Anybody can make up backroom horror stories, seeing connections where they don't exist. But what evidence have you got? None of it rises to the level of malfeasance."

"I don't know about that. You're the expert. But judges disagree. It might not be enough for a court. But it's enough for me."

47

"Tough talk. But what did you do?" asked Maggie Malloy, when Jack returned to the house in Hancock Park.

The girls were watching *Deadwood* on satellite cable. When Trixie the Whore picked up her skirts and shot George Hearst with Sol Star's derringer, the women around the flat-screen hooted and clapped.

"That's the way it is with them," said Rosalind to a woman in spandex sitting on the ottoman. "One look and they can't see anything else."

"You can't figure she shaved her pussy, either," said Ms. Spandex, "not in those days." That touched off a general debate about straight razors and disposables, razor burn and shaving creams.

From across the room, Jack watched them, until Maggie tapped him on the knee. "I see you have your vision back. But something's gone wrong with your hearing. I asked, *What did you do next?*"

"At the funeral? I'll tell you what I did. Newman came up to the grave to toss in a shovelful of earth. When she finished, I called her to one side and told her the same thing I had just told Judith about Annie and Hoeffler."

"All of it?" Jack nodded, and Maggie laughed. "After all your hard-nosed detective work, defending Her Honor on a murder rap? You turned her in for what? Busting the balls of a cop?"

"I don't know … malfeasance of office. Peddling her influence. I'll let the Lieutenant figure out the charge."

"But they won't prosecute a sitting judge."

"The D.A.? Don't be so sure. Newman will push for it. They tend to get itchy about judges selling out the legal system. The prosecutors spend a lot of time in those judges' courtrooms."

"They still need evidence, don't they? What do you have to give them? A broken heart?"

"This and that. Between the Hoeffler case and the opening of Annie's adoption file, they can probably establish the pattern they need to indict Judith Frick. Maybe Harold Spinnaker too."

"Did you ever see a banker go to jail?"

"Not personally," he conceded. "But they tell me it's a pretty sight."

Maggie took Jack's hand. "Come with me."

"Where are you taking me?"

"I'll give you a hint: you won't need your pants."

"To your room? Why? Because I rescued your daughter?"

"That was nice of you. But she's your daughter too. It's the least she should expect from you."

"Then why? Because I turned in Judith? You can't be catty as that."

"Not because you turned her in, you idiot. Because you were willing to. You're over her, Jack. You've finally opened your eyes. Which means you might actually see somebody else lying on the mattress next to you."

"Don't you think I saw you there?"

"I'm pretty sure you didn't, the first time. But we'll see what we can do."

THE END